FLORENCE ERWIN'S
THREE HOMES

FLORENCE ERWIN'S
THREE HOMES
A Tale of North and South

The Black Heritage Library Collection

BOOKS FOR LIBRARIES PRESS
FREEPORT, NEW YORK
1972

First Published 1861
Reprinted 1972

Reprinted from a copy in the
Fisk University Library Negro Collection

INTERNATIONAL STANDARD BOOK NUMBER:
0-8369-9008-0

LIBRARY OF CONGRESS CATALOG CARD NUMBER:
77-38650

PRINTED IN THE UNITED STATES OF AMERICA
BY
NEW WORLD BOOK MANUFACTURING CO., INC.
HALLANDALE, FLORIDA 33009

FLORENCE ERWIN'S

THREE HOMES.

A Tale of North and South.

BOSTON:
CROSBY AND NICHOLS.
1862.

ELECTROTYPED AT THE
BOSTON STEREOTYPE FOUNDRY.

FLORENCE IN THE COUNTRY.

THE THREE HOMES.

CHAPTER I.

IT was just at sunset, on a bright March day, that a carriage was seen slowly passing along the high, narrow road, which lay between the rice fields on a plantation, in the southern part of South Carolina, and approaching the small patch of live oak trees which hid from sight the plantation house and its surroundings.

Although still half a mile distant, there was no mistaking the easy, careless trot of Dick and Rob, the two carriage horses, or the white hat, with its long crape band, of Cato, the coachman; and no sooner had the recognition taken place than little knots of negroes began to gather together, and form their various plans for the "reception," which was evidently expected.

"Dere, now," said a large, fine-looking mulatto, — John, the head serving man, — "all you whole heap of little niggers! cut sticks and run! Dat Jupiter and Sambo, gwine to go!" A step forward, among a clustering group of children, with a large stick in his hand, scattered them from right to left like the sudden upsetting of a pail of blackberries. Some hid behind one tree, some behind another. Some dropped into the centre of a bunch of bushes, from which their dark eyes, with their bright, white settings, glowed out like black fireflies. A half dozen boys climbed up into the wide-spreading branches of a mimosa tree, and curled down among the delicate, quivering leaves, like the imps of him whom Milton tells us once "squat like a toad" in the bower of the sleeping Eve.

Others stretched themselves out on gnarled, knotted branches of the live oaks, the acorns from which grow the time-defying trees of southern liberty, while Dinah, and Rose, and Chloe, and all the other descendants of African princesses, sank under canopies of broad fig leaves, or unconsciously wreathed their woolly heads with chaplets from the laurel tree.

The house servants, dressed in their best, each wearing some small badge of crape, were carefully drawn up by John in the order in which they ranked as members of the household; not even little Dick, whose only occupation was to tend "the bantams," was missing; and while he was busy arranging them in "fust rate style," the carriage was coming nearer and nearer; so near, now, that the rattling of the loose wheels, and the cracking of Cato's whip, could be distinctly heard.

They have entered the drive; and at the opening through the trees, from which may be caught the first view of the house, the horses are checked, while Cato, pointing to it, says, proudly, —

"Dat Massa George's house!"

"Indeed!" said Mr. Erwin, the only occupant of the carriage, in that slow, northern tone which falls so ungenially on a southern ear. "It looks vastly like a barn."

Cato rolled his eyes for an instant over the stranger in silent contempt, then said, with a shrug of his shoulders, —

"Barn! *barn!* eh! best house in South Carlina Barn! Bress de Lord! eh!"

"You never saw our barns at the North," said Mr. Erwin, conciliatorily.

"Bress de Lord! no; neber wish dat are," said Cato, decidedly. "Barn! eh!"

"They are handsomer than many of the houses I have seen," continued Mr. Erwin, "as I came up on the railroad to-day."

But Cato only uttered a contemptuous ejaculation by way of answer, and gave his horses so hard a cut with his whip that they both acknowledged the indignity with a spring, which scattered, at some distance from the wheels, the swarm of young negroes, whose curiosity overcame their fear of John, and who began to drop out of their various places of concealment, and follow behind the carriage in as close proximity as they could without touching it. On dashed the horses through the long, winding avenue, without giving Mr. Erwin time to observe with how much taste and care the whole was arranged and kept.

Now, the branch of a laurel tree put its shining leaves for an instant through the window, and now, the swinging, graceful moss hung itself in drapery over it. A bunch of yellow jessamines, withered and waiting for some rude touch to remove them, were jostled off, as the wheels rolled by, and fell like stars on the black cloth which was festooned inside the carriage; or a climbing rose scattered its rich crimson leaves all over the vacant seats. Where the avenue ended, the drive took a semicircular form; the space between it and the house being occupied by a large flower garden. This Mr. Erwin saw at a very brief glance; for his attention was immediately arrested by the line of negroes who, on either side of the road, were bowing and courtesying, with such rows of shining white teeth and glistening eyes as surely never were bent on him before.

"Huddye, massa!" "God Almighty bress you!" Such were the words which seemed to pass from mouth to mouth as they moved more slowly on. Cato, having now expended a little of his indignation, reined in his horses, and nodded from right to left in a most approving and knowing manner.

"Finest lot of niggers in South Carlina," he said, turning his head for an instant into the carriage. "Massa George good massa; good massa make dem dere good niggers. Lord bress him! eh! eh! neber see his like again — neber."

Cato's tone evidently implied that Mr. Henry Erwin was very far from "his like," even if he was his own mother's son; and perhaps it was these tones, more than the personal appearance of Mr. Erwin, which, reaching the assembled negroes, made them join the procession behind the carriage with sober, almost sad faces, and sent the whisper round from John, "dat Massa George's brudder no more like, dan like dese tother white folks. What we gwine for to do now? Jist tell me dat are — will you?"

"Trust de Lord," said old Rachel, leaning heavily on her stout cane. "He take care of us so far; he take care of us all de way long."

A general groan followed this speech, not loud, but sufficiently so to send into Mr. Erwin's mind stories which he had read of sudden insurrections on the part of the slaves, and the murder of every white person in the family of their owners. He looked uneasily at the house before which he had now stopped. Every thing was so strange, so unlike the northern home from which he had come, and the necessity which had brought him was of so sad a nature that he should be forgiven for the feeling of distrust which crept over him. The dwelling was a long, one story building, raised high upon posts at its corners, but perfectly open underneath. It seemed to have been altered and enlarged from time to time, until it had as many sides and angles as a child's block house.

Along the entire front, with turns and twists to match the house, ran a broad piazza, also raised some ten or twelve feet above the ground, and supported by rough logs. Long windows, it seemed to Mr. Erwin within a foot of each other, reached down to the piazza, and numberless outside doors opened in every direction upon it.

A "barn," Mr. Erwin had called it; on nearer inspection he felt inclined to call it an "air castle;" for certainly before never was there a building so devised to catch every breath of heaven; but he had not time to indulge very long in these observations, for, as he looked up the broad, wooden steps, — they almost seemed like stairs, — he saw a little girl standing at their top awaiting him.

Her small, delicate figure was enveloped in a full, black dress, which was covered with crape folds to the waist, and there met a tight, very low-necked bodice, fastened in front with a long, flowing sash of crape. Short sleeves were caught up to the shoulder by more long, crape bows; and the child's bare neck and arms, as they shone out from their dark envelope, looked almost like alabaster. Her face was round and full, and as Mr. Erwin met the large, blue eye which was fixed steadily upon him, he saw the very look which he remembered in the boy's eye of the dead brother. The long, dark curls, which fell in such rich luxuriance till they were lost in the crape folds, were the same he had seen flowing over the shoulders of the fair, young, southern bride, and as the sign of recognition, a faint, hardly perceptible smile played around her lips, he thought again of those he had seen, so full of life and love, ever ready with this welcome, but cold and still now.

"Are you my uncle Henry?" asked the child, after her careful survey was over.

"Yes; and you," said Mr. Erwin, springing up the steps and taking her in his arms, "are my little niece, Florence."

"Yes," said Florence, simply, struggling to get down. "I am very glad you have come; my father said you would, and it is not a long time. I thought, perhaps, it would be."

All this was said in such a womanly, collected manner, that Mr. Erwin felt he had made a mistake in treating her like a child, and with a hearty kiss, and a slight apology, he set her down.

Florence restored her dress instantly to order, then

offering her uncle her hand, led him into the house. A slight shudder passed over Mr. Erwin as he crossed the threshold. It seemed to him as if he had come to meet the spirits of the dead who were there awaiting him; and as he passed on through the long, broad entry into the empty parlor, the feeling increased every moment. In that large, vacant room he held a little, warm hand in his, and beside these two there was no other.

"Florence," he said, as he became certain that they were alone, "is there no friend staying here with you?"

"Friend!" said Florence, looking with surprise into his face. "O, yes, indeed, mauma is here, and Maum Hannah, and Cato, and John, and all of them."

"But any white person, I mean, Florence; any one to have the care of you?"

"Mauma has the care of me."

"Who is mauma?"

"Mamma and papa called her Rachel; but she is only my mauma."

"Is she a negro?"

"Of course she is, uncle Henry!" said Florence, now looking at him in most undisguised astonishment.

"A slave, I mean, Florence?"

"She belongs to me," said the child, quietly; "so do Cato, and John, and Sam, and Juno, and Hannah, and Rose, and Clito, and all of our house servants."

Mr. Erwin involuntarily dropped the little hand he held. The tie of consanguinity was lost in this

knot of slavery. Here was a child, scarce ten years
old, talking of owning human beings — immortal
souls — in as easy and nonchalant a way as a
northern child would of owning dolls in her baby
house.

Florence seemed glad to have her hand released;
the new uncle looked not unlike her father; but how
very different he was! She felt it in the sudden
checking of those eager longings with which she
had looked forward to his arrival, and as he seated
himself upon the sofa she sought a distant chair,
placing it as much out of his sight as possible.

"What a queer little thing she is," thought Mr.
Erwin, as he observed her movement. "So much
for being an only child, an heiress, and, worst of all,
a Southerner."

How heavy and tomb-like was the stillness which
now gathered over them! Florence sat in her chair
with her eyes fixed upon the bright fire, which, composed mostly of light wood, sent up its sparkling
flame, now into the broad mouth of the chimney,
which opened at some height above it, and now, out
into the deepening twilight which was fast settling
down into the dark, distant corners of the large
room, as if it felt itself the only warm, living thing
there, and knew there devolved upon it the duty of
keeping up the hospitality of the hearthstone, never
wanting to a stranger before.

Mr. Erwin was not imaginative, very far from po-
etical; but there came instantly into his mind those
beautiful lines of Longfellow, —

> "When the hours of day are numbered
> And the voices of the night."

Slowly he repeated it to himself, word by word. It almost seemed to him as if the writer must, sometime in his life, have been situated precisely as he was to-night, with those very

> " Shadows from the fitful firelight,
> Dance upon the parlor wall."

Memories of him, the young brother, cherishing all those

> " Noble longings for the strife,"

who so early

> " — fell and perished,
> Weary with the march of life,"

came thronging back upon him; and there he sat, with his hat still in his hand, and the quiet little figure near him, so quiet that she might have been one of the throng who were visiting him, until the twilight had deepened into darkness, and the entrance of John, with candles, and the immediate announcement of dinner, recalled him not only to the novelty, but to the unpleasantness, of his situation.

John moved his master's chair, at the head of the table, as a signal that he was expected· to occupy it; and Florence, quiet and womanly, as if she were accustomed to the position, which indeed she had been of late, assumed her mother's place, waiting, before she took her seat, for the blessing which her father always invoked, while his family and servants stood with bowed heads and folded hands; but Mr. Erwin never asked God's blessing. So far, in his life, he had worshipped but one deity — that of Money; and so distant from his thoughts, even in this house desolated by death, was the " overruling Providence," that he looked at Florence, in her attitude of devotion, with hardly a recognition of its meaning; and it was not until she said, as he seated himself without the customary form, "You have forgotten to ask the blessing, uncle Henry," that he understood her.

Ask God's blessing? He had never done it in his whole life, that he could remember. Could he do it now? Impelled, he could never tell by what influence, he rose, uttered a few words of prayer, and, confused and disconcerted, sat down again, with those deep-blue eyes, a child's, but still not a child's, fixed inquiringly upon him.

But he was a man too much accustomed to self-control to yield long to these mysterious, silent influences. Shaking himself free from them, he began to draw from Florence such particulars of her father's last sickness and death as he had not been able to learn from any other source; and the information that the child was unable to give, John, who was standing behind his chair, supplied, with an accuracy and intelligence which surprised Mr. Erwin; nor did he fail to notice that John's language was almost entirely that used by the whites.

"I will take him north with me," he said to himself. "He will do credit to my handsome establishment in New York;" and so, having formed this one link between this strange present and his future, Mr. Erwin began to feel a little more at home, and to make the arrangements with John, for his short stay upon the plantation, quite in the manner of one who felt he had a right to command. He became more familiar with Florence, and even won the affectionate child to the place upon his knee which had always been hers upon her father's; so that, when the tall, noble-looking negro woman came, with her smiling face, to take " Miss Florry away for the night," uncle and niece parted with a warmer feeling towards each other than their first meeting had promised. This was much enhanced by some kind words, which made Rachel say, after she had closed the parlor door behind her,

" Dat dere Massa George brudder for true, bress de Lord! He gwine to take care of us, after all."

CHAPTER II.

MR. GEORGE ERWIN, the father of Florence, was born in one of the most sequestered and beautiful villages of New England. The youngest of a large family, he had always been the object of peculiar affection. His mother died of that common northern scourge, consumption, a year after his birth; and his father, a lawyer by profession, and deeply engaged in the most active duties of the bar, instead of bringing another wife home to assist him, devolved the entire domestic duties upon his eldest daughter. Though but seventeen years old at the time, Jane Erwin immediately accepted the responsibility, considering it God-sent; and no one could have more faithfully and efficiently executed her trust.

Child after child grew up in the discipline and happiness of a well-ordered New England home, and went out from it to take an active, useful part in life.

George always was petted, and more so from the peculiar delicacy of constitution which he evinced. Struggling on through a sickly boyhood, he reached the age of twenty-one, completed his college course, taking the first honors, and showing what place he was destined to occupy in the future; but, having chosen the ministry for his profession, was allowed to pursue but one year of study, when the symptoms which had in part, during these last years, disappeared, returned with increased strength; and the physician ordered him to a warmer climate, and another mode of life.

Wandering sadly away from his past and present, George Erwin found himself among strangers; but, carrying with him those true, infallible passports to kindness and attention, — good manners and good principles, — he made friends wherever he went; and, occasional but severe hemorrhages of the lungs preventing his return to the north, he attached himself to a young southern girl, married, and settled on a plantation.

His wife, Catherine Lloyd, was the only child of rich parents, both of whom died young; and at the time of their death, Catherine, or Kitty, as she was every where called, was sent north for a "finished northern education," and, especially, with the hope that she would contract habits of activity and energy, which should make her better fitted for the responsible place she was to occupy when she should be of age.

Her parents' wishes were more than fulfilled. She became so entirely northern in her feelings and prejudices, that it was only as a matter of stern duty that she could bring herself to desire the southern life which was awaiting her. The whole burden of slavery, as an hereditary and necessary evil, weighed heavily upon her heart. She could not, even though the possession of the property was legally hers without any restraint, free herself from her duties by selling her one hundred and fifty human beings; for if they still continued slaves, how was her responsibility in one "jot or tittle"

2

diminished ?   She could not free them; for she well
remembered how fondly old Nero clung to his log
cabin, and how old Dinah had begged and prayed,
when it was proposed that she should be sent north
to wait on "Miss Kitty," that she might "neber go
to dat place, where there nothing but dem free niggers. Me no want to be free. Who take care of
me, massa, when me be old?"   "Who will take care
of these helpless beings when they are old ? "   This
was the plea which drowned every other voice, and
brought Kitty Lloyd back again to the desolateness
of the long winter residence on her rice plantation.

Kitty enlivened the first winter with a houseful of
young friends, matronized by that most invaluable
of all property in every family, a maiden aunt; and
the second winter, before, it must be owned, Kitty's
duties and responsibilities had weighed too heavily
upon her, George Erwin came to share them with
her.

Kitty's few relatives made no objection to the
agreeable stranger.   It was then not a crime to be a
northerner; and Mr. Erwin, with something of the
feeling of a young missionary, in a quiet, unobtrusive, but effective way, sure always of the cheerful
coöperation of his young wife, went to work to make
a little Christian settlement of the long-neglected
plantation.

" I can serve my God here as well as elsewhere,"
he said often to himself, when the obstacles he found
he must encounter were always of a nature most
trying to his active temperament.   And so, for
twelve long years, with only an occasional visit to
his friends at the north, he had staid, labored faithfully, and God had blessed him.

The limits of our story will not allow us to linger long upon the plantation, or it would be very interesting to mark the progress of the good he did. From the most depraved, ungoverned set of slaves, he brought out, at last, a disciplined, faithful body, — men and women, who rose so rapidly from the condition of brute beasts to that of intelligent beings, that, marking the change, not only in the slaves, but in the condition of the plantation, and the average yield of the crops, many of the neighboring planters, seeing no occasion for jealousy or distrust of the northern man, began to " go and do likewise."

In the midst of this usefulness and happiness, death came. Mrs. Erwin, always contented upon the plantation, delayed the customary move into a large town too late in the season, and fell a victim to that deadly misama which has always proved so fatal to the whites upon the rice plantations. At her death she left one child, the little Florence of our story; and for two years after her mother's death, Florence had proved the only comfort left in life to her mourning father. The light of Mr. Erwin's southern life went out in the grave of his wife. It was in vain to strive to rouse himself to old exertions by former motives. He could no longer remain where he was. His little girl must not be left with the same cares, perplexities, and anxieties which had distressed her mother. Twelve years had fitted these slaves better for freedom. He would remain a short time longer, and finish the work which had been so promisingly begun, then, giving them their liberty, would remove them from the state, sell the plantation, and, with his restored health, provide for their child's future by his own exertions at the north.

Perhaps it was well he did not live to test the soundness of these plans; but he was working busily towards their completion, when the sudden return of his early complaints left him no hope of prolonged life ; and he had hardly time to form a hasty outline for Florence's future life, when he died from the rupture of a blood-vessel of the lungs.

His wishes had been made known to his brother Henry, who, being but a few years older than himself, had always seemed nearer to him than the other members of his large, scattered family — nearer than all but the sister-mother, to whom he clung now, in these desolate, dying hours, so far away from her, with a tenacious fondness, which God only attaches to those who bear to us this dearest relation.

His orphan child Mr. Erwin left, with his large property, to the care and guardianship of this brother, stating it as his express desire that she should live one year with his family in New York, and another year with his sister's family in the New England town where she, having married a clergyman, now resided, and then should be left to her free and unrestrained choice of a home, remaining with whichever of the families she should prefer, until she should be old enough to return south, or to remove to a house of her own.

Mr. Erwin provided himself an overseer, a man whom for years he had been training in his own method of taking care both of the negroes and the plantation, upon whom the management of all southern business should devolve, making him strictly accountable in money matters to his northern brother, but allowing no influence from this brother in plantation affairs, should such become necessary, — devolving the responsibility entirely upon a number of southern gentlemen, in whose superior knowledge of the circumstances of the case he had full confidence.

Every business matter was found, at the event of his death, arranged with the utmost clearness and precision ; and when, upon the sudden summons, the nearest neighbors — those upon a plantation eight miles distant — were called in, they found there was nothing left for them to do but to follow out Mr. Erwin's expressed wishes.

In accordance with these, friends of the family staid at the house until after the funeral ; then Florence was removed, to remain with them until her uncle could come to her from New York ; and the day upon which he was expected the child had insisted upon returning home, in order to be there to meet and welcome him.

In putting so much of her future into her own hands, Mr. Erwin had shown his appreciation of his daughter's character. Always accustomed, from childhood, to the society of her father and mother, and seeing very few white people besides, Florence had early developed uncommon maturity and judgment. If her parents could have foreseen the life that awaited her, they could hardly have adapted her education better, in many respects, to it. Simple, earnest, and trustful, she mingled the quiet, affectionate, impulsive character of the South, with the cool consideration and thoughtful vigor of the

North; and, it must be confessed, as she inherited
so many of the virtues, she had her due share of
the faults of both sections of the country. She was
often arrogant and obstinate, high spirited to a
fault, and unforgiving if any act took the form of
a personal injury. Poor little Florence! she was
only now, at the time of her father's death, a child
of ten years; and yet marked, weighed, and used as
the reason for regulating her future life, were these
half-formed, half-slumbering natural traits. But Mr.
Erwin did the best and only thing he could. We
shall see, as our story progresses, with what discern-
ment he read the character of his child.

Mr. Henry Erwin had obeyed the summons south
with all possible speed; and being previously informed what directions his brother intended to leave,
had come prepared to carry them fully, and immediately, into execution.

We have already shown him to our readers on
the night of his arrival at Myrtle Bush, Mr. Erwin's
plantation; we must now pass over the few days
necessary for his arrangements, and come to that
on which, accompanied by Florence, he took his
departure for her new home in New York.

CHAPTER III.

MR. ERWIN disliked scenes. Perhaps it was because they were not of unfrequent occurrence in his home; perhaps it was because his New England blood had retained enough of its Puritan source not to like to be hurried by any cause beyond its own control. Certain it is, he always avoided them when he could, and never more determinedly than during this visit south. It seemed to him that if he did but put his foot over the threshold of the door, some black face started out upon him with a demonstration. Now it was a little basket of eggs, with only a "God Almighty bress you, massa;" and now it was a curious fish, which a negro had caught in the "back water," and for which he looked to receive an equivalent. One morning, a fine large deer lay dead in the woods near by, and "massa" was waited for, to draw the knife across the throat; and perhaps, that same evening, a live alligator had been hunted from its hole in the marshes, and was opening his wide jaws for "massa's" edification in the back yard. Mr. Erwin was not allowed to behold these southern sights without a crowd of other spectators. The whole plantation, from Daddy Tom to the least bit of a black baby, turned out — some to see what was to be seen, but almost all to catch a nearer view of "Massa George brudder."

Mr. Erwin had, from the first, a presentiment that a set of human beings who were capable of showing so much attachment for the dead, would cling with much tenacity to the living; he had, therefore, devised every expedient for withdrawing Florence as quietly and speedily as possible. He would have been glad to have spirited her away in the dead of the night; and inwardly fretted over the necessity which compelled him to use precisely those means which would almost certainly excite the negroes, and bring out, in a most unbearable form, one of these dreaded scenes.

As he was sitting, the night before they were to leave, alone in the large, desolate parlor, wondering what could have become of Florence, and really longing to hear her light step in the hall, his ear was attracted by a sweet voice, so sweet, that at first it seemed hardly human, close under his window. Going softly to it, having put out the candles, he found the yard filled with negroes, — one, a girl, having approached the window, and seeming, by the motion of her hand, to be directing the rest.

A momentary fear of insurrection and assassination crossed his mind, as it had on the first night of his arrival; but certainly the men were not armed; and, if he mistook not, that little figure moving round among them was Florence.

Leaning against the window, but so as to be half hidden by the drapery of the curtain, he heard the same person, who had evidently been awaiting his movements, commence in a low, sad tone, what he soon found was a dirge for his dead brother. After chanting six lines, of unequal length, but of perfect rhythm, she changed her tune, and a heavy band of voices chimed in with a full, rich recitative chorus; the last few words of which, only, could Mr. Erwin's ears, untutored to the negro dialect, comprehend. These were invariably "Glory! glory! glory!" accompanied with a sudden clapping of hands.

As the improvisatrice — for such Mr. Erwin soon distinguished enough to consider her — went on, the feelings of her audience seemed to become more and more under her control, and the voices which had not been heard excepting in the chorus, began now to interrupt her from time to time.

After describing, in words which, could they have been translated into pure English, would have been found replete with true poetry, the coming of Massa George and his young bride among them, she went on to repeat what they had done for their slaves; and as she recounted, one by one, the changes which had taken place, some voices sung, "God bress him foreber and eber, amen." Others cried aloud so piteously that the listener felt his heart growing warmer and warmer towards the poor, down-trodden, grateful African; and when, at last, the songstress described the death of the mistress, such a wail went up from the crowd as Mr. Erwin never forgot to his dying day. Then came those years when "the bird had flown, and its weary, wandering mate was seeking it in vain, until he went for it, up beyond the blue sky, way, way beyond those deep, silent stars, and there he found her, young, and a bride again."

"Glory! glory! glory!" chimed in the excited

chorus. But the song went on. "Massa George took none of us niggers dere; neber, neber, neber see him any more."

Another groan, deeper, louder than before, and then, as if conscious that neither her audience or auditor could bear more, she slid gracefully into a description of "our little missus, our white lily, our bridal rosebud, our pearl of all pearls, the apple of our eye, and the light of our life."

Mr. Erwin ventured to glance out to see what had become of Florence. There she stood, in the centre of the group, swaying her light figure back and forth, in time to the music, and clapping her little hands in the chorus with the others. It was so dark that he could not discern her face; but he was quite sure that she turned, from time to time, as she would in the mazes of a dance, and bowed to the negroes as they expressed their approbation of some endearing name by which she was called.

At length she glided up to the singer and spoke a few words. The effect was instantaneous. The whole voice and manner changed, and turning so as to face the window, she commenced a series of compliments upon "Massa George brudder," which it was well, with his dislike of scenes, that Mr. Erwin did not wholly understand.

As he stood there, listening, he was startled by feeling some hands placed in his, but before he had time to be conscious how small they were, Florence's voice said, —

"Uncle Henry, open the window, please, and go out and thank them; they will wait for you. Papa always did."

"And did your papa give them money?" asked
Mr. Erwin, recalling the gift which was always expected for such an out-door performance at the
north.

"I think not," said Florence; "if we were going
away, he ordered John to give them a soup in the
yard, or an extra allowance of hominy. Should you
like to have him do so now? I should, very much."

"Certainly, if you wish; I see no objections. Will
you call him, and tell him what to do, while I step
out and thank these people?"

Florence glided away again, and with much reluctance Mr. Erwin raised the window and spoke a few
kind words to the negroes; every one of which was
received with so many and such warm blessings,
that their very fervor seemed, as he sat, after a few
minutes, alone in the parlor, to breathe warmth and
life into its cold, tomb-like atmosphere. For hours
afterwards Mr. Erwin heard the sound of the same
voices in song and chorus; indeed, the last consciousness he had, as he closed his eyes, was of
the long-drawn, emphatic "Amen! Glory, glory!
Amen, amen!"

"Thank fate, last night used up all the excitement
even these negroes can summon. We shall go off
quietly at last." Such was Mr. Erwin's first thought
as he waked on the following morning. "Now, if
the child will only behave as much like a woman
as she has all the time since I have been here, we
shall soon be safe in the cars, out of the way of
scenes."

It was a soft, spring morning when Mr. Erwin
opened the door and went out to examine the state

of the weather. That afternoon, at four, they were
to take the steamer at Charleston for New York, and
in going to sea one looks anxiously at the clouds and
the vane.

It was very early; the gray daylight was just
stealing up over the tall, pointed forest trees, and
glancing down into the large flower garden directly
before him. Mr. Erwin had lived too long in the
city not to enjoy, with peculiar freshness, the par-
terres of choicest flowers. In a moment their dewy
beauty took him back to boyhood, — to the old New
England home, — and to the little pet brother whose
taste had laid out this scene. Soft and genial as this
early dawn, came back that other brighter dawn;
and impelled by a crowd of memories, which came
thronging on, he walked out into the garden; then,
with hardly a consciousness of where he was going,
further on in the well-known path which led to the
negro quarter of the plantation.

Never before had he marked, with such close observation, the peculiarities of this southern scene.
It seemed to him almost as if his brother was by his
side, and was pointing out this and that thing, with
that attachment which came to be so strong for his
adopted home.

He saw the long, folded leaves of the mimosa tree
beginning to open as the fingers of the day gently
touched them. The rich perfume of the white blos-
somed bay tree laid itself on the still air, making it
almost heavy with its weight of fragrance; and
down upon him, as he walked slowly on, fell golden
showers of the climbing jessamine. Tame birds just
hopped a step or two before him, turning their pretty

heads constantly towards him, and singing all the time a song, in which there mingled not one note of sadness on parting.

Fawns looked out from between stately trees at him as he passed, but, missing the familiar voice to which they were accustomed to answer, shook their graceful necks, and darted away.

Fully occupied by all these sights and sounds, Mr. Erwin, almost before he was aware, found himself among the negro huts. This was not his first visit; but all his others had been hurried, doubtless looking at each cabin, not to see how comfortable and pleasant it had been made, but to assure himself that human beings had this portion allotted them with no home of a frame house ever rising above them, labor perseveringly, faithfully, and savingly as they might. This morning he was struck with the extreme neatness and order of every thing.

The cabins, some forty in number, were built around two open squares which had been cleared in the middle of the old woods. They were all made of logs; but so neatly whitewashed that Mr. Erwin was obliged to confess the logs were rather pretty as ornaments. There were very few windows, and the doors were so slight they looked as if a touch would burst them open ; but before every house ran a light fence, and within the small enclosure were every kind and variety of herbs which could be made to grow in the climate ; some few flowers — here and there a rose in its fullest luxuriance and beauty; but as a general thing, it showed that the negroes, in their idea of cultivating their ground had much more of the practical and useful than of the ornamental.

"This is George's work," said Mr. Erwin, as he satisfied himself that his observation held good. "No black ever, for himself, chose what would do him good."

But early as it was, the walk was not destined long to be an uninterrupted one. First, the dogs — and every cabin owned one or two — came out with a very noisy good morning; and then one little negro after another put his woolly head and glistening black eyes out of the opening doors, grinning at Mr. Erwin as only a happy plantation negro can grin.

Very decidedly he turned away from them. He had quite enough of negro developments on the previous evening; and, more than half regretting that he ventured so far, he was hurrying home, when his steps were at once arrested by sounds proceeding from one of the largest and most respectable of the cabins. It was a voice, not a man's, and certainly very unlike a woman's, engaged in earnest prayer; and as he caught the first words, there was no mistake. It was praying for him.

Drawn, by an irresistible curiosity, to the opening in the side of the cabin, he saw through the chink four old negro women kneeling on the hard ground, which made their floor, with Florence in their midst. One, the oldest and most singular looking, was praying aloud, while the others were uttering, during every pause of the prayer, the most fervent ejaculations.

What a scene it was to northern eyes! The

light of the cabin was still the dim gray of the early morning, and mingling with it in a strange, weird way was the leaping, sparkling flames from the sticks of light wood which burned on the hearth, under the open spot that served for the chimney. The women were dressed in the blue homespun, so great a favorite with the older negroes, all with coarse white half-handkerchiefs crossed over the front of their dresses, and blue and white checked turbans brought closely down to their heads and tied with a tight, small bow.

It seemed to Mr. Erwin that never before had he seen age and decay so visibly written upon human beings. Their faces were shrivelled and wrinkled until they had hardly a vestige of cheeks or chin; but out from all shone the never-dimming black eye, and the thick, protruding lip seemed to have more prominence from the deep indentures by which it was surrounded.

"Now," thought Mr. Erwin, "there is not a child of ten, north of Mason and Dixon's line, who would not be afraid of these old hags, and run from them as it would from a brownie; and here is this southern girl, long before even this daylight, sitting down with them as easily and as contentedly as if she had come to see her own grandmother. Turn and twist it whichever way you will, this matter of slavery is a strange thing enough."

Riveted to the spot, Mr. Erwin heard the prayer ended, and saw the old negroes rise slowly, and with much difficulty, from their knees. Then Florence, dropping down before one, laid her head in her lap, while the woman, putting both of her skinny, yellow

hands upon the clustering chestnut curls, invoked
such a blessing on her "little missus" as brought
the tears into the hard, worldly eyes which were
gazing so curiously at the group. "Amen," echoed
the others; and then Florence knelt to each one
of these, and from each came the same warm, fond,
trembling blessing.

As the last was ended, Florence moved into the
centre of the circle, and in a position which immediately reminded Mr. Erwin of the statuette of
little Samuel, with which, a few years ago, the
streets of New York were filled, folded her
hands, and, in sweet, childlike, but very audible
tones, began herself to pray.

"O God, please to bless Maum Rachel, and Dinah,
and Rose, and Chloe. Take good care of them all
the long time while I am gone, and send some
beautiful angel to come and see and talk to them
when I am far, far away. Do not let them die until
I come home again : for Christ's sake. Amen."

"Amen, amen," chimed in the voices; and Mr.
Erwin, afraid of being discovered if he staid any
longer, walked softly away.

The bright sun came out as he left the woods,
and laid itself like a sheet of gold over the springing
grass and the glad flowers. It rested on the old
plantation house, gilded the eastern windows, and,
prosaic as Mr. Erwin was, reminded him irresistibly
of that city which was "of pure gold like unto clear
glass," and of the brother who a short time ago
treading as he trod now on these "sands of time,"
had exchanged them for the "foundations which
were garnished with all manner of precious stones."

FLORENCE IN SOUTH CAROLINA.

It was a matter of serious congratulation to him, when, upon entering the house, he saw every arrangement for an early leave-taking had been already made by the efficient John.

This servant Mr. Erwin coveted. He would willingly have paid his market value twice over, could he have bought him and taken him north; but the words of the will were positive: "No negro upon the estate shall, on any account, be sold, unless in compliance with their own wishes, and then not without careful scrutiny on the part of the executors, to insure there being no mistake as to its being the free and uninfluenced choice of the slave."

John felt quite insulted when Mr. Erwin offered to buy him, take him north, and make him a free man, provided he would agree to remain in his service, on reasonable wages, for the next five years.

"Ky, ky! Massa Erwin!" he said, with a contemptuous shrug of his shoulders, "who you tink, den, stay in South Carlina, and look after little missis's tings? Me no want other freedom than she gives, de Lord bress her!"

And so, reluctantly, wonderingly, hardly feeling that he should dare to repeat the story when he should return home, Mr. Erwin gave up all hope of removing John, and felt his regard for abolitionists sink down to freezing point.

Rachel, Florence's nurse, was to accompany them. This had been decided long ago; and Rachel was, in Mr. Erwin's words, "a very capable, superior negro." She was an elderly woman, having been maid to Florence's grandmother — afterwards, nurse and maid to her mother; and descending, as such

3

dignitaries do, maid and nurse to the little Florence. The hereditary attachment to such members
of the family is very strong, and mutually so. Florence loved her "mauma" — the negro name for
mother — better now than any other human being;
and Rachel loved this foster-child better than Cato,
her husband, and better than those six, half-grown
boys, who, standing between plantation negroes and
house servants, promised to make such first rate
hands, that even Rachel and Cato, proud as they
were, and anxious that all the "hands" should do
the best, were not ashamed of their children.

Parting with them all was a great grief to Rachel;
but not so great as it would have been to have
parted with Miss Florry. She was left at liberty to
return south any time after Florence's first two years
at the north were over, and the freedom which was
to be her "unalienable right" as soon as she touched
northern soil, was made by legal rights hers, to use
as she should please, when she should return south;
and Rachel, unlike John, was glad to be free. Accustomed from her earliest life to associate intimately
with the whites, she had early imbibed a love for
freedom, as peculiar as it was strong; for never had
Rachel known what it was to be a slave; and those
deprivations and disgraces, so synonymous to northern ears with the very name, were to her simply
impossibilities.

Yet her life was always saddened, always tinctured by the memory, that in deed and in truth, she
was not her own; that if her master and mistress
should die, she, in common with all the rest, was
liable to be bought and sold like cattle.

Her education was far above that of the servants generally. She read eagerly, through many days and weeks, and, take her life together, years of easy labor; and beside her own reading, she listened to a great deal while she was busy minding the baby, — listened intelligently, and at the time of Mr. Erwin's death, Rachel was a well-educated woman. She could write really a fine and bold hand; and it was her fingers which first guided Florence through the labyrinth of pot-hooks, and to her teaching, that the child owed her practical lesson in "Reading without tears." With this increasing intelligence grew the desire for freedom, and though Rachel was too sensible "to make it ever a subject of conversation" with the other negroes, she often told her missus she felt as if she could not die a slave; as if her very soul were not her own, and she had no power to say, "Here am I, and the children thou hast given me." It almost seemed to Mr. Erwin, that the more developed and sincere Christian Rachel became, the more slavery weighed upon and oppressed her. The constant burden of her mourning was, "I cannot hold up free hands unto God." This made a peculiar phase in Rachel's religious character. She seemed always struggling, by the greatest faithfulness, the most austere penances, to make up for the imperfectness of the offering. "I am only, after all, a poor, miserable slave," she would say; "but for me, too, Christ died." Her piety had more than the usual negro imaginativeness, more fervor, more warmth. Perhaps it had imparted a touch of its life and vitality to the whole house. Even the young minister, dying with only this faithful nurse and his little child near him, may have caught from her glowing words some nearer, more perfect idea of the rest and beauty of heaven. Certain it is, that when George Erwin closed his eyes for the last time on earth, no other voice prayed with him but this poor slave's; who, kneeling close beside him, with his head pillowed in her faithful arms, repeated verse after verse of those precious words whose meaning the passing spirit seems better to comprehend than ever before; for are they not the language of that country into which he is silently entering?

It may be supposed from these traits of Rachel, that she would not be deficient in the qualities which would make her a good, useful nurse; a watchful, efficient person to be intrusted with Florence. Indeed, so very reliable did she seem to Mr. Erwin, that he occasionally cast a troubled thought to his not very well regulated domestic establishment at home, with the wonder how so systematic and nice a person would mingle with the elements she should find there. She used only occasionally the negro dialect; almost never in speaking to a white person, unless it was as an expression of affection towards her "little missis," as she loved to call Florence. This was well; and would be quite an assistance, Mr. Erwin saw, in accustoming her to northern life. Upon the subject of her freedom Mr. Erwin was sedulously silent. In his heart he hoped she did not know it; but would consider herself, during her northern stay, a slave. He preferred so much the respectful, ready obedience of the negroes, to the impudent, sulky way of receiving orders, so common among the servants in New York. He thought the best thing in slavery was the prompt, cheerful manner in which the " chattels" went about their daily tasks.

Would all this disappear when Rachel, landed on that noisy wharf in the distant city, should know herself *free?* It was a problem which Mr. Erwin could not solve, but which gave him considerable anxiety as he thought it over.

Breakfast, this parting morning, is punctually served. Rachel is at the back of Florence's chair, only a shade more sedate and respectful than ever. She is dressed in a neat, gray travelling dress, for which Mr. Erwin feels very thankful; he had dreaded the peculiar plantation dress, and now has only to hope that a snug bonnet will cover that spotless white turban. Florence is pale, very pale; her uncle wonders, as he looks at her, whether she has not been up all night, and his guess is not far from the truth. Florence had many last words to say to the negroes while the soup was being given out, and long after the majority had gone to their cabins a few of her favorites lingered, to be near her as long as they could. Then, after a few hours of troubled sleep, she had wakened to make her early farewell visits to the negro quarter, and had already been there a full hour when her uncle saw her. Rachel wisely allowed her to have her own way. "She will be better there," she said to the expostulating Cato, "than fretting here; let her go while she can."

And so now, Florence, too much exhausted to be keenly alive even to the coming separation, sat pale and silent, replying to her uncle's cheerful remarks only in monosyllables, and turning from the untasted food almost with loathing.

Taking the first opportunity after the meal was ended, Mr. Erwin said to Rachel, "Can you not see that there is no assembling of the hands; nothing to excite this child any more? She looks more than half sick now."

"All very quiet, massa," said Rachel. "John told them last night no one must come near little missis to-day — never fear."

"And Rachel," continued Mr. Erwin, in his most conciliatory tone, "now you are going to the north, perhaps it would be well for you to change your forms of speech. You speak with remarkable correctness; but if you should call me Mr. Erwin, and Florence Miss Florence, it would attract less attention, and be a little more proper."

"Yes, massa," said Rachel, dropping her head.

"You will remember it!" And Mr. Erwin's eye ran keenly and quickly over the bowed face of the negro. He thought he saw a defiant expression there; but she answered simply and gravely as before, "Yes, massa."

In a short time the carriage was at the door; the trunks had gone before in a large open lumber box; and, walking silently down the long flight of steps, Florence preceded her uncle. Rachel, in the white turban, followed; and Mr. Erwin, as he glanced hastily around, saw no one but John. This was well. Now, a few minutes more and the dreaded parting would be in the past.

Rachel, without a word, took her seat in the carriage, by the side of Florence. Mr. Erwin never had ridden so near a black person in his life. For an instant his northern antipathies rose strong within him. He hesitated; but Florence had already thrown her arms around her "mauma," and buried her face in her lap. Any thing to avoid a scene; so Mr. Erwin, with a slight shudder, took the empty place; and Cato, springing upon the box, snapped the whip as if the very noise were an outlet for his excitement. The horses dashed away, in a manner which would have led one to imagine they were partakers in the scene; and, with her buried face, stifling her sobs so that even Rachel could not hear them, Florence left Myrtle Bush, in its glad spring beauty and with its beating human hearts — all her own — for the far distant northern home; and Rachel, as she glanced back through the long avenue, saw one after the other of her six boys come out from their hiding-place in the woods, and wave her a long farewell.

CHAPTER IV.

At Benton Crossing the party were to take the cars. Mr. Erwin had not been aware that Cato was Rachel's husband, and that here another parting was to take place, or the satisfaction with which he had ridden over the last five miles would have been considerably abated. When they stopped at the rough wooden house which served for a station, he was agreeably surprised to see Florence raise her head and speak cheerfully to her "mauma," and no less so to see the eyes of the negro, for the first time, dimmed with tears.

Perhaps Rachel was afraid to ride in the cars, and he began to reassure her in his kindest manner. But Cato also was silent, and, as he stopped, seemed to find an unusual difficulty in making the horses obey his command.

Mr. Erwin bustled about with that peculiar excitement so necessarily a part of every American traveller. One would think, to see them on the eve of starting for a long journey, that they have every arrangement to make for the conducting of every train of cars, or steamboat, from the start to the end. Mr. Erwin made more stir in looking up his luggage than the station master had ever seen made before. The very negroes about the establishment looked after him, as he flew from one trunk to another, as if they thought he had certainly gone mad. Nor could they, for some time after they were assured that he was "only a northerner," feel quite safe near him.

Cato and Rachel had gone apart from the others. This only added to Mr. Erwin's uneasiness. Suppose the cars should come, and Rachel should take that opportunity to hide herself until they were gone, what could be done? She was now exhibiting more unwillingness to go than she ever had before, and negroes were so proverbially false.

"Florence," he said, approaching the child, who was sitting on the corner of the steps, looking with much interest at the preparations that were making, "you will keep your eye upon your mauma, and see she does not go away far; for the cars, you know, do not stop but a moment."

"Yes, uncle," said Florence; "I will speak to her." And Mr. Erwin was relieved by hearing Rachel say,

"Don't fret, Miss Florry; I neber leave you, neber. No fear of your old mauma."

Fortunately for all, the cars were unusually punctual to-day; and never was sound more musical to Mr. Erwin's ears than that of the long, shrill whistle, as it echoed through the pine hills at their north.

"There they are, Florence. Take hold of Rachel's hand, and don't be in a hurry. I will put you in after I have seen the luggage all aboard."

As he turned for his trunks, he saw Cato throw his arms around Rachel's neck, and the sobs of the two were distinctly audible. Florence stood like a statue near them, and he heard her say,

"Go back, mauma — go back; I can do without you."

"Bress her heart, no," faltered Cato. "What

would missus, what would Massa George, say? Dat
dere must neber be. De Lord be thanked that
Rachel can take care of little missus; and de God
Almighty," continued Cato, spreading out his hands
over both, "bress you, and keep you as de apple of
his eye, foreber and eber. Amen."

"Amen!" responded Florence and Rachel; and
any other parting words were lost in the rattling,
noisy train, which came thundering up, with its great
iron heart, all unconscious how many trembling human souls listened to its sound as to a knell.

The delay was very brief, but long enough for Mr.
Erwin's purposes, especially as he heard Rachel say,

"Remember, Cato, you neber see me a slave again.
Look at Rachel, dat ting dat can be bought and sold!
Next time, Cato, no one buys, no one sells. I gwine
to be"— and Rachel drew her fine figure up to its
entire height — "dat bressed ting our Lord made —
a *free woman!*"

"Dat for true, Rachel," and the sadness of Cato's
voice Mr. Erwin never forgot, "but dem dere boys,
and Cato?"

"Little missis will make you all free too, Cato,
neber fear."

"I will," said Florence, raising her hand solemnly,
as if sealing a covenant.

"Den de God of Abram, Isaac, and Jacob bress
you, little missis. As you do unto us, so may he do
unto you, foreber and eber; and when you go to
heaven in de golden chariot, may Rachel, and Cato,
and Dick, and Pompey, and Sam, and March, and
Juby, and Cæsar be there to push along the wheels,
foreber and eber. Amen."

The last word was drowned in the fast rush of steam and the renewed motion of the wheels. Florence and Rachel bent far out of the car window; and there, until the rapid motion hid him from their sight, stood Cato, with hands outstretched, as if still imploring the blessing.

Mr. Erwin drew a long breath. The dangers of the sea were nothing in comparison to those which he had already passed; and as the cars bore them swiftly on, such a sense of relief came over him as to make him fully conscious how intense his previous annoyance had been.

It was but a few hours' ride before they reached the seaport of Charleston; and driving directly to the wharf, they went on board the large steamer upon which their passage had been previously taken.

Mr. Erwin saw with pleasure that there were a large number of white turbans there besides Rachel's; and he could not but notice, even amid the bustle and confusion, with what quiet dignity she bore herself, and how superior she seemed to any of the negroes by whom she was surrounded.

The steamer was not as large or luxurious as those which are used in the present day. Every thing was wet on deck; every body was intent on jostling and inconveniencing to the greatest extent in their power.

The captain, a northern man, uttered his commands so clothed in oaths, that it almost seemed as if he was invoking curses upon his ship. White and black sailors were running about indiscriminately, executing them; while the passengers who were crowding on board, after being helped over the wet, slippery plank which connected the ship with the wharf, were left to find their state rooms the best way they could.

Holding Florence tightly by the hand, Rachel, as much at home as if she had always been used to such circumstances, descended into the crowded, littered cabin, and looked around for the door which should bear the number of the card Mr. Erwin had given her.

It was one of the best berths in the steamer, central, and larger than any of the others. It had, therefore, been appropriated already by a family of southerners, who were making an early northern move for the summer, and who, with their characteristic carelessness, had chosen the best, without regard to the ticket which assured them their lot had fallen into far less pleasant places.

Rachel looked from her number many times to the one upon the door, until she became quite assured that they were one and the same, then, calling the stewardess, pointed out the mistake.

"All right," said the huge negro woman who filled this important station. "How many óf you are there? You shall be in in a minute."

"Only my little missis," said Rachel, holding up the small white hand so tightly clasped in hers.

"Only that child!" repeated the stewardess; "why, this is the largest state room on board — large enough for a dozen of her; but if she has paid for it, it is hers just the same, I suppose. Wait patiently; it takes time to deal with such folks;" and she cast her head, with an expressive twist, in the direction of the state room.

In a few minutes Rachel heard a warm altercation

proceeding from there, which gradually increased in noise and bitterness until the attention of the whole cabin was directed towards it.

"Go, mauma," said Florence, half frightened, "and tell them it is not any matter; we can take another room. I am sure these little bits of rooms are all ugly enough. I had as soon have one as another."

But obedience to "Miss Florry" was not a part of Rachel's servitude; so she shook her head, and, as if a sense of rights was coming with these first movements towards freedom, said,

"It is yours, Miss Florry; you must have the best, when you gwine paid for it already."

"But, mauma, I don't care; I don't like the best. Please let them have it."

"Hush you, now, Miss Florry. Dem dere folks must come out; and if dat big woman can't do it, why Rachel shall soon be dere herself."

True to her word, Rachel was soon in the midst of the affray; but in a very efficient and novel manner. Entering swiftly, she first seized the baby, and, notwithstanding her kicks and screams, carried her and deposited her triumphantly in the state room which belonged to her parents. Returning, she carried off the next youngest child, and would have proceeded so with the whole family of six, if she had not been violently stopped by the angry and excited mother as she took up the third. Gathering her armful of bundles, she hastened to transport them; and by this time the two children who were left in their new quarters began a scream, which was in no danger of being unheard; and as the nurses were busy hunting up lost baggage on deck, the mother was obliged to leave her borrowed quarters for the far less convenient one belonging to her.

"Eh? eh?" said Rachel, returning, in her wrath, to the negro dialect. "Dat dere woman tink she gwine to take my little missis' room, eh? eh? She no know her old mauma. What for I gwine to dat north for, if not to take de best care of her? — jest tell me dat, will you, eh? eh?"

While Rachel was busy removing — it must be acknowledged, not in the most careful manner — every intrusive article out of the way, Florence had stolen to the state room where the crying children refused to be pacified by the angry mother, and, taking from her travelling basket some of the tempting candies with which she was liberally supplied, was endeavoring to quiet, or rather to make friends with, the worsted party. As the lady did not know Florence had any connection with the servant who had so summarily removed her, she received her more graciously than might have been expected, and was not a little annoyed, when Rachel had put every thing to rights in the state room, to find that it was for this very child she had been obliged to give up such nice accommodations.

Rachel, too, was not pleased to find Florence here. She tossed up her white turban with the air of much-offended dignity, and took Florence to her own quarters almost as quickly as she had crossed the cabin with the other children. Indeed, she felt quite inclined to express her sense of what she thought Florence's want of spirit; but there was a quiet dignity about Florence which repelled all querulousness; and Rachel had to content herself with uttering sundry heated ejaculations, which if they did no other good, served as a safety valve for her own excited feelings, and helped to calm her. By the time Mr. Erwin found their state room the storm had entirely subsided; and so ended Rachel's first protective, aggressive act in Florence's northern life. It was well all this occurred before the steamer had weighed anchor; for certainly if those wheels had made a first revolution, Rachel would have had something else to think of besides Florence's "rights."

Mr. Erwin wished Florence to go on deck, that she might see the city and harbor of Charleston as they sailed away; but no inducement could make Rachel accompany them. The slight motion of the steamer, as she got under way, seemed to fill her with mortal terror; and no sooner did they disappear up the steep, narrow stairs, than, falling upon her knees, she began to pray, it must be confessed, not without some misgivings as to whether her petition would be answered as readily as if she had not indulged in the anger of a few hours before.

When Florence reached the deck with her uncle, the noise and stir of departure was at its utmost height. She clung to him, much more alarmed than interested in the city they were so quickly leaving behind them, and while he was imagining her receiving images of the seaport of her native state, which long years would not efface, she was in reality only carrying away a picture, dimmed with tears and frights. On they sped, now passing a large, dark ship, which lay still upon the water, like the pictures Florence had often seen of a whale; and now going close up to a small brig, whose outspread sails reminded her of the doves which flew so tamely about her father's yard at Myrtle Bush; and again a small black steamer, with its high chimney and its volume of curling steam, darted by them like the finny fish in the distant breakwater. In spite of her fear, Florence gradually became interested and amused; and her uncle was ready to tell her the name and properties of all the strange inhabitants of this new world of waters.

The land soon faded from view, and as they stood out boldly to sea, Florence lost all fear, not only of the noisy sailors, but of the roaring, trembling ocean, which only seemed to her, as it dashed up against the side of the vessel and darted back, to be playing with her.

So deeply engaged was she in this new scene that she forgot Rachel; and it was not until the gathering twilight began to hide even the white-crested waves from her, that she remembered how long and lonely the time must seem to her below.

"Come, uncle!" she said, with one of the quick, imperative movements, which were natural to her, "mauma will wonder where I am."

"Stop a few minutes longer, Florence. I want you to see how strangely the stars come out when there is no land. Sometimes I have seen it look as if there were two heavens, one in the sky and one on the sea, and the stars were the same in each."

Florence looked eagerly up. "How beautiful it must be, uncle. I should so like to see it; but I cannot stop now. Come, please."

"Very soon, Florence; wait a moment longer." But Florence, without another word, slid her hand from his, and threading her way through the busy sailors, over the large coils of rope, by the piles of uncared-for luggage, she found the cabin stairs, and swiftly descended.

"What a queer child she is!" said Mr. Erwin, half aloud, as she disappeared. "I hope she will one day be a little more like other children. Just compare her, now, with my Ida—and there is not half a year's difference in their ages!" Then Mr. Erwin slowly followed her, mentally wishing the voyage over, and the child safe under the care of a woman, but not just such a woman as Mrs. Erwin. Florence, as soon as Rachel was remembered, became almost alarmed to think she should have left her so long; and with a presentiment of evil, she flew along the cabin, hardly noticing the uneven motion of the vessel, until she reached her state room, and then her first look at her mauma told her her fears were well founded. Poor Rachel had crawled into the lower berth, and with teeth chattering from fright, and eyes dilated to an unnatural size, was endeavoring to hold herself in the berth, while the vessel rocking gently from side to side, seemed to her threatening every moment to roll her out.

Florence made a place instantly for herself by her side, and nestling up close to her, put both arms around her neck, endeavoring by every gentle, loving word she could use to soothe her.

So Mr. Erwin found them when he entered their state room, and immediately surmising that Rachel's fears were much increased by the premonitions of sea-sickness, he took, perhaps, as good a way as Florence to allay her trepidation. He poured out

4

a large spoonful of brandy and compelled her to
swallow it, telling her at the same time that there
was danger of nothing but sea-sickness; and thus, by
dint of a little physical aid and wholesome authority,
restoring her from a state of suffering, which had
really been more intense than any thing she had ever
known before.

Mr. Erwin then saw them both made comfortable
for the night, and left them; but he had been gone
only a few moments when the vessel, getting farther
out into rough water, began to roll and toss; all
Rachel's fears returned with double force, and at the
same time her sickness. Such groans and prayers
as she interspersed Florence had never the power
of forgetting; and growing more and more terrified
every moment herself, she crept down from her upper
berth, and kneeling by Rachel, joined her prayers
with hers. In the midst of this scene the door
opened, and the stewardess made her appearance.
No sooner did she divine what was the matter, than
she burst into a loud laugh, which mingled most ungenially with the other sounds, but had the effect of
instantly arresting them.

"Ky," said she, using negro words, — she had
herself once been a slave, — "dat great nigger —
Lor me! what's all this awful fuss? Ky, ky! Never
saw a tub of water afore — frightened to death!"
Here came another loud laugh. "Get up, dere,
darkey; you not gwine to Davy's locker this time;
havn't spoke for dat passage, nor paid for it either.
You're gwine to York, so stop that caterwauling, and
sit up, or — " (Here she grinned most emphatically.)
" I'll call dat woman from number 64, to see how big

you are now. Ky, she'll have the laugh her own
way, reckon, and no mistake."

Rachel stared at her as if all her senses had left
her, and she had no power of understanding a word
she said. The stewardess took hold of her arm, and
giving her a good hard shake, soon restored her to
herself. "Dere," said she, "now wake up; shame
on you; you a mauma? and dis little Missis sittin'
here like to take her death a cold, a praying over
you. Dat de way you take care? I reckon your
massa teach you better manners when he catch you
near a sugar house."

"Go away!" said Florence, stamping her foot
angrily upon the floor; "go away this instant!"

The stewardess only laughed. "We will teach
you better ways than this, my little lady," she said,
"before you have been north long. We never have
any one put on airs there; so, perhaps, it will save
you some trouble if you begin to learn here."

"Go away!" reiterated Florence, stamping her
foot only the more angrily. "Go directly, when I
speak!"

"It isn't much to us northerners," said the negro,
good-naturedly, in different language. "Well for you,
little girl, you are to go where you can measure yourself, now and then, with other people. But come,
mauma! have courage. You are as safe here, this
moment, as if you were in your cabin, on your plantation at home. I have been over this same sea
more than a hundred times, and you see I have not
gone to the bottom yet. Come, I'll give you notice
in time to say prayers enough for yourself and me
too before we go down. Get your senses about you,

and look a little after this child. That is what you are here for."

Encouraged by her words and by a lull in the motion of the vessel, Rachel sat up in her berth, and the stewardess told her what she was to expect, and how she should behave, promising to look in herself every now and then, " to see every thing was going on right."

Florence, pacified by the peace which was made with her mauma, was once more lifted to her novel quarters; and Rachel, now understanding that the vessel did not go to the bottom every time it gave a lurch, and that sea-sickness was not one and the same thing with drowning, lay quietly struggling with her doubts and fears, and finding, after all, the greatest power of soothing came from the measured breathing of the little sleeper above her.

All through the long hours of this first night at sea, Rachel tossed with the ship; but shining for her, down in her dark room, as well as for the sailor who watched on deck, was the bright northern star. It led the sailor to his destined port; it led Rachel to that beautiful land where the shackles must fall from every slave; to that port where the very air should give her that long coveted, much dreamed of, boon of freedom.

With the light of the next morning came an entire cessation both of sickness and fear; and Florence, finding the old smile on Rachel's face, as she stood by her berth and wakened her, sprang up to a keen enjoyment of the excitement of a short sea voyage. Children are almost never sea-sick or timid. Florence was naturally fearless, and keenly sensitive to

the passing pleasures of any scene in which she was
a partaker. Now, she hurried Rachel so summarily
through her toilet, that, what with Florence's impatience and the rocking of the vessel, which never
allowed her to find any thing where she expected,
the nurse's patience was sorely tried, and Florence's
too.

"Now, mauma!" she said, not so good-naturedly
as she might, "you see, I am not a little girl any
longer, and am going to the north, where every child
dresses herself. I shall just begin to-morrow, and
you must make all my clothes fasten in front, so I
can be quick."

"Miss Florry gwine to be an old woman for true.
Where you get dat idea, say? Mauma go back in
the next ship. No want her any more. Lord bress
de child, what notions she does take into dis little
curly head."

"But, mauma, it is true. I am a large girl, and I
can't be made a baby of any more."

"Eh, eh! Little missis grown so big!"—and Rachel lifted up her hand as high as she could,—"since
she left Myrtle Bush; gwine to be a great lady."

By this time Florence was ready for the deck, and
with much persuasion, as her uncle had not come for
her, she induced Rachel to venture up with her. It
was early morning, and hardly a passenger besides
themselves had arisen; so they went softly through
the silent saloon, and up the stairway,—a matter of
much more diffeulty to Rachel than to Florence.

The negro was in much doubt whether she was on
her head or her feet. Now she was sure she was
close by the large mirror, which covered the side of

the saloon, nearest their state room, and at the very same instant she found herself close by, and holding on to the white handle of the state room door, at the very opposite end.

"Dis is just no place at all, Miss Florry," she said, in much bewilderment. "I am dere and here, and ebery where, in the same time."

As if to verify her words, the vessel gave a lurch, and Rachel, slightly losing her balance, went rolling down the bending side of the vessel, dragging Florence with her, and not stopping until they came violently in contact with the side of the saloon.

"De Lord hab mercy! God Almighty forgive me all my sins, and little missis, too!" groaned Rachel, in a sepulchral tone, as the blow was received; but hardly were the words uttered, when the return motion of the ship began to slide her, as it would a loose piece of furniture, over the floor to the opposite side. Florence nimbly regained her feet, and Rachel, seeing her stand alone and unhurt, once more gathered courage, and with many groans and fervent ejaculations, climbed slowly up. Willingly, now, would she have returned to her state room; but Florence pulled her resolutely along, and with more authority than she had ever used before, made Rachel ascend.

It was surprising to see how fear restored to Rachel the attributes of the negro race—docility, and obedience to the white. She would have resented the manner in which her "little missis" spoke at any other time, but now she followed as quietly as she could; and a good-natured sailor stood ready to help her over the remaining obstacles, to a pleasant seat on the side of the deck,

How the appearance of things had changed since last night! Such perfect order and neatness prevailed over the deck, that as Florence glanced around, it hardly seemed as if it could be the same place. All the luggage had been removed to the hold. The ropes were neatly coiled up; the boxes and barrels all out of sight; and floating above them, like the wings of Florence's dove, were the broad, white sails. The wind had freshened during the night, in the right direction, and the vessel was now flying along with all the speed of steam and sail. The sea was curled by the breeze into small rolling waves, and the long line of foam which followed in their wake was blending with the white caps, as if it were in reality the parent of them all.

The sun was just rising over the distant sea; and as its first beams struck across the water, they seemed to be opening a golden door down into the glistening depths below, and the vessel to be going with all haste in there for a voyage of discovery.

As Florence and Rachel cast their eyes upon it, it may be questioned whose soul was filled in the greatest degree with wonder and delight, — Florence, with her quick, asking, child's mind, or the negro, with the imaginative fervor of her race; seeing not the world of waters, but a clear, white, glowing expanse, over which dim and shadowy fancies floated, making it the sea of glass mingled with fire, and standing upon it those hallowed, blessed ones, who, having gotten "the victory over the beast, have the harps of God;" and louder than the roar and dash of the waves, came to the ear of the listening negro, and trembled as if in concert

from her lip, the song of the Lamb, saying, " Great
and marvellous are thy works, Lord God Almighty."

Mr. Erwin, when he came, at a much later hour,
on deck, found the two still there; and though a
little annoyed at their close proximity and affectionate intercourse, he wisely resolved to allow them to
do as they pleased, at least until their arrival at
New York should make his interference less ques-
tionable.

The day proved boisterous, but not sufficiently
so to induce Florence to go below; and Rachel, no
longer timid, and dreading to repeat her former ex-
periences in locomotion, staid closely by her, though
she suffered more from the cold, as the keen sea
breezes swept over them, than she had in all her
previous life.   At night there was every promise
of a storm; but it was not until the large drops of
rain began to fall that Florence could be induced
to go below.   There was an intense gladness to
her, child as she was, in the increasing waves.
Always accustomed to the level scenery of the
south, the very undulations of the water became a
source of growing pleasure; and when she saw a
dark, heaving mass approaching them nearer and
yet nearer, and then felt that they were tossed, like
a feather, for an instant on its crest, she clapped her
hands, and laughed merrily, in an outburst of childish glee and excitement.

But it was a very different thing when they were
shut up within the four walls of the narrow state
room, with nothing but the dismal creaking of the
vessel and the rolling of every loose thing on board.
It seemed like a tomb to Florence; and she actually

shuddered, as she laid herself down in the long, narrow berth, so like the place upon which she had, a short time ago, seen them lay her father. Fortunately, as Florence's fears increased, Rachel's seemed all to leave her; and now, as if surmising the troubled state of " little missus'" heart, she stood close by her, holding firmly on to the side of a berth, and suiting herself to the motions of the reeling ship, in a manner which would have made it impossible to recognize in her the terror-stricken being of the night before. As she stood there, she repeated many hymns aloud. One might almost think these lyrics fraught with inspiration, so strong is the hold they have upon the heart and mind of those who have been educated to love them. They were uttered to-night to this little orphan, as she lay there at the mercy of the winds and waves, not only by the good, faithful nurse, but by those silent voices who had so often repeated them over and over, that they might be to her in her future life what they were now — sources of simple, trustful comfort. And it was singular with how much judgment Rachel chose her hymns; none of those warm, exalting rhapsodies which she loved so often to repeat, but "Jesus, lover of my soul," and "Rock of Ages, cleft for me."

"Sing, mauma," said Florence, nestling closely to her; "please sing."

Then Rachel, with a clear, sweet voice, which was heard in the pauses of the storm, and startled the occupants of the surrounding state rooms, — as it had something strange and almost supernatural in its tones, — sung, one after another, of those "holy songs," until the child, lulled by them, sank to as quiet a sleep as she used to when Rachel murmured them as a lullaby over the infant cradle in her pleasant home. Then Rachel thanked the God who had sent the sleep, and sat herself down to watch by the slumbering child with a care and vigilance rendered only more intense by the increasing violence of the storm.

The lights were all put out at a very early hour, and the darkness of the state room was, as Florence had felt, like that of a tomb. Cold and darkness are the two evils against which the black race seem to have the least power of resistance ; and as- Rachel sat to-night, with her body becoming gradually more and more incapable of motion, from the intense chill of the air, and the darkness so heavy that it seemed like a real, palpable presence, she was showing the strength of that character which last night seemed like "a reed shaken with the wind."

Towards midnight she heard a crash, which she supposed was only one of the many strange noises which she was constantly hearing ; but in a moment after, Mr. Erwin opened their door, and in a voice which was so altered that she hardly recognized it, told her the vessel had struck; that they must be in imminent danger ; that she must take up Florence, and be in readiness for the long boat at a moment's notice.

"Den may that blessed Jesus, who walked on dem waters, take my precious lamb and carry her safely over in his arms," answered Rachel, in as quiet and calm a voice as if she had only been answering to a common order. " Dere is no use to frighten the child, Mr. Erwin; I will bring her, the moment you call."

"There will be no time for that," said Mr. Erwin. "Take her now, and follow me quickly. It will be a push for life or death. I will wrap her up, and carry her myself as she is."

Rachel groped around for a few articles of clothing, which Florence, having wakened at the crash, and heard in silence every word her uncle said, hastened to put on; but before she had succeeded, there came another crash, and another, in quick succession, — and catching her up without any regard to the nurse, Mr. Erwin hurried, with her, on deck. Rachel followed them, with much difficulty, a few steps; but before she was half through the crowded saloon, the passengers, all having taken the alarm, and crowding now, as best they could, towards the stairway, blocked up every avenue, and in the hurry and desperation, pushing each other frantically in every direction, sought in vain, with oaths and prayers, the passage out, which they themselves impeded. In the very centre stood Rachel; but so soon as she found how she was situated, as motionless as if she had been changed into stone. Through that darkness came a vision again of the sea of glass; and amid the din of groans, and prayers, and imprecations, she heard the "song of David."

But this excited state lasted only a few seconds; and then came to the negro a sight of the cabin under the spreading branches of the live oak, and she heard children's voices and little feet pattering round on the hard ground, and small, dark faces looked lovingly into hers; and mingling with them,

came blue eyes, and rosy cheeks, and long, waving,
chestnut curls. And then Rachel felt, in very truth,
a child's hands lay themselves on her dress, and
naturally, as she had to the children of the vision,
she stretched out her arms and took this living child
up. It was a tiny thing— a mere baby; and good,
kind Rachel shuddered, as she thought of what
might be in a few minutes before them. She felt
the warm cheek laid against hers, and she seemed
to know, as if by instinct, that it was one of the
same children whom she so summarily dismissed
from Florence's state rooms.

"God will forgive me, then," she said to herself,
"for having been so angry ; for, if I can, I will save
this child's life." And there, amidst all that mortal
agony, Rachel stood pressing the loving little face to
hers, and whispering words which the baby seemed
well to understand.

How long this lasted, no one who was present
could ever tell ; and the scene must be imagined,
rather than described. It seemed a lifetime to
many of them, during which, they thought over and
over the whole of their past lives, with a fidelity and
quickness which left upon them forever a sense of
the nearness of eternity, and the truth of the existence of a "worm that never dies." At last, their
situation, even amid the terror of the storm, excited
the notice of some one on deck ; and, partly by
threats and partly by persuasion, the crowd were
made to move so that the door which opened above
could be pushed back. Then came dashing in a
wave, so cold and sudden that nearly all supposed
the ship was lost, and they going fast to their

watery grave. Then arose one more last, long, loud, wail, followed by a moment's silence, which was broken by the voice of a negro, saying,

"Lord Jesus, bress my little missis, and take her mauma with her, to glory."

At this juncture, the stewardess, who had been busy at the pumps, came below, holding a lantern in her hand, which she cast around from time to time, not answering any of the many questions which were asked, until its light fell upon Rachel.

"Come," she said, pushing the others unceremoniously to the right and left. "I told you I would give you warning when we were going to the bottom in time, so that you could pray for both of us. Come, and pray as hard as you can; we haven't a moment to lose, and the Lord knows I have been wicked enough to need something before I can reach heaven. Come, hurry! we can count the years of our future life by seconds now."

Seizing Rachel, to whom the child still clung, she pulled her with a strong, steady hand up the stairs, along the side of the deck, where wave after wave was breaking in unceasing fury, and pushing her into a more sheltered corner just under the wheel house, she said, impatiently,

"Pray, pray for the worst sinner that ever lived. Say that if God will spare me this time, I promise to do and be better in future." And so Rachel, held up by the stout stewardess, prayed. And the prayer went up through the dark, heavy night air — shall we doubt it — to the mercy seat.

At a time like this, money takes its true value. Mr. Erwin, as soon as he became convinced of their imminent danger, had offered thousands of dollars to be insured a seat in the life boat for himself and niece; but the captain laughed him to scorn, telling him, briefly, that at such times there was but one single rule, "First come, first served." But Mr. Erwin had been too often at sea, not, on the previous day when the sky was threatening, to make himself acquainted with the ship, and no sooner did he hear the first crash than, starting up, as we have seen, he seized Florence, and easily secured a place on the deck which would command immediate access to the long boat, should it become necessary to lower it.

It was not until he was securely in this place that either Florence or himself missed Rachel. To do him justice, we must say that it was a matter of sincere regret that he had lost her. He valued her life more than he did that of any white person on board.

Even in this moment of extreme peril he did not lose the cool, considerate judgment which had always marked him. But there was no returning to look for her, and Florence, after she had made herself pretty certain that she was not with her, seemed to resign herself without any farther struggle to the fate which was so directly before her. Indeed, the cold and fright benumbed her sensibilities, as they did her body, and it was not until she heard Rachel's voice in prayer, not far distant from her, that she made any effort to leave her uncle in pursuit of her.

Dashing so suddenly away that he had no time to restrain her, she went in the direction of the voice to the spot only a few feet from her, but which the howling of the storm had made seem so much more distant, and while Rachel was still fervently praying,

Florence interrupted her with a loud, glad shout of recognition.

The day began at last to dawn, and the fury of the storm to abate. The stewardess, who knew every sign of the weather as well as the captain himself, told Rachel she was sure " she must be the prophet who prayed that it might rain, and it did — or certainly his sister; for never had such a tempest been stopped by human voice before; " and declaring emphatically, " that all danger was past," she hastened away to resume, as well as she could — perhaps a shade more hardened and wicked than ever — the work which belonged to her.

Her predictions were true; the storm gradually lulled, the wind died away, the waves rolled less and less mountainously, and by and by a bit of blue sky, no larger than a man's hand, told that God's smile would beam again over the vast deep.

The vessel, driven from her course, now slowly resumed it, and, after another day and night, the ship rode as proudly into harbor as if she had not, so few hours before, threatened to be recreant to her trust, and leave those she bore far away in those starless graves, which shall never give up their dead, until the summons of the last trumpet.

Perhaps thoughts of this event went with many of the passengers to their homes; certain it is that upon the minds of Florence and Rachel it left an ineffaceable impression.

CHAPTER V.

"WELL, Florence, here we are safe in New York,"
said Mr. Erwin, as the carriage he had hired started
slowly away from the wharf. "You are very welcome to the North."

Florence looked out of the window upon a street
crowded with bales and boxes, drays and vehicles of
every description; men and women, dressed and
looking as she had never seen them before; dogs,
pigs, and boys, wallowing in the mire; girls with
tattered clothes, without bonnets, and without shoes,
and yet white; heaps of refuse piled up at every
corner; long, high buildings, way up, Florence thought
as she tried to see their top, as high as the tower of
Babel.

She looked at her uncle in dismay, her eyes asking
what the good manners she had been taught prevented her tongue, "Is it possible I am to live in
such a dreadful place?"

Mr. Erwin was so accustomed to the business as-
pects that he never suspected how it would strike a
child used only to the quiet and cleanliness of plantation life. For himself, there was something delightful in all this stir and bustle. The very dray-
men seemed like friends; and the marks of thriving
enterprise betokened the kind of earnest, active life
best suited to his taste.

On they drove, and still the streets were filled with the same kind of people, the same kind of boxes. Florence's heart died within her; she would willingly have shut both eyes and ears, but she could not; there was a fascination in it all, and so with straining eyes she rode through the almost endless thoroughfares of the city, until they reached Broadway, just opposite the City Park.

"There are some green grass and trees, almost as large as at Myrtle Bush, for you, Florence," said her uncle, as they were passing it. "You shall come here whenever you like."

"Is this in New York?" asked Florence.

"Of course it is, my dear; and we have a great many other just such parks besides; you didn't suppose it was all streets and shops, did you?"

"I was afraid so, uncle!"

Mr. Erwin laughed, and saying a word to the driver, he turned his carriage towards the pleasantest side of Broadway, and Florence was soon lost in astonishment and delight at the beautiful things she saw in the shop windows.

It was amusing how soon, when once more in New York, Mr. Erwin forgot the peculiarity of having a black woman with only a white turban on her head in the same carriage with himself. Indeed, he had become already so accustomed to it, that he was hardly conscious what it was made so many of the passers by stare into his carriage as it drove slowly along.

Up, up, what a street! would it never end? Florence's eyes and head began to ache, and even Rachel, all astonishment as she was, began to be impatient to have it close.

5

At length they turned into a fine street, and Mr. Erwin said, —

"Here we are at home, Florence. It is early in the morning, but I hope your aunt and the children are up."

Early in the morning! Why, the sun rose before they left the steamer. It seemed to Florence almost as if it were time for noon.

The carriage stopped before a large, handsome house, with a granite front, and the driver asked, in a tone which struck Florence as being very unmannerly, "if this was right."

"Yes," said Mr. Erwin, pushing open the door and springing out; "all right — home at last."

The door was immediately opened by a white man. Florence thought he must be some gentleman staying at her uncle's, and was surprised to hear orders given to him, as she had heard them given to the servants.

"Mrs. Erwin and the children down yet, John?" her uncle asked.

"All at breakfast, sir," said John; and at this moment Florence saw peeping out, timidly, from behind the door, the sweetest little face, with bright blue eyes and short light hair. The eyes of the two children met, and seemed to know each other at once.

"Ah, there is Georgy!" said Mr. Erwin, seeing him too. "Come here, my boy, and take cousin Florence's travelling bag."

The boy sprang from behind the door, and down the steps to the carriage before Florence had time to get out; and though only a little fellow, he held out his hand to assist her, with the manner of a perfect gentleman.

"This boy is your father's namesake, Florence; you must love him for that reason, if for no other," said her uncle.

Florence looked at him as if she thought that would not be very difficult; and as she bent down to kiss him, George threw both arms around her neck, and gave her what he told her afterwards was "a good hard hug, brimful of love." But no sooner had Rachel descended from the carriage than his attention was entirely absorbed. Running back to her, and fixing his eyes curiously upon her turban, he said, "You forgot your bonnet. Wait a minute, until I bring it."

"No, no; Rachel has her bonnet on," said his father, catching hold of him. "That white cap is her hat; a very pretty one, too — is it not?"

"I don't think so," said George. "It looks queer."

"Well, never mind how it looks now, my boy. Take your cousin into the breakfast room; I will come in a minute."

Hand in hand, the two children went in through the small hall, down such a narrow, crooked flight of stairs as Florence had never seen before, into the breakfast room.

"Here they are! I told you I heard a carriage stop," said George, as he threw open the door, "and this is Florence."

A lady, still young and quite pretty, in an elegant morning wrapper, was sitting at the head of the breakfast table. On her right hand sat a girl about Florence's size and age, and in his father's place a boy some years older.

The lady pushed her chair back slightly, and held out her hand.

"Ah, Florence," she said, "how do you do? I am very happy to see you north."

She imprinted a very formal kiss upon Florence's glowing cheek, at the same time running her eye coldly over the deep folds of crape which Florence wore upon her dress. Florence was chilled in a moment. She stood quite still, with her eyes cast down, until her aunt said, —

"Ida, this is your cousin Florence. You must be very good friends, you are so near the same age, and both little girls too."

Ida rose with the primness and precision of a dancing school, and advancing a step, held her hand out, with a patronizing air, to the stranger cousin.

Florence laid hers, with its small black glove, coldly in it, and again the keen blue eye ran over her face, as it had over George's. A slight expression of pity passed over it. "How very plain you are!" it said; but fortunately no one could know what it meant, for Ida's homely, ill-natured face was a point upon which Mrs. Erwin was specially sensitive, she considering it a sort of family disgrace, only the more keenly to be felt because it was so irreparable.

Henry, the boy, waited until his sister had passed through her formal introduction, then, with a manner extremely like his father, held out both hands to Florence, pulled her towards him, and kissed her three or four times, so loud and hard that Florence was almost frightened.

"Don't be rude, my son," his mother was saying when their father entered the room, bringing Rachel with him.

His reception was hardly more hearty or less formal

than Florence's; and as for Rachel, the stately frigidity would have chilled a much colder heart than hers.

Mrs. Erwin rang the bell. "Show this woman to the kitchen," she said; and Rachel, with a despairing look at Florence, followed a good-natured Irish girl to the kitchen.

"You will like breakfast, I suppose," she said to Mr. Erwin. "I will order fresh toast and an egg, if you wish."

"By all means," said Mr. Erwin, contrasting the scantily-furnished table with that he had seen at Myrtle Bush. "Our little visitor would hardly feel as if she had any thing to eat, with this."

Mrs. Erwin's face said very plainly that 'our little visitor' must be contented with what was put before her, and not expect any extras on her account; but she ordered a slight repast, and Florence was taken to her own room "to change her dress," her aunt said, glancing again at the unfortunate folds.

But the baggage had not yet come from the boat; and Florence, not knowing what to do, or how to call Rachel, sat down the moment Ida shut the door, and began to cry. Not a glance did she give around the room, which was to be hers for a long, long year. She hid her face in her hands, and felt tired and miserable.

But she was not allowed to sit thus long, for the door opened softly, and before she could wipe her eyes to look up, two soft arms were round her neck again, and George said, —

"Don't cry, cousin Florence; breakfast is all ready, and papa said you should have a nice one. After you were gone, he made mamma send for ever so many nice things; and I tell you what, it is first rate. Come — I wish they would let me eat over again with you; but they won't, I know."

"I don't wish any breakfast," said Florence. "I wish my trunks and mauma."

"What is a mauma?" asked George, wonderingly. "I don't think I ever heard of such a thing."

"Why, my nurse, Rachel," said Florence, smiling in spite of her grief.

"O! is that black woman a mauma?" asked George, laughing very merrily. "Why, we call them negroes, or" — he whispered this softly — "niggers, in New York. I never heard any thing so funny as a mauma. Well, come to breakfast, and then you shall have her; but" — he whispered again — "don't say any thing about 'mauma' before Henry, he will plague you so."

Pulling her gently up, Florence could not but go down with him. She was glad to think her uncle was in the room; there would be a security in his presence.

Her aunt was still at the breakfast table, but Ida was busy in one corner of the room with a piece of worsted work, and did not look up, or take any notice of Florence as she passed her. Henry had gone. This was a relief, for the roughness of the kisses had made Florence a little afraid of him.

"And this is what George calls a nice breakfast," thought Florence, as she seated herself by her uncle. "Where is the hominy. I don't see any thing but toast and two eggs, with a little bit of beefsteak. How queer!"

Mr. Erwin would have been glad to have made

this first breakfast a pleasant meal, but no one seconded his efforts. Mrs. Erwin was not in the best possible mood, for two reasons, and Mrs. Erwin's moods were very important things in the happiness of the family. One was, that she had been obliged to alter her breakfast — a kind of deference which she disliked paying to a child; and another, and far more important one, she found the little southern girl quite a beauty, therefore, by contrast, making her own plain daughter seem plainer still.

"Now for the baby, Susan!" said Mr. Erwin, pushing back his chair with a sense of relief, as the meal was ended. "Florence and I will go up to the nursery and see her, if she is awake. She is the pet of the family," he said, addressing Florence, "our little sunbeam. Come, I think she looks something like you." Ida glanced up from her bright worsteds as Florence passed her, but made no offer of accompanying them; and as she found herself alone on the stairs with her uncle, she ventured to say, —

"Where is Rachel? May she come to me?"

"Certainly!" her uncle answered, pleasantly. "We shall have to establish her up stairs here somewhere. Shall we not? Perhaps she will like the nursery and Grace as well as we do."

Opening a door at the head of the stairs, Mr. Erwin called out to a little chubby thing rolling about on the floor, —

"Papa's baby! Come and see him."

The bundle of clothes gave two or three quick turns over, and then coming out head uppermost, Florence saw a round, full face, with two large blue eyes, and a few dark locks of hair hanging over a broad, high forehead.

"Come," said her father, holding out his hands; "this is your new cousin; come and kiss her."

Grace, without standing upon her feet, sidled along towards her father, putting one thumb far into her mouth, and opening her great eyes wider and wider, the nearer she approached Florence.

"What a funny little thing she is, uncle!" said Florence, laughing. "Does she look like me? How mauma will love to see her!"

By this time Grace was safely ensconced in her father's arms, and taking her thumb from her mouth, began pointing it at Florence. As Florence came up nearer to kiss her, she drew back the wet hand, and gave her a sudden slap upon her cheek.

"O, for shame, Gracie!" said her father, while Florence's cheeks reddened with anger. "This is your dear cousin Florence. Kiss her now, and say you are sorry."

The round face was held out in an instant towards Florence, and Grace lisped, "Thorry, Gracie thorry;" but Florence moved away quickly, and still looked angry.

"Come and let her kiss you, Florence. That is a naughty trick Henry has taught her; but only see how sorry she looks."

Grace's neck was bent over towards Florence, her lips moving in a series of impatient smacks, and the offending hand opening and shutting in the quick way so peculiar to nervous children. Florence could resist these pleadings but a moment longer, and one good hearty kiss made the cousins friends for life.

"A South Carolinian don't like to have her face slapped. Learn that, my little Gracie, once for all," said her father, tossing her up and down, to the child's great delight. " There now, that will do. I will go and send Rachel up here; then you will amuse yourself in your own room, or here, or wherever you please, Florence, until your cousin Ida comes home from school."

When Rachel came up to the nursery, she found Florence busy on the floor making block houses for Grace, while the latter knocked them down and tossed them about, as if that only added to the zest of the play. Here Rachel was at once at home, and would gladly have joined with them; but no sooner did she approach Grace than the child screamed, struck at her, and sidled away to the pleasant looking Irish nurse, who, busy with her needle, sat watching the group with much amusement and curiosity.

And now Florence began to exert all her arts to make the two acquainted, and by much show of her own affection for Rachel, every act of which was as warming to the chilled heart of the negro as a ray of southern sun, she at last won the baby to come near enough to lay her little white, dimpled hand in the broad yellow one of the negro. This Grace did more readily as the inside of Rachel's hand was almost white; and once there, it seemed as if the love with which the nurse's heart was filled stole down her arm, and magnetically held the baby fast.

Certain it is that Grace had allowed herself to be taken up, and after putting her round thumb first into one of Rachel's eyes, and then into another, as she had been used to in the large glass eyes of her wax doll, she began pulling away most vigorously at the neat bow of the turban, and would certainly have pulled it partly off the head of the unresisting negro, had not Florence, who had early been taught that this belonged to that world of "No, no, not touch," prevented her.

While the group were thus busy, the door opened, and Henry made his appearance. Grace struggled out of Rachel's arms, and ran as fast as her little feet would carry her to her nurse, Bridget; and even Florence, with the memory of her rough reception by the boy still fresh, made a step or two nearer Rachel. But of these unmistakable signs Henry took no notice. Coming directly before Rachel, as if he saw her now for the first time, he made a very low bow, and said with mock gravity, —

"How do you do, Mrs. Othello?"

"Her name is not Othello," said Florence, with the color mounting into her cheeks at the boy's manner; "it is Rachel."

"Ah, I beg ten thousand pardons. I thought she must be Othello's second wife, and I was wondering," — here Henry drew himself up, and assuming a theatrical attitude, made a plunge at the left side of Rachel, as if he held a dagger in his hand, — "I was wondering if he would try to put out that light — it being somewhat dark already. I tell you what, Florence, with that great white turban, and standing up so straight and tall, she looks like an Egyptian queen, such as I have seen very often at the theatre. You shall go to the theatre soon. Mamma said you should as soon as she could get you out of all that rigmarole of black crape."

Three things about this speech displeased Florence. She felt Henry was laughing at Rachel. She had no idea what a theatre was, and did not like to hear her dress called "a rigmarole;" so she stood still drawn up by Rachel's side, with very much the look of one who expects every moment to be called to spring to the defensive.

Grace, too, hid her face under Bridget's arms, and well it would have been if Bridget had allowed her to do so without taking any notice of her; but this was not her way; so she called Henry's attention by the very means by which she had hoped to divert it.

"Indade, Mr. Henry," she said, "I think it is a sin and a shame that you have been and made this darlint so afraid of you, that every time you come nigh she trembles like a leaf. An sure, if I were a big boy, most thirteen, I should be so ashamed of it I never would come nigh her."

"Stuff and nonsense, Biddy!" said Henry, crossing the room to where Grace was; "she is no more afraid of me than you are. It is only your way of making a fuss to keep me out of the nursery if you can; but that ain't so easy, you will find. Come here, Gracie," he said, adopting some very coaxing tones. "Come to Harry, and see what beautiful candy he has for you in his pocket."

Grace looked out from under Bridget's arm, but did not move.

"Come!" continued Henry; "I've some red candy, and white, and lots of pretty sugar plums. Come quick, or I shall go away with them all."

Grace sat, and looked full in Henry's face, and Bridget said, —

"Don't be for fooling her, Mr. Henry."

"Come, Gracie!" said Henry, rattling something

in his pocket with a very confectionery sound. "If you don't come quick, I shall go away, and give them to some other good little girl." Then Henry stepped towards the door. Grace immediately slid out of Bridget's lap, and ran towards him; but no sooner did he turn than she made a quick retreat to the nurse. However, the game was fairly open, and Henry was never so persevering as when bent upon mischief. Now he drew Grace towards him, until he could catch her up, which he did in no very gentle manner; but the child, in anticipation of the candy, bore it very patiently.

"Candy! .Harry! Candy!" she said, putting her face close to his, and opening and shutting her hand impatiently.

"Candy? O, Gracie don't want candy," said Henry, evasively.

"Gracie do," said the child, struggling down towards the pocket. Henry allowed her to put her hand in, and draw out, first a penknife, which she flung across the floor, then a ball of cord, which followed the knife, then some small screws, and a marble, which she tested with her small, white teeth, much to Henry's amusement; but at last the pocket was emptied, and not a particle of candy to be found. Grace's face turned very red; she doubled up her fist, and struck her brother with all her strength in his face, saying, —

"Notty, ugerly boy; Gracie don't like you one bit."

Henry laughed as if the whole was an excellent joke; and Grace, on hearing this, seemed to lose what little temper she had left, and burst into a long, loud scream, which brought Bridget immediately to her rescue.

FLORENCE IN NEW YORK.

"There, now, you are always after mischief, some way or other. If you don't come to the gallows one day, it won't be your fault; indade it won't. You never come nigh us, but you stir up a row; and I'll tell your father, as true as my name is Bridget."

Henry made a series of very low and respectful bows, every one of which tended to increase Bridget's anger; and, amid such a shower of abusive words as Florence had never heard before, he at last closed the door behind him.

For a moment she stood too astonished by the scene to attempt to move; but turning to Bridget, she asked, at length, "Didn't he say he had candy in his pocket?"

"La, yes, miss," said Bridget; "he don't think any more of telling a lie than he does of telling the truth. You will find, before you have lived with him long, that he is the worst boy in New York, if it is Bridget that says it. I hate the very sight of him."

"Come, Rachel," said Florence, almost frightened by the quick utterance of the excited Irish girl, which she could only imperfectly understand. "Come, let us go away."

"Go where, little missis?" asked Rachel, yielding to the impatient haste of the child.

"Away, back to Myrtle Bush."

"Bress de chile," said Rachel, soothingly; "one would tink dis world wasn't half good enough for her, to see how quick she runs when dat dare wicked boy tell dat falsehood — eh, eh! Dat be northern childrens. Me go back to my own little

niggers quick; dem no lie, not dey. Cato half kill
um for true."

So saying, half in soliloquy and half to Florence,
Rachel accompanied the child to the small but
cheerful room which was to be their home for the
next twelve months.

However unpropitious their first introduction had
been, a few hours here alone, busy in unpacking the
articles which had been placed in the trunks in dear
Myrtle Bush, made them feel quite at home; and it
was not until a tap at the door brought Mrs. Erwin
to investigate the condition of Florence's wardrobe,
that their pleasant dreams of contentment were disturbed. With the eye of a severe critic and con-
noisseur, Mrs. Erwin looked over the different articles as Rachel exhibited them.

Every thing had been prepared with much care
and taste, by the same kind friend with whom Florence had resided during the interval between her
father's death and the arrival of her uncle; and, in
accordance with southern taste, the style of dress
was much more decidedly English than that of New
York. Indeed, if Florence had been fitted out in
London, the wardrobe would have been almost precisely similar to what. it was; but she must have
come from Paris, to be *a la New York.* Mrs. Erwin, after some shrugs of the shoulder, had good
sense enough to find this out, and to determine to
allow the child to remain a little *distingué* in her
style. What with her own pretty face, her own
colored servant, her many slaves, and the funded
property, which Mr. Erwin assured her was not inconsiderable, she certainly had the elements with

which quite a show might be made ; and this process
no one understood better than Mrs. Erwin. Rachel,
too, should remain unmolested, white turban and all.
She would give *éclat* to the establishment, should
she happen to be seen by chance visitors. Very
happy conclusions these for Florence and Rachel,
and happier still, when, in accordance with her sud-
denly-formed resolution not to interfere with or
change their habits more than was necessary, Mrs.
Erwin gave a ready consent to Rachel's occupying
the couch in Florence's room, instead of the small,
dark attic which had been prepared for her.

The truth was,—though Mrs. Erwin did not know
it,—Florence had never been separated from Rachel
a whole night in her life ; the custom at the south
being, generally, to have the nurse occupy the same
room with the child ; if she be young and strong,
rolled up in her blanket, lying upon the floor ; if
older, and of more dignity, like Rachel, finding her
bed upon a chamber couch. To have been separated
here would have made them both thoroughly unhappy, whatever else might have been done ; but
this Mrs. Erwin did not know. It was a matter of
convenience to her ; for Ida had insisted before
Florence came, that no inducement should compel
her to share the same room.

All these matters were satisfactorily adjusted before Mr. Erwin came home to his late dinner ; and,
when, as he entered the parlor, his eyes sought anxiously for Florence, he discovered her sitting in the
bay window, under the shadow of the heavy curtains, very busily engaged with a new book, which
George had given her.

Ida was at a little distance from her, with that basket of endless worsteds; and Mrs. Erwin was "resting"—an occupation of which she was very fond—in the large easy chair; and the boys, Henry and George, were building a ship out in the small back yard.

"All going on nicely," Mr. Erwin said to himself, with a great sense of relief; "if I only can get Florence over the first home-sickness without any scenes, there will be no great trouble in the future."

To have Florence happy and contented, to have her choose this for her future home, became every day more of an object to Mr. Erwin. The large property, of which she would one day become the undisputed possessor, was by no means a matter of small moment to a man whose whole life was wrapped up in dollars and cents. He might, if he managed properly, and yet within the bounds of the strictest honesty, use a portion of it very much to his own advantage in his mercantile business. Besides, the annuity allowed by his brother to the family in which Florence should ultimately reside, was very handsome, and would go far to meet those many bills which Mrs. Erwin seemed to have the power of increasing from year to year. Altogether, it was a desirable matter, more so than Mr. Erwin chose wholly to confess to himself, that the southern child should be happy with them, and his morning experience of breakfast troubles had made him fearful that his wife would not prove more of a helpmeet in this matter than she had previously in so many others.

If he had any other doubts and fears, they were

about Ida; but she was his own child, and should, sooner or later, do as he desired. There was, also enough of the father about him to see and feel that Florence was, in many respects, superior to Ida, and might be of much use in bringing the ill-tempered, selfish child to a more proper appreciation of what "*good* child" really meant. *If* — that was a very important word in this connection — he could only bring them pleasantly together, could induce Ida not to be jealous of, but to love her fair southern cousin, one great point would be gained. How could this be done? Mr. Erwin was deeply engaged, thinking it over, feeling that the very first steps, in this case, were those of the most importance, when the dinner bell brought the various members of his oddly-constructed family around him.

Florence stood behind her chair, and folded her hands as she had that first night at Myrtle Bush; but Mr. Erwin was at his own table now, and there, never, excepting when some clergyman had happened to be present with them, had a blessing been invoked.

Henry's quick eye caught Florence's position, and understood in a moment its object.

"Father!" he said, "Florence wants to say grace; why don't you give her a chance?"

"Be still!" said Mr. Erwin, turning sharply round upon his son. "You will never know your place."

Henry laughed; and Ida, for the first time since Florence had seen her, smiled, too; but George asked, —

"Papa, why don't you say grace? Uncle Niles always does; and I like to hear him."

"Your uncle is a minister, George, and I am not."

"O, then it is only ministers who pray, is it?" asked George, in much surprise.

Ida laughed again; so did Henry. Florence could not understand why they should; and perhaps the wonder which her eyes expressed was even more disagreeable to her uncle than the criticism of his boys. The dinner certainly began as uncomfortably as the breakfast; but home discomfort Mr. Erwin was accustomed to. He exerted himself to make every thing pass off as cheerfully as he could; then proposed to take the children out for a drive, as the pleasantest ending of this first day.

But no one cared to go; and Florence was so fatigued that she gladly availed herself of the opportunity to run away to her own room and Rachel, especially as Henry, for whom her aversion was every minute increasing, showed an inclination to stay where she did, and, in his own words, "make friends at once, and have the job over." Friends with a boy who had that day told a falsehood! Florence could not understand how this could be. She watched him keenly, as she would some wild animal, of whom she stood so much in terror that she did not even dare show her fear. When she found herself on the stairs, going to her room alone, she kept constantly looking behind her, as if she was afraid he would be following her; and at last, reaching her own room, where she found Rachel waiting for her, she shut and locked her door so quickly and violently that it brought from the nurse the reproof, "What for dat, Miss Florry? Sure dem dare doors no done nothing, that you should bang dem so. Eh, eh, — gwine to be as rude as northern childrens. Sure, what Massa George say to dat ? "

So ended Florence's first day at the north.

CHAPTER VI.

"Your cousin Florence has been here more than a week, Ida Erwin," said her mother to Ida, one morning; "and I have never yet seen or heard of your doing the first thing to make it agreeable to her. Your father says he shall not allow you to behave so another day; that, now your vacation has commenced, he shall insist upon your devoting a part of your time to her. You may go now — there is plenty of time before dinner — and ask her to go with you through Broadway; and mind, we shall both insist on your showing her every thing, and doing all you can to make the walk pleasant to her. You understand me, do you ? "

Ida shook her head, or rather her shoulders, in her dumb manner of expressing her dissatisfaction, but said nothing; neither did she put up her work; while her mother stood by her, looking on with an expression which told of any thing but maternal affection.

"Do you understand me ? " she repeated, at last, very sharply. "I should think you were a block, by the way you take things. Go at once to your cousin's room, and ask her if she would like to go out with you."

Ida lifted her dull gray eye for a moment to her mother's, and seeing there the something which she knew it would not do to disobey, she began, very slowly, to put away her work.

"Ida, you are the most disagreeable child I ever saw," continued her mother, in the same tone. "Henry is bad enough; but there is nothing even as redeeming about you as there is about him."

Here Mrs. Erwin saw the color coming slightly into Ida's face, and, as if glad to have elicited some sign of emotion from the "stone," she went on in the same tone.

"I don't see why I, of all mothers in the world, should have had such children. No other one takes half the pains, in bringing theirs up, that I do; and yet their children are much more grateful and obedient than mine! It is a sin and shame to you."

Ida smiled — an unpleasant smile, which only irritated her mother the more; and one of Mr. Erwin's dreaded "scenes" was undoubtedly about to occur, when Ida made a quick retreat, but not as her mother had directed her, to walk with Florence. Stealing, on tiptoe, softly up the stairs, she was about locking herself in her own room, trusting that her mother would, as she had so many times before, "forgive and forget" as soon as she was out of sight, when she heard the door of Florence's room open, and led by an irresistible curiosity, she hid herself, and listened.

"Come, come, little missus," said the peculiar voice of the negro; "you take tight hold of your old mauma's hands, and we'll go right down where we saw all dem dare beautiful things. Rachel's eyes wan't put in her head for nothing. You tink she no see. She see every thing. Come, come, little missus."

"But, mauma, it is so noisy, it frightens me to think of it."

"Dat dare Massa George's girl, for true," said Rachel, forcing a laugh, "'fraid of noise! Ky, ky! and she South Carlinn, too!"

"I do so long for the fresh air and the sunshine, mauma! Do you suppose it is clear and bright to-day at Myrtle Bush?"

"You jes stop talking about Myrtle Bush, will you, dare?" rejoined Rachel, with a slight tremulousness in her voice. "Prehaps dare ain't no sun dare at all. Prehaps it rains, and dem dare ditches are run way over de top with de water. "Prehaps"— and Rachel's eyes dilated at the awfulness of the thought — "prehaps dare come thunder and lightning, and earthquake, and dare ain't no sich place as Myrtle Bush no more. Don't be all the time a thinking of what you can't hab. Come here, now, — hold up your head, and let me tie on this new hat your aunt bought. For true, if you don't look like mauma's little southern rosebud, now, and no mistake."

And then Ida saw Rachel, with nothing on her head but her turban, come out, leading Florence, who, as she said, did "look like a fading rosebud."

"If mamma knows I have let them go alone," thought Ida, as she saw them close the hall door behind them, "she will be very angry; so will papa. I had better follow them. But I will keep on the other side; and in the crowd, they will never know me."

So Ida put on her bonnet, and went hastily out after them. As they had gone but a short distance, she easily overtook them, though on the opposite side.

As might have been supposed, the pretty white girl, in her peculiar mourning, and the fine-looking, turbaned negro, — even in this city, where every peculiar object under the sun seems to congregate, — began to attract attention; and while Florence and Rachel were walking quietly on, Florence so much amused as to lose all fear, a crowd began to gather behind them; and Ida saw, with much concern, that if they were allowed, with their retinue, to reach Broadway, they would be in danger of collecting a mob.

There was no time for hesitation. She must cross the street, and take them into the first shop they came to, where they must wait until the crowd dispersed. So, much to Florence's surprise, she joined them, and opening the first available door, she told them, quite authoritatively, that they must come in.

Florence hesitated. A tone of command, for some reason, always raised her temper. But Ida pointed behind her, and said, in a whisper, "See there! sometimes they mob black people in New York."

Florence turned, and saw, with much alarm, herself and Rachel the centre of the eyes of the boys, and ill-dressed men and women who were behind them. So far, however, they were respectful and quiet; but no sooner did the shop door close behind them, than they uttered a short, sufficiently expressive groan to call the police to the spot.

Rachel, entirely unconscious of their share in the matter, stood at the glass door of the shop, looking eagerly out, to see what the noise could mean;

and the police officer, supposing, when he saw her, that it was some fugitive slave rescue, immediately opened the door, and ordered her to leave the shop by a back entrance, which was much better known to him than to Rachel.

Rendered perfectly helpless by the man's manner, and the knowledge, from his uniform, that he spoke with authority, Rachel, trembling and bewildered, started down the narrow lane which the anxious shop-keeper pointed out to her, followed by Florence, and for a step or two by Ida. But the latter, seeming to recollect herself, called to them to stop, and going back, beckoned to the officer, who immediately coming, she told him who they were, and requested him, with as much dignity and self-possession as if she were many years older, to call a carriage and see them safely home.

By dint of some very summary threats, he dispersed the crowd; then seating himself upon the box of the hack, which fortunately was passing, on the lookout for passengers, he conducted the party safely to Mr. Erwin's house; cautioning Ida, before he left, not to allow the negro to go again, turbaned, into the streets, while the "peculiar institutions of the south" were matters of so much excitement.

All this Ida explained, clearly and sensibly, to her cousin and Rachel, as she found herself once more safely at home. Florence could not understand it; but to Rachel, with her love of freedom, the whole affair was clear in a moment. The turban was a badge of slavery. She was now in a land where all the living human beings were their own; they could not endure even the sight of this badge

— this type of the great sin. As Rachel thought it all over, the shout, which she recalled, as they entered the shop, seemed to her the most musical sound she had ever heard, and that ill-dressed, miserable crowd to be the happiest of all the happy — those who enjoyed and appreciated being free.

They were both grateful to Ida; and with a warmth and affection with which the child had never been addressed before, they thanked her, in no stinted words, for her timely interference. Ida said, briefly and coldly, that "it was nothing; they must never go out again alone. Rachel must at once buy a new bonnet, and dress like the northern colored people;" with a variety of other good, sensible advice, which made the plain northern girl rise rapidly in the estimation of the nurse, and called forth from Florence so many and such warm thanks, that at last Ida grew bashful and silent, and a suspicion began to take possession of her that Florence was laughing at her. This was not decreased by Florence throwing her arms around her neck, and whispering, "Please, Ida, do love me a little."

Ida threw her arms roughly off, and left the room; while Florence, vexed at her own impetuosity, and grieved at the reception her advances had met, hid her face on Rachel's great broad shoulder, and began to sob.

"Now," said Rachel, raising her up, "dat what I call being a baby. I tink you was gwine to be a lady; and here you be, Lord bress me, what a child! Look at dat Miss Ida, — why, she 'have more like an old — old negro mauma, dan like a little bit child! Eh! — for shame, little missus!"

But Ida carried away from Florence, perhaps, the warmest feeling which had crept into her young cold heart for years, and for this early iciness Ida was certainly not to blame.

The first time her mother's eye fell upon her new-born babe, she saw that the child had inherited from her, what had been a family peculiarity of feature, a very large nose. This nose was by no means a common large nose; it was neither Roman, nor pointed, nor pug, but indisputably what is known as the bottle nose. The upper part of the feature was small, like the neck of a junk bottle, then it seemed immediately to dilate, and to round off, with a flat place directly in front, precisely like this same bottle. It was, moreover, *the* feature of the face, which expressed, beyond the power of the owner to conceal, every emotion; even the workings of the intellect, made themselves visible representatives here. In short, it was the family idiosyncrasy, and like all such peculiarities, a source of great family sensitiveness.

Mrs. Erwin and one brother, alone of a family of six, had escaped it. It made her the pride and boast of the nearer relatives, and with her really pretty face, she passed for a much greater beauty than she would have under other circumstances.

When, therefore, she saw this nose upon the face of one of her own children, no one can tell how annoyed and chagrined she was, or how immediately, with her weak mind and vain heart, she conveyed the feelings to the little innocent thing that lay beside her.

"What business had she, and a girl too, to have

such a nose? She had no such thing herself; it was
a sort of imposition in the child; she did it on purpose to make herself unpleasant and trying."

So fretted Mrs. Erwin in her secret heart, but of
course she did not express it in words. She only
steeled her heart against the child, and went through
the routine of a mother's duties as if it was somebody's else baby, who, by some mysterious and unjust dispensation of Providence, had been sent to
fret and worry her.

As Ida grew from the baby, the ill-starred feature
seemed to increase in very undue proportion. Mrs.
Erwin only yielded to her having the sweet name of
Ida because her husband insisted that she should,
and it began to be rumored round among Mrs. Erwin's fashionable friends, that the last baby was deformed or an idiot, before she presented the new
comer to answer to her many calls.

It need not be said that of course Ida looked better to every one than to her own mother. One old
lady very sensibly remarked, " that she was glad to
see the Norris nose coming back into the family
again. A broad, generous nose, always showed cap-
ital good sense, and if this baby was the plainest, she
had no doubt she would in time be the most sensible of the family."

This lady happened to be fully aware of the fact,
that in losing one distinguishing attribute, Mrs. Erwin had lost the other; and that Mr. Erwin, after
only a few months of married life, had found the nose
and the sense wanting together.

How well Ida might have verified the good lady's
predictions under proper influences, no one can say;

but certain it is, subjected to cold looks and cold
words, an unloved child, she grew up unlovely. No
wonder that by the time she had heart and head sufficient to see that in some way she was different from
other children in the child world, she had become
obstinate, selfish, and ill-tempered.

Her father did all that a man, who has very little
interest in home and a great deal in his business, can
do to counteract the evil; but it was so little, when
so much was needed, that Ida never learned to distinguish him in his treatment of her from her mother, and never, really and truly, loved either of her
parents.

Of course she was troublesome, a real "thorn in
the flesh," until even her mother began to consider
the nose more as an index of her actions than as a
homely appendage, and really dreaded the deep crimson, which, tipping the rounded and swelling end,
indicated a coming burst of temper, more than the
untastefulness of the look.

But in the face of all these disadvantages, Ida,
perhaps even the more for the many quiet, uncared-
for hours which belonged to her, learned to love her
books, and any employment which afforded to a very
active mind, pleasant, independent occupation. When
at last she was sent to school, she mingled very little with other children, and soon became disliked by
them, and was as uncomfortable at school as she had
been at home.

Such was Ida when Florence came to live in her
father's family; and perhaps no inmate could have
been introduced, who, so far as external appearance
was concerned, was more fitted to aggravate the al-

ready existing evils; for Florence, as we have before
said, was singularly pleasing and attractive, with delicate, classical features, and the rather peculiar mingling of the northern and southern faces.

Whether Ida had grown to a consciousness of her
peculiarities, it would be difficult to say, for she was
silent, and never confidential; but Florence had never been told, excepting by her own negroes, from
whom words of praise were as natural as the words
themselves, that she was beautiful, and so innocent
was she of attaching any special importance to the
gift of beauty, that very probably flattery would at
present have been entirely lost upon her. She had
now much to be thankful for in the ignorance of the
actual state of affairs, for whatever progress she was
to make towards Ida's affections must be made without that self-consciousness which would have de-
stroyed at once her influences.

It must be confessed, that for several of her first
days at her uncle's, had Ida been only prettier,
many little antipathies would have been spared
her, for the short face, dull gray eye, and large nose
were constantly objects of criticising study to her,
though she was unconscious of it.

The first time these children had ever actually approached each other was, as we have seen, on the occasion of this walk. To Florence it seemed to end
most disastrously for their future; but Ida found herself thinking of her fair cousin with a smile every
now and then, and recalled the fact of her arms
thrown so suddenly around her neck, very often, with
a strange, new feeling.

The next day the children went out together for

a walk, and Florence found, much to her surprise and delight, that Ida could talk, and could say very pleasant things too, if she only had a mind.

"I am very glad to see the girls are beginning to take to each other," said Mr. Erwin to his wife, as he saw them pass the window together.

"Ida never 'takes,' as you call it, Mr. Erwin," replied his wife, "to any thing or any body. She is certainly the most peculiarly disagreeable child I ever saw, and only seems the more so to me in contrast with Florence; though, to be sure, Florence's face is just like a wax doll's — no expression, no more than if it was painted."

"I think the children look enough alike to be cousins," answered Mr. Erwin, without taking any special notice of the general spirit of his wife's remarks. "George and I were always said to resemble one another very closely, especially when we were boys."

Mrs. Erwin hummed a line of a song significantly. It was an unpleasant way she had of answering her husband when she was slightly displeased. And then the conversation glided on, as it will sometimes, from one unpleasant topic to another, until the whole range of domestic grievances was made to pass in rapid review before the head of the house, ending in a somewhat sharp contest about the habits of Mrs. Erwin's pet, the wilful, strong-headed Henry, — a conversation which the hopeful youth himself interrupted.

CHAPTER VII.

FLORENCE'S fear of Henry increased from day to day, and from week to week. If she was alone in a room and he entered, she was sure to make her escape as soon as possible. If he spoke to her, she answered quickly, with her eyes cast down, and often with visible trepidation; and if he approached her, even with others in the room, she took refuge nearest the person who seemed most able to defend her.

At first, all this was rather gratifying than otherwise to Henry. It made him feel his importance; he was by nature tyrannical, and all such natures seem to rejoice as much over an exhibition of fear or distrust as a nobler one does of love and confidence. It was, in his words, "great fun" to see a delicate girl shrink from him as she would from a wild beast; and he liked to watch the color come and go, indicating dislike and fear. It gave him very much the same delight as it did to see the index of Ida's feeling glow with its intenser expression of annoyance. But Henry soon tired of this avoidance. It deprived him of all opportunity to practise his mischievous feats; and besides, in spite of himself, the bold, bad boy was becoming conscious that there was something about this little child which disarmed him — which made him feel not ashamed, but awkward in saying or doing what was ungentlemanly or improper. He had seen the look of horror which the falsehood he had told Grace about the candy had called up, and he had striven to make Florence forget it, by ostentatiously bringing the child the very confectionery some days afterwards. Grace was contented, and could easily forget; but there was one look from Florence's eyes, quick, and instantly covered by the drooping eyelids, but it said to Henry that she had not forgotten.

Unfortunately for his plans, Mr. Erwin had warned him, if he found him meddling with or annoying his cousin in any way, he would punish him so that he should not soon forget it, and he well knew this was a kind of promise which his father always kept; so he bore for a longer time than usual the inconvenience of having a subject for his amusement kept out of his reach, but all the time he was making his plans for bringing about another state of things, with as much secrecy and despatch as possible. To begin with, he changed his manner entirely both to Florence and Ida. He began to be gentle and thoughtful, and almost affectionate. Ida understood that there was something behind it; but Florence came directly under its influence, and was as blinded as the baby Grace. Even George was heard to say, as he was won into giving up one marble after another,

"If you would always be so pleasant, Harry, you would be a right clever fellow."

Nor, in this new scheme for success, was Rachel forgotten. "Love me, love my dog," Henry knew was emphatically southern; so he never omitted any opportunity of saying a kind word to the negro, and, once or twice, brought her home some southern fruit

which he found in the markets. But Rachel was
wary. She was not to be bought by a bunch of ba-
nanas, nor a basket of large oranges. The candy in
that pocket — why, it seemed to spread itself out
over every thing Henry did or said. It lay on the
top of the tempting fruit; it curled itself up over
the long stems of raisins; it sprang from the small
covered box of figs; in short, for the first time in his
life, Henry had become conscious of having committed a moral offence, which had been received as such,
in its full force, by those before whom it was acted.

He tried to call it " green," " Methodistical,"
" southern notions," "pious," and a great many other
names which a bad boy knows how to use; but he
could no more forget it than could Florence or Rachel. It stood up before him constantly, offering
him battle. He would have given almost any thing
he possessed to undo it; not because it was wrong,
but because it stood in his way — because it annoyed
him.

According to the maxim that "it is an ill wind
that blows nobody good," this change in Henry's
home life began to have a most beneficial effect upon
every member of the family, excepting himself. He
grew more hardened, more scheming, losing every
day some of the freshness and youth of an already
premature life. It is a wise dispensation of Providence that, while the guiltless must often suffer with
the guilty, by far the greater punishment always falls
on those most deserving it. Thus far, Henry was the
only one injured by his duplicity and double dealing.
Even Mrs. Erwin, rendered less nervous and irritable
by the absence of his former pranks, became less fault-

7

finding. Indeed, sunshine seemed ɯ have found
its way through the opening Henry had made.

And now, as if to be in unison with the domestic
sunshine, the beautiful summer came quickly on,
springing out of the rains and fogs of April like a
child's smile from amidst its showers of tears. Florence saw with delight the long, low windows of the
city house opening one after the other, admitting the
soft, delicious air, and the shadows which the flying
clouds sent in the place of the dance and play of the
budding leaves, to say to city children that they had
come. The very bricks and stones of the long streets
caught some of the sheen and quiver of the glad
time, and Florence knew summer was there. Mr.
Erwin had always been anxious to have his family
remove into the country through the warm months ;
but Mrs. Erwin, having unwillingly complied with
his wishes for one season, refused to make the effort
again ; so, with the exception of an occasional drive,
the children were as ignorant of the whole world of
flowers and birds as if they had lived in some stricken
planet where no such things had been created. It
was in vain that Mr. Erwin used every argument in
their behalf. A peculiarity of Mrs. Erwin's was,
never to give up a point when she could bring experience to prove her judgment correct ; and, very
unfortunately for them all, the summer in the country
had proved an unhealthy one. "If the children ever
went again, Mr. Erwin would take them, and the
entire responsibility."

This summer Mr. Erwin made a new attempt. "It
would be so good for Florence ; indeed, he doubted
whether he had any right to keep a child accustomed

to the freedom of plantation life shut up within four brick walls. It would be better to send her to his sister, Mrs. Niles, at once."

"Florence could do as he thought best," was Mrs. Erwin's constant reply; "for herself and children, the matter was settled three years ago."

Mr. Erwin thought, with a sigh, how pretty Grace's curly head would look peeping up from amidst the clover tops; but his experience told him that nothing was to be gained by combating the point; so he planned an excursion, for all but the baby, about twenty miles up the Hudson; and, not being able to leave his business himself, he determined to intrust every thing to Henry, whose age and experience made him perfectly competent to take the charge, if he would.

He was even more delighted than the others, for at last it gave him an opportunity to carry into execution a scheme for some "great fun" which he had been revolving in his mind for some time past.

All were to go but Grace; and, very unwillingly, Mr. Erwin allowed her to remain at home, especially as the morning dawned, bringing with it one of the most perfect of all summer days.

Having carried her own point with regard to the detention of the baby at home, Mrs. Erwin gave herself no trouble about the other children. For the time, they seemed only to belong to Mr. Erwin; and she saw and heard every arrangement made with the greatest unconcern. All well for Henry, for she had a certain shrewdness which led her often to suspect and put her finger on the very point which he had chosen as the one for his pranks.

What a gleeful party they were, as they hurried through their formal breakfast! There was something absolutely contagious about it. Mr. Erwin felt himself growing younger as he heard the children's merry anticipations. He had many stories to tell them of the time when he was a boy, and always lived in the country, away in the beautiful New England home; but no one heeded him much, but Florence. She had heard of that same home often from her own father; and it wakened, though the child knew it not, many memories of the dead parent.

Rachel was to accompany them. This was Henry's proposition, and Florence thought it very kind and pleasant in him. Ida was not so well satisfied. Her experience with Rachel in the street, on the morning of their first walk, was quite a warning to her — one which her good sense prevented her from wishing a second time. Mrs. Erwin had bought Rachel a neat black bonnet; but as the negro never had put one on, no inducement could prevail upon her to do so now. She would stay at home from any sight-seeing rather than wear it. Indeed, the only time she had even tried it on, Florence had put it over her tall turban, and, peeping under it, with her own face full of fun, had been suddenly sobered by finding Rachel's covered with tears.

Ida wished Rachel should wear the bonnet to-day. Nothing was more common than for the city children to make excursions into the country, under the charge of colored nurses; and as George was quite small, and they had neither of their parents with them, Ida thought they should probably escape any

observation or remark. The great trouble with Ida's
good sense was, that it was continually kept out of
sight by her intense reticence. If she ever expressed
an opinion, unless under the influence of temper, it
was done in so quiet and unobtrusive a manner, that
very few seemed to know she had done so at all;
and thus it happened, this morning, that, in spite of
her expressed opinion that Rachel should wear the
new bonnet, or remain at home, the negro was not
only allowed to go, but put on a turban a little high-
er, more spotless, and prominent than ever before.
For this Henry was responsible. He had whispered
to Florence that Ida was nothing but "a fussy old
maid," that he reckoned "he had not lived in New
York so long, not to know a thing or two," and that
it was "most likely they should find the cars half
full of nurses with the same head rigging."

Florence was delighted; so was Rachel; and it
need not be said that Ida's wiser counsel was reject-
ed. Mr. Erwin was too busy to remember any such
little peculiarity of dress, or, if he had, the matter of
appearances was about the only one which he felt he
could safely leave to his wife, and he would not have
thought of interfering.

George eyed the white pyramid suspiciously, then
said, "Mauma," — he always called her so now, and
Rachel loved dearly to hear him, — "you must wear
a bonnet. Why, the bees will sting your ears if you
go out into the country so; they will think your
head is covered with a bran-new white hive."

"Eh, eh!" said Rachel, good-naturedly. "Dat
boy tink bees no know turban from hive; dey seen
Rachel's white head many time off down in South
Carlinny."

" Tell me about them south, please ; " and George,
sitting down close by Rachel, ended the dispute, as
they were all apt to end, in asking eager questions
of that southern home, which, if Florence and Rachel's glowing stories were true, was so much more
beautiful than any fairy land.

The longest part of an excursion day, to children,
is always that of waiting for the carriage ; and
though Henry sang " Wait for the Wagon," with
much spirit and no inconsiderable music, over and
over again, it was a tedious half hour which preceded
the actual start ; but at last they were off, rattling
over the street to the station, with much more enjoyment in the very noise and bustle than either Florence or Rachel would have thought possible when
they landed, so few months before.

The train they were to take was an early one, and
the scenes around the station were of a much quieter
description than those near the wharf. They were
soon sitting in the neat saloon ; and Henry left them,
to " procure tickets," as he said, and see " that all was
ready."

The four children — for Rachel, with her great,
questioning eyes, seemed as much of a child as either
of the others — sat watching every new comer, every
motion before the door and windows, with as much
intentness as if they thought the safe arrival of the
cars depended upon them. They noticed — Ida with
much dissatisfaction — that their party attracted
more than the usual share of attention. Women
dropped in, conversed in whispers, then went out, to
come back with a fresh supply of gazers ; and now
men began to join them ; their party still being the
centre of all observation.

THE THREE HOMES. 103

These "impertinent people"—for such the glowing color of Ida's nose very plainly said she considered them—at last amounted to about twenty, reminding Ida, though they were so much better dressed and perfectly quiet, of the mob which began to assemble before.

She looked around impatiently for Henry, and was sure she saw him once peeping in through the door, with the sly, wicked look which always betokened mischief. As she sat there uneasily, a lady, really a lady in her dress and appearance, approached them, and sat down by Rachel. Taking the hand of the astonished nurse in her own delicately-gloved one, she said in a gentle, pleasant voice,—

"My sister, you are very welcome to the land of liberty."

Rachel's great eyes dilated with her amazement; but she said, immediately withdrawing her hand,—

"Thank you, missus."

"We have no mistresses here," continued the lady. "You are now at the north, and as you came, not as a fugitive, but of your own free will and accord, if such a misapplication of terms may be allowed towards a slave, you will be happy to learn that you are now a free woman, made in the image of God, redeemed by the blood of his precious Son; an immortal soul, who, having burst the bonds which once chained it down to earth, shall dare to be, in deed and in truth, *free!*"

"Yes, missus," said Rachel, a little frightened, and dropping a retiring courtesy, which said very plainly, "I have had all I can understand; please let me alone."

"Dear sister," said the lady, making a step or two towards her, quickly, as if she would embrace her, "we are all one in the brotherhood of Christ; and again we welcome you to that freedom for which our glorious ancestors bled and died."

"Thank you, missus," repeated Rachel, making a hasty retreat. "Massa George made me free before he died. I am very thankful, indeed."

"Your master never made you free," continued the lady, her voice rising as her feelings grew warmer. "He has only deceived you, as all southern masters do. You are, in his eyes, nothing but a chattel — a thing to be bought and sold. He would separate you from all your family; from your fond and devoted parents; from your noble, affectionate, and faithful husband; he would tear your children from you; even the baby at your breast he would not spare; and while drops of blood are flowing down your lacerated body, if you dare so much as to utter one word of complaint, to shed oné tear, wrung from you by the agony of your riven nature, he will command the lash to be plied harder and yet harder, while he stands by, — inhuman monster that he is, — and smiles."

During this harangue Rachel's face had assumed all manner of expressions; but the epithet with which the lady ended, seemed to concentrate her astonishment and consternation, for she burst forth with, —

"Missus, missus! for the bressed Lord's sake, missus, what dat you say?"

"Calm yourself, my sister;" and the lady put that kid-gloved hand once more on the trembling, shrinking black. "You are perfectly safe; no tyrant's power can reach you here. Never again, no, never, never, shall your broken-hearted sighs ascend to the ear of an offended God. You shall sing the glad, new song, and the key-note of your happy strain shall be — Freedom forever!"

"But, Massa George ——"

"Don't name the cruel, wicked wretch; he is no longer your master. You shall henceforth serve but one Lord; and that you may know that we, who love every drop of your precious blood as dearly as we do that within our own veins, — yea, you are, in deed and in truth, nearer to us than even ourselves — we offer you ——" Here the lady's voice sank to a whisper; but if every word had been a red-hot ball, it would not have produced greater effects upon Rachel.

Her countenance became pale, flushed; the muscles worked convulsively around her mouth, and her protuberant eyes seemed literally bursting from her head. One after another of the collected party joined her, and each one seemed to have something to say, which only added to Rachel's discomfiture, particularly as the whispered words were difficult for her to understand.

In a few minutes all Florence and Ida could see of her was the white turban, which seemed bowing up and down, as if some one had a wire in it, and was jerking it. The whispers were soon exchanged for low, confused, but earnest tones of conversation, and rising above all the indistinct answers, in the most perfect plantation tones and words, Rachel having forgotten every thing else in her fright.

The children heard, as, too astonished to interfere, they sat watching the scene.

"Neber leave little missus — eh, eh! Who you tak this nigger for? Free! free! Ky, what muama want it free, but to tak better care of Miss Florry? Massa George a wretch! De Lord forgive you. Free! Massa George! missus! Eh, eh! I jus wish Cato here, with dem dare six little nigger; you see, then, if slave not happy. I no gwine to be free. Let me be. I'm gwine back to South Carlinny. Neber leave little missus. De Lord bress her, and bress old massa, and tak Rachel back, and make her and Cato, and dem dare six boys, slaves foreber and eber. Amen."

Then followed more earnest conversation on the part of the abolitionist; and again Rachel's voice, so agitated that no one but Florence could understand what she said : —

"Money — money! God Almighty forgive you. Massa gone; missus gone; what dare old mauma want of money? Tink little missus let her want money? Ky! for shame! You neber live off down in South Carlinny."

Rachel's habitual reverence for the white would not allow her to make that violent retort which her eye and motions indicated was so easily within her power; but she stood in the centre of her circle of white friends, a perfect impersonation of the noblest qualities of the colored race. There was not now a shade of fear in the flashing, dauntless eye, which rolled itself around from one strange, excited face to another. With her arms crossed proudly over her heaving breast, and her fine figure erect, every nerve and muscle instinct with swelling pride, she might have taught a lesson to both north and south; for she could prove to the south what noble creatures those are capable of becoming, whom despising, as only a little better than the "brute beast that perisheth," they hold in a bondage so often worse than death; and to the north, that, depressed and down-trodden as they think the race, there are yet those whose cherished, almost cultured life would contrast well even with members of their own too often neglected household.

Rachel's unconscious influence, at this moment, was holding at bay the well-laid scheme for her abduction; or, as her would-be friends termed it, her liberation. The lady who first addressed her, — some dim foreshadowing spirit, in whose person was faintly gleaming forth the bright light which was so soon, like that of those God-sent angels, to burst the prison doors and proclaim liberty to the captive, — seeming now to be losing either her temper or the warm affection which so whimsically embraced the "dear sister," said, abruptly, and in rather a different tone, —

"Brother Foster, if this poor, benighted heathen does not know what is good for herself, God has appointed us her guardians, and we must force her to accept that boon of liberty which she so ignorantly and obstinately refuses. You and brother Jones must lead her to a place of safety."

Two very meek, women's-rights-looking men approached Rachel and laid their hands upon her arms. Then, with a shake which sent them both reeling from her "like cotton buds,"—Rachel said

afterwards — she freed her arms, pushed the whites
unceremoniously to the right and left, and with every
feature distorted by sudden and violent passion,
walked up to Florence, and, seizing her hand, said, —
"Come! Back to South Carlinny."

The whistle of the cars at this moment scattered
the philanthropists; but they did not leave Rachel
triumphant, nor wholly unscathed. No sooner did
she see the last one disappear, than she sank down
in a chair, trembling, cowed, half frantic with fear
and excitement. It was of no use to tell her that
the cars were waiting, that Henry was beckoning
for them at the door.

She neither stirred nor spoke; and Florence, scarcely less excited, clung to her with a fondness which
drew from the curling lip of Ida an expression of
contempt.

There was too much gratified fun in Henry's face,
when, afraid to wait another moment, he came in to
the saloon to hurry the party, for Ida to doubt that
he was at the bottom of the whole affair; so she
said, quickly, "You may order a carriage, Henry
Erwin! You have, for once, burnt your own fingers.
There is no one to go into the country to-day, and
father will very soon hear what the reason is."

There was an obstinate look about Ida's face, which
Henry very well knew how to understand; and one
glance at the half petrified negro, and the pale face
of Florence, told him that for once he might have
gone a little too far; but, at any rate, this was no time
to stand arguing the matter; the bell was ring-
ing, the train was already in motion; should he go
himself, or — it was a sudden bright thought — could

they wait for the next train? and by that time would this excitement be all over, and nothing left but the story of the "glorious fun" to be repeated to the boys, who had already been informed of what was expected to take place.

But here again Henry was mistaken. Ida insisted — and so, recovering from her fright in a short time, did Florence also — that they should immediately return home. George was sent, very reluctantly, and with great tears running down his red cheeks, to find the carriage which Henry refused to order; and soon the once happy party were on their way home, disappointed, angry, sullen. Poor Rachel, with her beautiful ideas of that promised freedom, all strangely mingled and lost in bitter words, gloved hands, white faces, and moving figures of men and women. Florence puzzled and unhappy, Ida angry and full of plans of immediate revenge, and Georgy, not trying even to act the man, but crying, sometimes to himself, and sometimes bursting out in a sharp, vexed way, which naturally brought Rachel's hand in a series of loving pats on the dimpled one which lay on her lap!

Henry was discomfited. This was an end of which he had never dreamed; and now it becomes necessary to go back a little, and see how all this happened to take place.

It would be very useless to say that anti-slavery movements were at this period very rife at the north, for there has never been a time since the manumission of slaves there, when it has not been. Owning slaves was no more a legacy to the descendants of the Pilgrims than being slaves. Sharp, shrewd, and with a deep religious basis underlying the whole

structure of worldly aims, profits, and ambitions, the
lesson was early learned, that prosperity was one and
the same thing with a "clean hand," and the rust
from the chain of a brother, be he white or black,
was a stain which prevented "the blessing."

From that day — the day of the freedom of all
northern blacks — until this very present one, a
negro face, any peculiarity of dress indicating southern life and southern servitude, was a sure match to
ignite the whole magazine of philanthropic powder.
Men and women always have been, and always will
be, found, whose business it is to agitate. Stray
straws they are upon the great ocean of life, caught
in every whirl and eddy, tossing and turning, now
up, now down, and never perhaps knowing that
their little circle is but one of the bubbles on those
restless, ever-heaving waters, and that, as they spread
farther and yet farther, it must inevitably be lost in
the smooth, onward current, "held in the hollow of
his hand," and "turned even as the rivers."

A few of these choice spirits were known to
Henry, and to them he had communicated the fact,
garbled, and suiting his own purposes, that a slave
was now a resident in his father's family; that she
had formerly belonged to his uncle, who, having
lately died, had left her, with one hundred and fifty
others, to be sold under the hammer, as soon as she
should return south in the fall; that she had the
most ardent desire for freedom, and it was at her
earnest intercession that he applied to them to assist
her to run away, and remain hidden in Canada until
this dreaded sale should have actually taken place.

He told them of the excursion which his father

had planned into the country, promised to make Rachel well acquainted with their plans for her release, and to have her ready to accompany them at a moment's notice.

How faithfully Henry kept his word to either party has been already seen. Indeed, he had promised himself as much fun with the rescuing party as with Rachel; and during the whole affair had been peeping in behind the door ready to seize and appropriate for his own future use any tragic incidents which might occur.

But now these were all over, and there were to come some after-consequences, never so pleasant to a bad boy. Henry's had already begun in the loss of the day's sport in the country; but his father — what would come from him? Henry asked himself this several times during his drive home, with a good deal of uneasiness; and well he might, for he knew that his father, if fairly roused, could be most unsparingly severe.

Mr. Erwin, on his return at night, found a sober family waiting for him. He had not expected them until a late train; so his first inquiries elicited from the impatient Ida the whole story. This he heard in ominous silence — a silence which even Mrs. Erwin dared not break, though she longed to throw in her usual supply of excuses for Henry's faults.

Henry himself had wisely kept out of the way; nor did he make his appearance until dinner was nearly over. Then he was authoritatively ordered to his own room — an order, the tone in which it was uttered did not leave him an instant in doubt must be obeyed.

The other children were sent away as soon as possible ; and if we were to judge from the sound of the voices of the parents, we could easily imagine a scene not at all in accordance with Mrs. Erwin's taste. The result, however, was made manifest early on the next morning. A threat which Mr. Erwin had often made before was now at last to be carried into execution. Henry should be sent into the country, to a strict boarding school.

There was not allowed an hour of unnecessary delay. Mr. Erwin himself superintended every preparation, and taking the reluctant boy almost by force, hurried him off as fast as steam could carry him, to a home where there should be fewer opportunities of doing mischief.

What a sense of relief it brought to the house ! A troublesome child can do more to bring disorder and real unhappiness into a family than any other one thing. Poverty, sickness, even death, fail to disturb its elements of peace and happiness in so constant and thorough a manner. Now, therefore, every one, even the mother, after her first vexation was over, had a sensation of rest, of ability to do what and when they pleased, without being subjected to the interference of a prying, quick, ill-natured, roguish boy.

Ida's long summer vacation wore slowly away. "It were a sin," Mr. Erwin said, "to confine the children to masters during these hot months. If they would keep themselves alive, and one ray of color in their white cheeks, shut up as they were in the oppressive city air, it were all he would ask of them." So both Ida and Florence were left to find amusement or employment as they fancied, without being under the supervision of any one. Ida was accustomed to this life, and found enough to do. She would spend hours in her father's library, reading books which seemed far too old for her, or practise over and over again the already well learned lessons on the piano. Of her needle, too, she was very fond. In short, active and energetic by nature, and never having the temptation of kind words and pleasant home life to amuse and occupy her, she had early learned to care for — and it must be confessed *only* for — herself.

Florence looked upon her with wonder. Never before having been left to regulate a day, hardly an hour, of her life, she found herself listless and unoccupied during these long, weary weeks; no garden to put her foot into; no negroes to see and talk with; no plantation to stroll over; no birds to hear sing, as she leaned so longingly out of her high chamber window; no green leaves to watch, as they danced and quivered in every lifting breeze; no lessons to learn, or sewing to do, or steps to take; in short, no one to take care of, or think much about, but a little girl, who, just then, proved herself a very tiresome companion — Florence Erwin.

Ida read, but always to herself; never told Florence even the name of the great books in which she was so much interested; and when Florence's good manners allowed her to peep cautiously over her shoulder, she always found it a book she had not ever heard of before.

Did Ida never play? Florence asked herself this question many times, but never with a satisfactory

8

answer. Once in a great while Ida came to the nursery, where Florence spent most of her time, and watched Grace's frolics with a droll old smile; but her expression always said to Florence, "I think *you* are very silly for so old a girl. Why, you seem almost as much of a baby as Gracie herself."

Sometimes, but very seldom, Ida would ask Florence to walk with her. As a general thing, she slipped out quietly by herself; and as Florence was now enough acquainted with those parts of the city nearest home to go safely, she left her to take care of herself.

In short, not being at all dependent upon Florence for her own happiness, or not knowing that she was, Ida forgot that it was possible Florence might need a kind word or action sometimes from her — a selfishness which no one pointed out to her, and which, from her education, the poor child could never have discovered for herself.

Fortunately, Florence had been so little with other children that she did not give the thing its right name. She only knew that Ida was always busy, while she had nothing to do, and almost always silent, when she had so much which she would love to have said to her.

She began, though unconsciously, to adjust herself to this phase of Ida's character — to love her in spite of her coldness and shyness; for to love was as natural to the little southern girl as to live. She could, when she was weary of the stillness and silence of the parlor, or the library, where she had sat watching Ida, take refuge with George or Grace, both affectionate and demonstrative, and both very fond of her.

With them, Rachel, too, as the summer wore slowly away, found her occupation and amusement. George — whether from his name, or a look in his eye like that of the dead master — was her especial pet. She spent hours reading to him, making him kites, and spinning his tops. Florence had grown too large for the seat that had never been long un-filled before — Rachel's good, broad lap; but George soon learned to clamber into it; and the greatest trouble the nurse had was to settle which had the right to it — Grace or himself.

Bridget found her place quite a sinecure, Rachel did the week's mending so much more quickly and neatly than she did. Disorder, and the whole list of nursery untidinesses, were so repugnant to the habits of the negro, that, after she came, the children's room kept itself clear, Bridget said. Then Grace never cried for her, if Rachel was with her; and Bridget's flirtation with the man-servants could be carried on very much at their leisure, in the small, shady back yard. In short, Rachel made herself useful in so many quiet, unobtrusive ways, that she was a blessing to the none too well ordered family, and in being useful, was growing more contented and happy herself.

The southern correspondence fell mostly into her hands; and perhaps we cannot convey to our readers a more accurate impression of the way in which northern life was received by her, than by opening for them the next long letter which goes weekly to Cato, — charging them to bear in mind that it is not written by an uneducated negro, but by one, of whose endowments many a half-educated white might be envious.

"My Dear Husband : —

"There is no use in disguising the matter to you
at all. I may write volumes of all the strange and
beautiful things which I see and do at the north,
and yet you will see, through them all, that I am
very far from happy. Even my own little missis
seems altered to me since we came. She has learned
to call me 'Rachel' — never says 'Mauma,' unless
we are alone, and the door is tight shut. For the
last week I don't think she has kissed me once.
She grows older, and begins to take airs upon herself, more like this strange child Ida than like my
little missis ; and yet sometimes she is the very
darling again, just as she used to be at Myrtle Bush.
Last night I was all alone in her room, waiting for
her ; and perhaps, Cato, there might have been some
tears on my cheeks — I don't know. I had been
thinking about my Dick, and how cunning the little
fellow was when I put him out to aunt Dinah to
take care of, when Florence came softly in. I
didn't hear her, for a wonder ; but the first thing I
knew, she threw her arms around my neck, and
said, 'Mauma, why don't uncle ever have prayers,
as my father used to ? Don't he believe his family
want God to take care of them, as much as we did
at Myrtle Bush ? '

" 'Your uncle, Miss Flossy,' I said, 'is not a
religious man, I suppose.'

" Then Flossy opened her great blue eyes, and
looked at me so strange like. 'What will he do,
then, mauma, when he comes to die ? '

" I told her I hoped God would convert and save
him before that time came ; but, Cato, I hardly

know what to say to a great many strange questions
she asks me. Nobody here seems to care or know
any thing about religion. Even Georgy, dear little
fellow as he is, is as ignorant as some of those plantation negroes at Mr. Crane's. And it is no wonder; for they have no Sabbath here, and no Sabbath school; and I don't believe the poor child ever
heard a word about those beautiful Bible stories
until I told him.

"When I say they have no Sabbath here, I mean
they don't keep it as we do at Myrtle Bush. When
Mrs. Erwin is well, — which is not very often, —
she takes the two children — sometimes George
goes too — and drives, in the morning, to a great,
splendid church, near by; I never knew any one but
the servants to go in the afternoon. Mr. Erwin stays
at home all day; I don't know what he does. He
spends his time alone in the library. Miss Flossy
says the church is so large, and it has so many
people in it, she can't hear or understand much that
the minister says; and I do really think, if I wasn't
here to keep reminding her of it, that the dear child
would forget there was any such day as Sunday.
Not that she has grown wicked; for she is just now,
as she always was, one of Christ's pet lambs; but
that every thing is so strange, so unchristian, so
worldly like, that it don't seem sometimes as if it
was the same world that we were living in at home.
O, Cato, Cato! it is a beautiful thing to be in a land
of liberty. But I can't help wondering, sometimes,
if people find it as easy to remember God, and their
immortal souls, here, as they do where they haven't
any particular care of their own bodies. Don't think

for a moment that I would ever be a slave again, or that I shall rest day or night until you and our boys are all free. But, after all, I don't know but what, if it wasn't for my little missis, I should rather be at Myrtle Bush; though I wouldn't be sold, Cato, — never, never.

"This north is a very strange place. You know I wrote you about those people that called me 'dear sister,' and wanted to carry me away; well, every time I go out, which is more and more seldom, people seem afraid of me. They get as far on the other side of the walk as they can, so not to touch me as they pass; and when I go into a store, they look at me as if a dog came in. No one speaks and bows to me, as the whites all do to us at home, whether they know us or not; and I haven't seen a smile on a white face since I have been here. The negroes, too, Cato, — the free negroes, — you can't imagine what a singular race of beings they are. But my letter is already too long. I wish I could show you George, with our Master George's eyes and pretty way of speaking, — and the baby Grace ; but none of them all are equal to our own little missis. The Lord bless her, and you, Cato, and our six boys, forever and ever: Amen. Let me hear very soon from that best of all earthly places, dear, dear Myrtle Bush."

In this long letter Florence enclosed one, written not so legibly but that Rachel felt it necessary to dot the *i*'s and cross the *t*'s, in order to insure Cato's reading it. Here it is.

"DEAR CATO : —

"I do so long to be back in my own Myrtle Bush! Tell Dinah, and Rose, and Chloe, and Hannah, and May, and Penelope, and Jane, and John, and Sambo, and Cæsar, and Peter, and Nero, and Sam, and Dan, and all the others, that I don't forget them ; that I am coming back to them some day, and then I shall never go away again.

"Send old Rachel my white pullet, and Hannah my three bantams ; let Cæsar have the two old pigeons, and Natty the four fan-tailed ones. I can't give away any more now, but will try to the next time I write. Don't let Fan forget me ; give her a handful of ground-nuts, and tell her her missis sends them to her ; and don't let her forget her trick of laying her ears back when I talk to her. I do want to ride her so much! Send me some jessamines, and a rosebud from the bush close by the front steps. Water my japonicas every day, tell Bob, so I may see them grown to great trees, when I come home ; and don't forget the little row of laurels papa planted for me, close under my window ; and tell every body 'How d'ye,' from this little missis, way off north.

FLORENCE ERWIN."

With such messengers passing weekly between them and their southern home, Florence and Rachel passed away the first few homesick months of their northern life ; and it was not until the brief summer was ended, that Mr. Erwin began to form any plans for the accomplishment of the object for which, in reality, Florence had been sent to him — her education. In this he had acted, perhaps, more kindly

than wisely; for the child had many long, weary
hours in the past to remember and weigh in the
balance, when the day of her final decision should
come.

She had not been, at any time since Henry left,
positively unhappy, neither had she been happy;
and it may fairly be questioned whether this nega-
tive state is not more trying to an active, sensitive
child, like Florence, than a little real misery. Certain it is, she became, every week, more and more
listless; and Rachel was distressed by finding idle,
tardy habits replacing those good ones, over which
her parents had watched with such untiring fidelity.

"Dis dare de north," she used to say, impatiently,
to herself. "Lord bress South Carlinny."

CHAPTER VIII.

Mr. Erwin could procure good masters; and with doing that, all his educational responsibility ended.

Ida at first refused to study at home, with Florence; and Florence herself shrank from competition with one who could read and seem so deeply absorbed in large books. But having made up his mind as to what was best, Mr. Erwin was unchangeable. Ida should leave her school, and share the home advantages of her cousin; and so the early fall months found the children with much more to do than they could with any thoroughness or propriety. An English teacher for primary branches, a French teacher, an Italian teacher, music, singing, and drawing, — why, they were enough to turn older and much wiser heads than either Florence's or Ida's, particularly as they were responsible for their lessons to no one but the teachers.

Poor Florence was utterly confused, and lost in the labyrinth; grammar and arithmetic mingling together without any dividing line, so that she used often to sit with her slate before her, and wonder by what rule of syntax she was to do this, that, and the other sum. The French and Italian verbs all belonged to one mode, and that was to the teacher the objective; while the straight lines of her drawing ran into crooked music notes; and she hummed her

songs, instead of playing her new exercise on her
piano. She had, moreover, never recited in her life
to any one besides her own parents, or Rachel; and
the patient, gentle affection, which brought out the
half-acquired knowledge, had done more to advance
her in her studies, than her study itself. There was
something embarrassing, almost to the degree of
stupidity, in those cold strangers' eyes, that seemed
counting her answers, not by their information, but
by the minutes of their own precious time, which
the slow utterance occupied; and so Florence, though
naturally quick and intelligent, came very near being
considered a dunce.

Ida, always accustomed to strangers' eyes and
the care of herself, was in no manner discomposed,
either by the variety or crowding of their day's
occupation. She always seemed to know her lessons; always gave a correct and ready answer, and
soon became the decided favorite of all the masters.
This was a kind of preëminence to which Ida was
accustomed. Her very silent, reserved habits gave
her the power of concentrated attention, and of
speaking to the point, when she spoke at all; and
now, it must be confessed, she took more pains
than usual with her lessons. Florence was prettier;
she was more amiable; she was rich. Every body
would love her better; every body would admire
her more. But she herself was the more intelligent;
she would rule every body, even Florence, by that
invisible power which, child as she was, she already
recognized as belonging alone to knowledge. She
never once thought of trying to assist Florence.
From surprise at her stupidity, she began at last,

with the teachers, to consider her a dunce; and the affection which Florence's sweet, winning ways had begun to awaken in the young, cold heart, was soon laid to sleep again, by the dull answers which the half-acquired lessons elicited.

Ida was ashamed of her, and in these reticent natures pride is the great source of all the feelings; even the very silence is only its outward and visible form.

Had Florence come out boldly as a rival, disputed with Ida the precedence in every inch of their progress, and been often the victor, she would, selfish as she was, have respected and therefore loved her more.

As it was, Florence grew day by day more unhappy and more stupid. Rachel shared with her all her anxieties, and very often, if any one could have looked into the room, they would have found the negro with the French Grammar in her hand, endeavoring to point out what it could be that troubled "little missus" so. Florence grew pale, thin, and fretful; no one observed it but Rachel. Her uncle had done his duty — provided the best and most expensive teachers; the responsibility now rested with them; and for the rest of the family, Florence might have been in the last stages of consumption without attracting their notice, unless Mrs. Erwin had found the sound of her cough "unpleasant."

Rachel devised every method in her power to check the evil, but every one failed.

One day she resolved to ask Ida to help her cousin; but even the negro's pride revolted over this tacit allowance that Ida was smarter than "little missus," and the next she would wait in the hall for

Mr. Erwin's return home from business, determined to point out to him the changes in her darling; but his cold, northern look was always like ice to the warm-hearted slave, and she would shrink away from the wondering glance of his sharp eye, as if it had contained a peremptory order.

George became now her only hope. So, one day, taking him up in her lap, and looking at him very seriously, she said, —

"Does Ida love you, Georgy?"

"No, not much," said the boy, promptly; "I don't think she loves any body. She never kisses me, or Gracie either, as Flossy does. I wish I could swap, and have Flossy for my sister and Ida for my cousin, so she would one day go way off south!"

"Would Ida do what you asked her if you were a very good boy?" pursued Rachel, without taking any notice of the boy's wish.

"I think not, mauma; she never does. I never ask her to do any thing. I always ask Flossy, now she is here."

"But some day, if you will try, I will tell you a great long, long story, about a big alligator that ran after a little black boy."

"Yes, I will," said George; "now tell me about it; did it catch the boy?"

"O, I can't tell you until you get Ida to do what I want her to, then it shall be ever so long, and all about the terrapins too."

George's face fell, and he immediately commenced the fretting process, which always brought about the desired result; but this time it was destined to fail, and George was obliged to wait until he had performed his part of the engagement. Rachel explained to him very clearly what it was; and with a child's impatience he ran away at once to do his best, not forgetting, however, after he had started, to come back, put his head into the door, and inquire if he should hear about the alligator if "Ida said she wouldn't." Rachel promised, and away he flew once more.

Rushing into the library, which Ida made her study during her father's absence, he found her sitting at the table with her Italian books before her.

Ida looked up, annoyed by the interruption; but George was too full of the alligator to care. So, walking boldly up to her, he climbed on the rounds of her chair, and peeping over her shoulder began to spell out the Italian words.

"Stop," said Ida, fretfully, "and go out quickly."

"I won't disturb you," said George, in his sweetest tones, and at the same time venturing to lay one of his fat, dimpled hands on her cheek. "I want to see those funny words. Read me a sentence, please."

Ida was not used to the silent language of the child's hand; it was in reality more unknown to her than that locked in the volume before her; but she leaned her cheek slightly towards the soft intruder, and read the sentence she was that moment translating.

"How pretty," said George, quite forgetting the object of his mission in the pleasant sound. "More, Ida, please."

Then came more and more — that never-ending child's plea; and in the midst of the sport George suddenly remembered what he had come for. With more than usual tact for his years, he exclaimed, —

"Flossy can't read this so pretty, I know. Why don't you help her, Ida? Rachel says she is sick and pale, and wants somebody to show her a little, only just a very little, as her papa used to."

"I don't see why she can't get her lessons as well as I can mine, if she has only a mind to study," answered Ida, with a toss of her head; "I never ask or want any one to help me."

"But Rachel says it is all so strange and new to her; she never had a single master before in her whole life."

"That is none of my business, I am sure," said Ida, still petulantly; "I wish you would go away, George, and let me study."

"And you won't help her a bit?" said George, sliding down, and putting the end of his two fingers in his mouth, his usual manner of commencing a good loud cry.

"Go away, quickly," said Ida; and taking hold of the little fellow's hand, she forced him out of the room, locking the door behind him; and George might be easily traced all the way to the nursery, by the noise of which he was not yet quite manly enough to be ashamed.

Whether Rachel took the attempt for the success, does not appear; but certain it is, the cries ceased very soon after the nursery was gained.

Ida, for some reason, could not go on with her lesson as easily as she had before the interruption. Florence's pale, sad face looked up at her from her book, instead of the printed words, and she could not help repeating to herself what George had said — "She never had a master before." As we have be-

fore said, Ida was by no means naturally bad hearted; she might have been selfish, but not to the extent which she was now, had her education been
different, or even the one unfortunate feature of a
nose changed. She could not, therefore, forget Florence, though she tried by every means to do so, and to
keep her attention fixed upon her lesson. At length,
growing impatient, she threw down her book and
took up her drawing. Still, on the clear white paper came out the long dark curls and drooping blue
eyes. It would not do; she must go and see what
Florence was doing. She had no doubt she should find
her working away at those arithmetic sums that she
herself had finished a fortnight ago.

Florence studied in the dining room. There was
always something going on there to distract her
attention, but this had never occurred to Ida, as she
appropriated the best and quietest room to herself;
nor did it now, though she found Florence endeavoring to be quiet, with the table girl busy in "setting the room to rights." There she sat, with her
slate and book before her, as Ida had anticipated, but
with such a vacant, sad look upon her face, that Ida
wondered, with a start, how any one ever could have
thought her pretty.

Drawn irresistibly towards her, she came to the table, and leaned over it. Florence looked slowly up;
she seemed hardly to think how unusual it was to
see Ida there.

There was something appealing in the look, though
Florence was all unconscious of it; and Ida took up
the Arithmetic, and in a minute, erasing the sum
which Florence had been so hopelessly performing,
she put it down clearly and correctly.

"Thank you," said Florence, with very little change of expression; "but I don't understand it, nor any thing else, I think, now I haven't my father to teach me."·

Ida looked up from under her light eyelashes, but did not say a word. If there had been a tear in Florence's eyes, she would have called her "baby," and given her up; but there was not — only the same settled, sad, stupid look.

"They are easy enough," she said, almost kindly. "I can do them as fast as I can say my multiplication table."

"How I wish I could!" said Florence, with a little more animation.

"You can; come, I'll show you. You have only got a little flustered, somehow. Mr. Crane is a miserable teacher in arithmetic. I have half a mind to complain to father, and ask him to get somebody else."

Ida drew her chair close up to Florence, and began to clear up some of the mist which had gathered around the sums, in a very intelligible and teacher-like manner. Perhaps it was this, but more probably it was a return to the old way — a kind look, a kind word, which made the difficulties vanish one by one. Certain it is, that when, after an hour's pleasant and very patient work, Ida left Florence to return to the Italian lesson, she saw a grateful smile look up from its pages, instead of the haunting one of an hour before, and Florence went through the morning's task with more heart, and consequently more success, than she had for a long time.

Rachel, with her keen, watchful eye, read the

change the moment she saw Florence; and if George had not heard the alligator story, he certainly had it in full length now, before he was put to bed.

If Ida had been both slow and selfish in waking up to a consciousness of Florence's trouble, she seemed desirous to make amends. Proceeding from one lesson to another, she quite constituted herself teacher; and if sometimes a little imperious, calling the blood quickly to the cheek of the young southerner, she was generally not unkind or dictatorial; and perhaps the most valuable lesson of all, she was learning herself, while she thus taught her cousin, to love — love naturally and warmly. Bending over the same book, drawing from the same picture, playing at the same instrument the same piece, the two little girls grew nearer and nearer to each other, and thus far Florence exhibited no claim to an excellence which could for a moment be considered as rivalling Ida.

Mr. Erwin saw, with pleasure, that the children were becoming attached. Mrs. Erwin noticed nothing but a spot, sometimes, upon their dresses, untidy hair, or some breach of good manners which happened to annoy her personally. She was fully immersed in a round of fashionable life, and had less to do with the true management of her house and children than Bridget, the nursery maid.

Sometimes she would call sharply to Florence, as she did to Ida, if she leaned her elbows on the table, kept her feet or hands in motion when they should have been still, swung her scissors on her fingers, or indulged in any of those thoughtless childishnesses

9

which require early and careful watching to prevent awkward habits in the grown person ; but
as for an inquiry into her studies, her habits of
daily life, or her moral training, it may be doubted
whether Mrs. Erwin ever remembered there were
such things.

˜ Mr. Erwin left no measures neglected which would
make Florence's residence in their family add to the
personal comfort of its mistress. To own a carriage
had always been the height of Mrs. Erwin's ambition. Now Mr. Erwin told her, as the cold weather
was coming on, and Florence would not be able to
walk as much as would be necessary for her health,
he had determined to buy carriage and horses, so
that she could go when she liked. While they would
be in truth and reality Florence's, he did not care to
have them called so, or to have the child know it;
he was afraid it might make her purse-proud; so,
with the strict understanding that Florence was to
have them whenever she wished, and go where she
pleased, he should consent to purchase them.

Nothing could be better suited to Mrs. Erwin's
taste and vanity; she even had a thought that day,
at dinner, of letting the children have a party, or
doing some little thing, to make Florence happy.

Ida was not informed of the terms on which the
new acquisition to the family comfort was made;
and great was her astonishment to be told that her
mother had at last reached the ultimatum of her
earthly desires, and rode, not in a hired hack, but
in her own neat and tasteful carriage — greater still
when day after day passed, and Florence and herself
were always allowed it for a long drive before the

morning lessons began. George, Grace, and even
Rachel to hold the baby, were often sent with them;
and those of the neighbors who took the trouble to
notice other people's business, wondered that the
fashionable Mrs. Erwin had suddenly grown so domestic, and ordered a carriage to give her children
an airing every day.

Florence had never become accustomed to the
noise, bustle, and being pushed about of the busy
street; and she enjoyed, perhaps more keenly than
any of the others, the ease and safety of the rides,
particularly if Rachel was with them. As the cold
weather increased, the increase of gayety in the
streets and in the shops was delightful to her. She
had no loss of flowers, or green and living things, to
mourn. The canaries sang as sweetly out of the
half-open windows, and the long, narrow strips of
blue sky were even deeper and richer than before.

Florence grew daily more and more contented,
more happy, and thought less frequently, and with
less yearning, of that far-off southern home. She
began to forget that there was such a thing as a
blessing invoked upon their meals, that there ever
could be family prayers any where but at Myrtle
Bush. All the religion of life lay far away, with so
many other things that had gone, with her father
and mother's grave, or with the negro cabins in the
grand old southern woods. To be sure, Rachel insisted that she should say her prayers every night
and morning, as she used, and would read to her
when she was so weary of the sight of a book, that
even the Bible her father gave her was not welcome;
but no one else troubled themselves about her; and

as for Sunday, if it had not been that there were no tasks, no masters, and church half a day, she would never have known when it came.

Poor Florence! she is in danger now of losing what to her is of more priceless worth than even the parents who are slumbering so far away. Rachel does her best; but she finds "little missus" often refractory, very often careless and thoughtless; and then the nurse begins to long for the six boys, whom she never knew she loved half so well before.

The cold weather creates in Rachel a kind of timid awe, as the sea did. Any new bodily sensation the negro race are peculiarly sensitive to, and shrink from, yielding, not resisting, as if this were the law of their being. George's little, cold, red hands elicited from her as much true sympathy as if they were actually injured; and it was curious how the boy, unused from babyhood to any other kind of petting than that of his nurse, clung to the soft, loving demonstration of the good negro.

"He is de only ting at de north, little missus," Rachel used to say, " dat is not afeard of your old mauma. De Lord bress de little soul, and make him jest like dat good Massa George who name for sure he got."

"I am half jealous of him, mauma," Florence would answer. "You love him better than you do me now, I think."

"Eh? eh? De Lord forgive you, Miss Flossy! What mauma here for, den? Why not go home to Cato and those six boys? Jes' answer me dat 'are, will you?"

And then Rachel had a glad, swelling sense of freedom, which lit up her eye, and made her heart bound with the knowledge that she could go back if she chose — that now, *now* she was *free*.   How it took away the chill from the cold, northern air!

CHAPTER IX.

CHRISTMAS was coming, that festival day both north and south. Florence proposed — almost her first request to her uncle — "that Rachel and herself might be allowed to send a box of presents to Myr. tle Bush." Mr. Erwin willingly consented, and, giv.. ing Florence a sum of money much larger than she had ever possessed before, told her the carriage should take them wherever they pleased to make their purchases. The long term of study was over, the masters all dismissed, and the children's time at their own disposal. Henry was to come home for the holidays; but he had been away now six months, and every one seemed to have forgotten how troublesome he was. They even began to speak of his return as something which would add to their merriment — all but Rachel, who never heard his name mentioned without rolling up her eyes, and uttering a most emphatic groan. But even she was too busy and happy now to trouble herself much about him. This box for home — it seemed to her like Jacob's ladder, and every little remembrancer that was put into it like the angels which descended and ascended it between herself and that heaven of a southern home. Florence, too — it seemed to recall her former life to her. The first thing in the morning was to plan some gift for an old negro, perhaps, whom she had not named for months; and the last thing at night was, to go

over, with a deal of satisfaction, every addition that
had been made to their treasures during the day.
No one was to be forgotten — not even the bits of
babies who had looked first, with their round, tawny
faces, upon the world since they left Myrtle Bush.
Ida became interested with them ; and though she
listened with a sort of contemptuous smile to the
expressions of ecstatic joy with which Florence wel-
comed each new gift, and could make neither beginning, middle, nor end to the plantation jargon in
which they seemed naturally to speak of plantation
matters, yet she brought to them, what they very
much needed — some experience in spending money,
and a good deal of common sense as to the value of
the articles purchased. What a task it was! Even
Florence's enthusiasm was beginning to flag; and
here, again, Ida's indomitable perseverance came to
their aid. It was play to her, as good as a Chinese
puzzle, to fit each gift to each person ; and so, with
only occasional interruptions, the work proceeded.

It must be shipped early in December to insure
its arrival on the plantation by Christmas. There
could be no delays after the day Mr. Erwin appointed. This Ida very well knew, but could hardly convince the somewhat dilatory Florence.

"To-morrow we will buy for Juno, and Sylvia,
and little Cato, and big Jim," she would say, as she
threw herself wearily back in the carriage.

"Not to-morrow," Ida would answer, "but to-day.
To-morrow we have more than we can do of the
things we arranged to buy then. We must keep on,
Florence ; don't be lazy."

Florence pouted, but kept on ; and ten days before

the appointed time, the box was ready to have the cover nailed on.

Of course this was the subject of conversation among the children and Rachel for many short fall days. Even Mr. Erwin was insensibly drawn into it, and showed more interest than he often did in any domestic affair; but to Mrs. Erwin it had become excessively tiresome. She thought it equal to Pandora's box, filled with all manner of evil, and was as anxious to have it off as the others.

Just as it was thus nicely completed, Henry came home. He had grown some inches taller, had a regular country bronze to his complexion, which quite improved him, and was much more like his father than he had ever been before. His voice, too, seemed to have strengthened or mellowed during his absence. Mrs. Erwin, looking at him with much pride, thought it would not be many years before he would be quite presentable; and if it did make her seem older to have a grown-up son, why, it almost made amends to have such a one. His father had paid some bills for him, during his absence, which he had not liked to mention even to his mother; so his reception was a little more in accordance with his memory of the past; and he could not but notice, with pain, that Henry's eye fell when his first rested upon him.

Ida was not glad he had come, and took no pains to appear so. Florence shrank away, as usual; but his pockets were filled with presents for the two little ones, and they alone seemed satisfied and pleased.

Henry was too old to take much notice of either of the girls; so he thought. He had many stories to tell of his country life; but they were for his mother, and the others might have the privilege of listening if they wished.

Of the box and its contents he was made soon aware by George; and Ida noticed the old, peculiar smile come back over his face as George enthusiastically described it, giving the name and quality of each gift, and the negro for whom it was intended, as if he had been in very truth southern born and bred. She tried to arrest the current of information; but George had a new, interested listener, and the box was soon emptied of its contents before him.

"Well, Master Henry," she thought, as he had at last heard enough, "if you are planning to play off any of your old pranks on this box, as I shrewdly suspect, from your face, you are, I am on the watch; so look out."

And Ida was as good as her promise. Henry never put his foot in the direction in which the box was, but, on some pretext or other, she followed him, putting her great nose, always red and glowing when she did so most unexpectedly, in his way, if his way led towards the store room. It would be difficult to imagine why Ida should have suspected him, to any one who did not realize how closely she could observe if she chose, and also how well she knew his old habit of never forgetting or forgiving an injury. She knew now that Florence and Rachel had to bear much of the blame of his long exile from the city, and that he would not be slow to vex and annoy them in any way he could, with the hope of escaping detection.

Nor was she wrong. Henry had, at first, been

miserable enough in the country, and had vowed vengeance, over and over again, against every one concerned in his being there, not excepting Ida. Towards the latter part of his stay he had found there was no place where mischief was not waiting for those who sought it; and he soon earned the character there, as at home, of being a very bad boy.

If he had at all, amid these new scenes, forgotten his intention of one day taking vengeance upon those at home, the sight of them, on his return, called up all the bitter feelings afresh; and he began, almost unconsciously to himself, to plan how he could most effectually annoy them. This Christmas box — no sooner did he hear of it than it seemed like a golden opportunity, worth coming home for — fun enough to consecrate the whole of the holidays.

He ascertained precisely the day, hour, and method of the box being transported to the express office, then took his measures in accordance; but he soon saw, also, that Ida suspected and watched him. This only gave the more zest to the thing. She was sharp, and to outwit her was double the fun that it was to provoke those at the south. How very rich vacation was opening! Why, it was equal to a night at the theatre, farce and all; and so, as was usual in former times, when he had any bad object to accomplish, Henry became very kind, cheerful, and merry; and again Florence's warm, unsuspecting heart went out to him, with almost a feeling of shame at being afraid of him, and not liking to stay long where he was.

There had been many visits and city excursions reserved for his children by Mr. Erwin until Henry should return. He thought him much too old to be playing any more pranks like the one upon Rachel at the station, as indeed he was; and that by taking Florence and Ida he could save him many hours for business, giving Florence what he felt his brother had intended she should have—an opportunity to see and hear city amusements and shows. Among the shows Mr. Erwin included all the galleries, and whatever pictures, statues, or panoramas happened to be on exhibition. Many of them his own children had seen before, but they never objected to going whenever they could, and, of course, willingly consented now.

The amusements Mr. Erwin chose from with much more difficulty. His New England home still lingered with him in what he had long since learned to call "early prejudices." The theatre, the opera, balls, he did not hesitate to attend if he wished; and Mrs. Erwin had no educational bias to prevent her free indulgence in them all. Still he found he could never take his own children to any such place without remembering, at least, how wrong he had been taught to think them; and now the question of Florence's accompanying them was one which seriously annoyed him. Florence's father had been strict and unbending in his own principles — "rigidly Puritan," Mr. Erwin thought to the last; and though he had never heard him express his opinion with regard to these city amusements, still he knew they were not in accordance with his ideas of right and wrong, and he doubted whether, if he had expressed a wish, it would have been to have had Florence attend them. This winter there were new stars in the theatrical firmament — world-renowned celebrities.

If Florence was to live in the city, and with them, as
he most sincerely hoped, she must get over many of
her father's religious notions, and this among them.
So, after much vexatious thought, he resolved to
give Florence an opportunity to go if she wished;
thus throwing, in part, child as she was, the responsibility upon her.

This fallacy one would have thought beneath so
sensible a man as Mr. Erwin; but it is strange how
our reason vacillates, even in the wisest of us, unless
we have stern, unflinching principle at the helm.
One would have thought Mr. Erwin might have had
some of his doubts solved by the effect which fre-
quent theatre-going had had upon Henry; but there
were so many other causes at work for the boy's
injury, that perhaps his father was not so much to
blame for not singling out this.

Since his return home now, every night saw him
out at some place of public amusement. Sometimes
his mother accompanied him; but he oftener went
alone, and as it was only vacation, his father silently
allowed it.

One way Henry had of endeavoring to make himself agreeable to Florence and Ida was, to tell them
of the wonderful things he saw and heard at these
evening resorts.

Ida had seen enough of them herself, to give them
more nearly their just value; but to Florence's vivid
fancy they were the stories of a place more enchant-
ing than any fairy land. She would sit with her
bright, inquiring eyes fixed upon Henry's face,
watching every word he uttered, as if she was afraid
she should lose one of all its wonders. Henry always

ended by promising her that some time, before he
returned to school, he would make his father take
her; and Florence's pleased smile was a ready enough
proof of her delight.

At last the invitation came. There was to be
one of Shakspeare's plays performed — Henry the
Eighth. "A most impressive and excellent way,"
Mr. Erwin said, in excuse to himself, to teach "Flor-
ence, so that she will never forget it, a lesson in
English history."

Florence was wild with delight when the night
was actually appointed, and dancing up to her room
with more of her old home life than she had shown
before since she had been north, she burst upon
Rachel with the astonishing intelligence that she
was to go, that very night, to the theatre, and she
must hurry and dress her just as fast as she could;
but Rachel dropped the work, and holding up both
of her hands, exclaimed, —

"De Lord Almighty forgive de chile. What dat
ting she be saying? Theatre! Theatre! Why, it
leads straight to de bottomless pit."

Florence looked in her face with her own as expressive of astonishment as the negro's, but did not speak.

"What dat ting, little missus?" said Rachel, in a
gentler tone. "What dat ting you say, eh, eh?"

"I am to go with my uncle to the theatre," replied Florence, with a slight tremor in her voice.

"Theatre! Theatre! Why, Miss Flossy, darling,
you are a poor little lamb, and don't know what a
dreadful wicked thing you say. The theatre is the
gate of hell, and no one walks in there that ever
comes out." Rachel was speaking in her voice of

authority, and her words at such times were always good English.

"My uncle goes, and Ida, and Henry, and George is to go to-night," said Florence.

"If every body in New York, and at this whole wicked north, go together," said Rachel, "Florence Erwin *must* not." Rachel's emphasis on *must* was unfortunate for the "little missus's" temper. Florence flew at once into a passion, and there followed such an outbreak of angry words as Rachel had never heard from her before.

During this scene Rachel had stood before Florence, moving her hands up and down, and rolling her eyes, while she uttered whispered ejaculations, as one burst of angry words succeeded another; but these only seemed to have the effect of exciting Florence the 'more, and had she not fairly worked herself into a torrent of tears, it would have been difficult to have told how the affair would have ended; for Florence, always betraying this sudden and violent temper, had been accustomed to having it controlled only by the authority of her father.

When the sobs came, Rachel attempted to draw her near to her; but Florence stood as if she was cut out of wood, and would not move, or be moved, and so Rachel left her, and sitting down in a chair, covered her face with her hands, and began to pray aloud.

It would have been difficult for any one less used to the peculiar forms of negro prayer than Florence, to have distinguished, in the strange mingling of words and figures, what she meant; but in spite of her anger, in spite of her sobs, she could not but hear every word, and before Rachel had half poured out her troubled heart, "little missus" began to relent, and to take a step nearer to her. Rachel neither saw nor heard her; the negro was really terrified, first at Florence's proposition to do what she looked upon as a deadly sin, and then at the violent anger which the child was showing. Prayer in an emergency was the natural tendency of her mind. "God, God." The thought of him as the only succor seemed to come to her as quickly as that of earthly friends to so many others. Florence stood now by her side, but still Rachel prayed. The child slid her hand into the two which were upraised and clasped, but no pressure recognized their being there, while the prayer grew more and more fervent.

Then Florence stopped her own sobs, and said, softly, "Mauma, dear mauma, don't be angry at your little Flossy. I will stay at home."

"And then," said Rachel, dropping the uplifted hands slowly upon Florence's head, "the God of Abram, Isaac, and Jacob — old missus's God — young missus's God — massa George's God, bless you forever and ever. Amen."

And she took the child in her great, loving arms, and sitting down, rocked her back and forth, and sang to her as if she were a baby again. So Florence sat, with her long, dark curls falling over the neat, crossed white neckerchief of the negro, and her round cheek pressed close to her heart, uttering only now and then a short, vexed sob, as the wind sighs after the storm is passed. Rachel could talk with her quietly and sensibly now, and told her much that she had heard or read of the wickedness of the theatre; how often she had heard her father speak of it in terms of condemnation, and how her own mother had never even wished to go.

Florence became slowly convinced, and before it was time for her to go down dressed, had run to her uncle's library to tell him "that she did not like to go."

Of course he was much surprised, and could not forbear a smile when he heard the reasons which Florence, in a very child-like manner, detailed as Rachel had given them to her.

"You shall do just as you please, Florence," he said, kindly. "Five years from to-night we shall hear a very different story, or I am mistaken."

The children were disappointed, and not a little vexed, at what they termed this "freak of Florence." They had promised themselves much amusement from her surprise over every thing she saw. Ida tossed her head, and took no pains to conceal a very contemptuous expression; but Henry burst into a coarse laugh, and said he had heard of being "tied to apron-strings, but never those that reached round a great blacky's waist before."

But, to Florence's credit, be it said, that she was proof against both contempt and ridicule, if she had once made up her own mind as to what it was right to do. Careless and thoughtless, as she had of late seemed, with regard to that religion in which she had been so strictly educated, the good seed was there, and though the tares had sprung up abundantly, it should yet bear a rich, full harvest.

She was grateful to her uncle for his pleasant

"good night" as they went out, and as unconcerned
about the coldness of the others as if they were
entire strangers; but no sooner did the carriage roll
away from the door, than, hiding her face in her
hands, she began to cry from the very bitterness of
the disappointment; but not long, for she knew
Rachel was anxiously waiting for her on the land-
ing of the stairs above. It was a sober, tear-stained
face that came looking up through the dim hall; but
Rachel knew it would be but a very little while before it was smiling and happy again; and so she saw
her "little missus" go quietly to bed, and long after
the child was asleep Rachel sat by her, and gave
thanks to " the good God who had saved her precious
one from the great sin."

It was late when the family returned from the
theatre. Rachel felt afraid Ida would come to tell
Florence what she had seen, and so awaken and
trouble her; therefore she had sat up, waiting to
prevent it; but she might have saved herself the
trouble, for that night, at least, all Ida's early contempt for her characterless southern cousin was in
full force, and she "passed her by on the other side."

When the house was once more still, Rachel had
been too much excited and troubled to sleep. She
seemed to feel with tenfold force the responsibility
under which the sole care of Florence laid her. She
began to lose all confidence in either her uncle or
aunt to direct her, and was fast taking the position
that she alone had the slightest inclination to even
look for the right and wrong in any of the matters
of daily life. The north was a great heathen land
to her; she saw no images of idols that they wor-

shipped, but she never heard any one speak of the one living and true God. No Sabbath, no prayers, no Bibles, no religious books. Could Africa be worse? Rachel grew very anxious and restless to-night, as she tossed about on her couch thinking over these things. She heard the city clocks toll out the hour of one, and weary of her bed, thought she would just steal down and take a last farewell look of the box, which stood ready to go on the next morning. That precious Christmas box! She almost had the feeling that she could put a share of her troubles into it, and it would carry them away, so near did it bring the days at Myrtle Bush before her.

Softly, so as not to disturb any one, and with her lamp shaded in her hand, she crept down the stairs into the room used as a store room. The cover of the box was not nailed on. It would be such a comfort to lift one by one those things again! Perhaps she could send a message of love in them, which the ready superstition of her race told her might be actually made known to those for whom it was designed.

She reached the door, and was somewhat startled to find it ajar, and to see that there was a light burning within the room. Bridget's stories of the dreadful housebreakings which were constantly taking place in New York immediately recurred to her, and her first impulse was to return as speedily and noiselessly as she came. This she had hardly done, when the idea of losing the contents, precious contents of the box, drove every thing else out of her mind, and she crept back, determined to watch closely and make no sound. Putting out her own light, and trusting to her knowledge of the house for a way of ready escape should she be discovered, she went down so like a cat, that surely a mouse would not have moved had it been in her way. The door was still ajar, the light there, and as Rachel came nearer and nearer, she was sure she heard a sound as of some one unpacking. The crack of the door was on the side from which Rachel had approached, and putting her eye to it, she saw a figure bent over it, as she had feared, busy rifling its contents. As if chained to the spot, without daring to breathe, Rachel saw bundle after bundle unrolled, the enclosed article taken out, and straw and paper, from a basket which stood near, put in to fill the place.

She could not turn her eye even far enough to try to discover how the robber looked. Now she saw that yellow turban for Nancy on the floor; next the queer pipe for old Dan; next the doll for little Biddy; and so on, until she felt sure the bottom of the box must begin to appear.

"Now or never," she thought, as soon as her paralyzed mind began to think at all. "What shall I do?"

She made a slight noise on the side of the door. The robber stopped and looked up, turning his light for an instant towards it. Rachel was still as death; she dared not even run away. Again the work proceeded, and again Rachel became conscious that in a few minutes longer all interference would be of no avail. Once more she made a slight noise, but this time no notice was taken of her; so, growing bolder, she tapped with a distinct sound upon the panel.

The thief started to his feet, and to her surprise and relief, she saw, as in his fright he turned himself and the light quickly towards the door, that it was Henry Erwin!

With great presence of mind, Henry immediately blew out his own light. Whoever was near him was evidently in the dark, and if he could only glide by them he might yet escape detection. Rachel, however, was too quick for him. No sooner had he opened the door wide enough to allow of his passing out, than she seized him by the collar, and without one word began to shake him, until Henry thought his head would drop off from his shoulders. Naturally Henry was a bold boy, and had he even at this moment had any idea in whose grasp he was, helpless as he would have been, he would have endeavored to resist to the utmost; but "conscience makes cowards of us all," and Henry Erwin, young as he was, had already done many things which would take true courage out of his heart.

Alone, in intense darkness and silence, he yielded to the strong hold of the negro, and without a groan or sound of any kind, found himself, now on his feet, now reeling over on to his head, now touching the side of the house, and then, with a quick jerk, pushed back within the store room. Back he went, unresistingly, until he stumbled, with a loud noise, over the box itself; then, as if the charm was spent, for the first time Rachel broke the ominous silence.

"Dare, den, you young, white tief, dare — dare" — (every *there* was accompanied with a fresh and more violent shake) — "you touch them gen. Shame on you. Eh, eh! you white boy. You young tief. No better dan very worst plantation nigger; dey steal, you steal. Henry Erwin, Scip Coal, all one; go to de same place, too good for dem both. Eh, eh! De Lord Almighty forgive you, you white boy — you north — tieving Christmas box! O my!"

Here Rachel drew her breath through her teeth, in the way of the negroes when they would express the most intense sense of shame and degradation. It sounded to Henry like the hissing of a room full of boa constrictors; but he was beginning to know in whose hands he was, and to collect his senses, which the sudden onset had driven away. Taking advantage of a pause which Rachel made in order to control the wrath which had mastered her, Henry stammered out, " Let me alone, you black dog, or I'll kill you."

"Kill me, kill me, black dog!" ejaculated Rachel; and Henry spun about like a top.

This was evidently a bad stroke on his part; and with the tact which never in any emergency long forsook him, he gasped out, as soon as he could gather sufficient breath for the effort, " Rachel, don't be so mad. I was only putting some new things into your box, — that was all, — some beautiful presents for them, you know."

"Liar, and tief too!" was his only answer. But the hand loosened a little from his neck.

" You'll choke me to death!" he said, with some difficulty; for indeed the lungs seemed to have shared in the general commotion.

" Good enough for you. Dat sin lead to de halter." And Rachel, as she said this, removed her hand to his arm, which she held as if she had enclosed it in an iron fetter. ⸱

"Let me alone, I say," continued Henry, endeavoring to shake her off.

"You just stand still, Henry Erwin. We will light a lamp, and you must put dem tings back just where you took dem from. Dat Massa George's nephew? Eh, eh! De Lord forgive him for having a tief for his own flesh and blood!"

There was something, however, in the idea which affected Rachel; for she drew Henry more gently towards the door, and was intending to take him with her to the kitchen, for a means of rekindling his light, when they saw a glimmer coming down from the second story, and in a moment Mr. Erwin, pistol in hand, made his appearance.

"Don't fire, massa," said Rachel, as soon as she clearly knew him. "It's no tief, but Henry, your own boy. De Lord forgive him, and comfort you, too!" she added, with true negro sympathy, as her eye fell on Mr. Erwin's pale and startled face.

"Henry! Rachel! why, what does this mean, at this time of night?" asked Mr. Erwin, as he became aware who was before him.

Henry hung his head, and preserved a dogged silence; and Rachel, after waiting a minute for him, told the story in her own way, omitting, of course, the summary punishment which she had inflicted. All this time she kept her hold of Henry, as if she feared he would make an attempt to escape.

"Let him alone," said Mr. Erwin, sternly. "Now, both of you follow me."

He led the way to the store room, and the appearance of things there corroborated at once Rachel's statements. Pointing to the heaps of scattered things, Mr. Erwin said to Henry, "What does this mean?"

"It was only a joke," stammered Henry.

"Joke!"—and Mr. Erwin unrolled the bundles of straw, and tossed them towards Henry, one by one.

"Yes, sir. I meant to put them back, after they found it out. I only did it to frighten them."

"Stop, boy!"—and his voice, Henry well knew, allowed of no answer. "Don't add a falsehood. It is contemptible enough, without another shade of your miserable, mean duplicity. Go to your room, and be up in season; for you return to Hampton by the earliest morning train."

Henry slunk away; and, strange as it may seem, Rachel, as she saw him with his head down, cowed and ashamed, felt sorry for the bad boy, and turning to his father, said, "Massa, p'raps he didn't mean to do so bad. Maybe old Rachel was too touchy like, when it came to de box, and Myrtle Bush."

"Silence!" said Mr. Erwin, "and put up these things properly, as soon as you can. The boy is bad enough for any thing, and will bring me to my grave, from very shame, for all that I know."

"God forbid," said Rachel, fervently. "Many a bad boy has made a good man. Neber gib him up. Blessed Jesus, he died for de tief on de cross. He save Henry Erwin yet, only ask him, massa,—ask him bery hard."

Mr. Erwin groaned,—the expression, for the first time in his life, of a father's heart feeling its utter incapacity to fulfil the trust which had been given to him in this boy. Did Rachel's words remind him of the time when his own mother had led him away from the other children, and kneeling down by his side, had asked God to forgive him some slight fault, and make him a better boy? Did he remember, that to this day, he had never prayed for, or with, this child? and in the helpless, hopeless anxieties now, did he miss the strong arm to bear upon — the trust in that unfailing wisdom, which giveth of itself only to those who ask? Perhaps he did; but his reply was this one groan; and it softened the already relenting heart of the negro, until she almost forgot her anger, and went to the task of replacing the disturbed contents of the box with alacrity and good will.

Mr. Erwin stood by, holding the light, until the last article was returned; then, nailing on the cover, said briefly, "Rachel, you will oblige me, as no one knows of this but ourselves, by keeping it a perfect secret. There is enough wrong in Henry, that all must see, to make it necessary to conceal what we can."

"Yes, massa," said Rachel. "If Henry does not tell, himself, me no tell long as my head knows what my mouth says."

The gray light of day was already coming in at the long windows, as Mr. Erwin passed them on his way to his room. He felt no inclination to sleep; so, going to his library, he shut the door upon himself and the heaviest of all earthly cares — that of an unruly, bad child. He perfectly comprehended Henry's motives for this act — revenge upon Flor-

ence and Rachel for their immediate share in his
being sent to the dulness of country life. Mr.
Erwin was himself so far above a mean action, that
the power of doing one was a great mystery to him;
and it was the most acute part of his punishment
for the early neglect of this child, that in almost
every piece of mischief in which he was detected
meanness of some kind bore a prominent part.

What Henry's own feelings were, when he found
himself alone in his room, may better be imagined
than described. He was detected, punished in a
way which he would not wish to have repeated, and
his punishment was not yet ended. To-morrow he
must return, disgraced, to school. His father seldom relented; he was very angry now, and there
was no hope. But it would have taken greater
trouble than this to keep Henry long awake; so he
slept soundly, without the least idea that his father,
walking up and down the library floor, was busy
with plans for changing the school for the vessel,
and the term's absence for two years before the
mast.

Rachel seated herself close by Florence's side,
watching her, with a sort of undefined fear that so
long as Henry remained under the same roof with
them there was no rest or safety for them.

And so passed the remainder of the morning twilight; and when the family once more gathered
around the breakfast table, it seemed as if a cloud
had rested upon them, which George's pleasant prat-
tle could do nothing to break; and as he was the
only one who seemed disposed to talk, all were glad
when they could separate to their various employ-

ments, Henry following a short, stern command of his father's, to prepare himself to accompany him to his office without delay.   Mrs. Erwin raised her languid eyes for a moment, but felt too tired, from the last night's dissipation, to make any inquiries.

CHAPTER X.

INQUIRIES with respect to the vessel proceeded much more slowly than Mr. Erwin had anticipated. Henry was pleased with the change of plans. Going to sea is always delightful in prospect to a wild boy; and whenever he had been punished, to run away and ship on board a vessel, never to come back again, was always his first plan. He hardly fancied being sent, but to go, after all, was the summit of his wishes. Mrs. Erwin objected — showed more natural mother's feelings than any event seemed to have elicited before; but Mr. Erwin was immovable, and used every exertion to procure a suitable vessel and voyage. In the mean time, the idea of the parting which was so soon and for so long a time to take place, made him kinder and more indulgent to the erring boy. Even Ida showed some concern, and as for Florence, being in utter ignorance with regard to the affair of the box, she became almost affectionate as the time passed on.

Every day of the holidays brought with it some delightful plan for enjoyment. The whole city was alive with gay, beautiful sights. Christmas trees stood in shop windows; Christmas gifts loaded every counter, and shone out fancifully from the very booths at the corners of the streets. Florence was almost beside herself with joy. She darted from one show to another, captivated and happy. Taking

tight hold of Rachel's hand, the two constantly attracted attention wherever they went; and it was not
an unfrequent occurrence for Rachel to be touched
by some elderly benevolent-looking individual, who
recognized — though Rachel had learned to wear a
bonnet — the tones and manners of a southern negro, and asked in a whisper, if she " did not wish her
freedom."

Rachel never heard it without a start of fear; and
indeed freedom and the loss of one's free actions
were fast becoming in the negro's mind so mingled
and confused, that she could not distinguish between
them.

Her invariable answer now was, with something
of a defiant shrug, —

"Thank you, I am my own mistress; I and this
little missus, it don't matter which." And then she
held up the small hand, and turned the child's lovely
face towards the questioner, as if she thought one
glance at that must settle the matter at once.

So passed the whole of these charming holidays.
Florence and Ida. were permitted on New Year's
Eve to give a party, at which were present many
very handsomely dressed miniature men and women
— a great affair, indeed, but not half as productive
of real pleasure to the children as a walk in the busy,
cheerful streets. Still the time flew by. Florence
could hardly believe it was the same world as the
one in which she used to be at Myrtle Bush, and
many an hour she spent, recalling, with Rachel,
every action of the last Christmas there.

A short time after New Year's, a vessel was found
for Henry, and he took his leave. There were no

heart-breaking farewells, though the day after he left Mrs. Erwin disappeared from the parlor, and was denied to callers; but in the evening she went to the theatre, and the next day vacation was over, and the round of lessons and masters continued as before.

The few months which remained of Florence's year with them, Mr. Erwin was doubly anxious should be made pleasant to her; and as they passed one after the other, he could not but see how much more contented she daily grew, speaking less frequently of the south, and acquiring, as fast as she could with so much to prevent her, northern manners and forms of speech.

Mrs. Erwin, too, was becoming dependent upon the changes which Florence's presence brought to their family for her happiness — Rachel was such a relief in the nursery and about the clear-starching; Florence kept Ida in better humor; and then, last and greatest of all, that carriage. It was a luxury of which she could never again be denied.

This second quarter of study passed quietly and much more valuably than the first. At the end of the three months, spring was again there. The time had come and passed, when, only a year ago, Florence's father died. Letters from Cato brought the yellow jessamine, and most glowing accounts of the coming on of the beautiful spring time.

Rachel felt heart-sick as she read; but Florence began already to think of her southern home as of some far-off fairy land, and with that child's happy faculty, found the present amply sufficient in its joys and griefs.

She was therefore very sorry when a letter came

from her aunt, Mrs. Niles, saying that as the year of
Florence's residence with her uncle was nearly over,
she should expect her at the parsonage in Grafton,
on the first day of the time which made her hers.
The letter was simple, affectionate, and earnest. If
Florence had been ten years older she would have
considered it an index for good; as it was, it was
only a source of annoyance to her. She did not wish
to go. She hoped her aunt would have forgotten her
father's request, or that she should be allowed to express the wish now which *must* be deferred for the
whole of another long year.

Ida had once been at Grafton, and gave her most
ludicrous accounts of things at the parsonage. She
hardly needed the shrug of disdain, with which Ida
finished her recital, to make her dread the new scenes
and the new life most keenly. Even Mr. Erwin
could not refrain from now and then drawing a picture, which showed, in striking and not pleasant contrast, the two homes.

Mrs. Erwin roused herself to more than usual interest, and related the conduct of the " help," who
was called in during her first and only visit, in a
manner which made a very strong impression upon
the child accustomed to the well-trained southern
slave.

As the last month approached, it seemed as if every
separate member of Mr. Erwin's family, in their own
way, did their best to increase Florence's unhappiness and dissatisfaction.

If they went to ride, Ida would describe the open
wagon of her uncle, with the board seat, and old
Billy to draw it along at his own pace — while in

place of the crowded streets and the charming shop windows, she declared all that could be expected was Mr. Barnes's red cow, the two pigs of Deacon Stephens, or the white-faced oxen of Mr. Phillips, the big farmer.

Throwing herself back on the luxurious cushions of Florence's coach, she would relate the scrambling over the rocks for berries, the falls, the great rough dogs chasing her and nearly biting her, and the "gawky" country children staring at her city dresses through the blinds of their straight white hair.

Florence's quick imagination took in all these scenes with quite as much graphic power as they were related, and her repetition of them to Rachel, when they were alone, puzzled and troubled the negro, as it had herself.

Rachel had most unlimited confidence in the judgment of "Massa George." Since he had sent them north, it was all right; but why and wherefore, Rachel spent hours in trying to make plain to herself.

Surely now, *this* was no home. In her heart constantly drawing comparisons between it and Myrtle Bush, she felt that it was a very different place — far more difference than her good sense told her need be made, by their being in two different sections of the country. Not in a single point could she make the north superior to the south. Masters in abundance Florence had here; but she was too intelligent not to perceive that she had derived more real instruction from her parents in half the time and with half the difficulty.

Was she a better child? Did she love to pray or read her Bible? Did she try to be less passionate here than there? These were the kinds of questions which Rachel asked herself, in order to test Florence's improvement, and she was startled to find how very decided the answer was. Florence had grown much older and more womanish, but far less lovable, with far less of the simple, sweet, child-like faith upon which her father had depended so much for the formation and guidance of her future character. Rachel dreaded this new home quite as much as Florence. There was no Sabbath and no religion in New York, where there were so many churches; how much, then, must there be in a small country town, where there was only one single minister and one meeting house.

Every night Florence wet her pillow with tears, as she mourned over, to the sympathizing nurse, the speedily coming change, and every morning she wished that it were the coming of yesterday instead of to-day, that it might not bring her nearer the dreaded time.

Ida was perfectly satisfied with the warm dislike to the country home which she so constantly and unreservedly expressed, and Mr. Erwin felt so sure of the result of the next year, that he announced to his wife his determination to keep the carriage, without the break which Florence's temporary absence would occasion.

Every one was so certain of the choice, that it was only like sending Florence, as Mr. Erwin said, "into the country to spend the summer." George was inconsolable. The summer was a forever to him; and to part with Rachel, if not with Florence, was a great sorrow. What should he do? Who would play with him? Who would tell him stories?

Day after day the little fellow went moaning out these questions around the house, until Grace learned them all by heart, and parrot like, repeated them whenever she saw either Florence or Rachel.

If there were any doubts on Florence's part as to her having been very happy here, she would have had them all solved now. Every body seemed so sorry to have her go, she must be very sorry herself. If she only might choose now. She ventured to ask her uncle if it would not be possible; but his refusal was couched in so many pleasant promises for the future, that it seemed like a consent. Her stay at her aunt's was to be only a visit — just time for her cheeks to grow red and her eyes bright, without any teachers or lessons to trouble her — nothing to do but to pick berries and run wild with the lambs over the rocks.

So comforted, Florence counted the days, then the hours passed, and at last the very morning dawned which was to bring for her the country parson uncle.

11

CHAPTER XI.

Just before the dinner hour of five, there was a
modest ring at the door. Florence and Ida were
alone in the parlor, and the instant Ida heard it, looking up from her work, she said, —

"Country! no mistaking that ring."

Florence was half amused and half frightened,
when the servant ushered in uncle Niles.

Mr. Niles was a man past the middle of life, tall and
athletic in his figure, with a large head covered with
thick white hair, which had even now an inclination to curl on his projecting forehead. He had
mild, full, hazel eyes, regular, rather small features,
the mouth expressing much sweetness, and the chin,
losing what in younger years might have been almost
effeminate roundness, in a large pair of mottled black
and white whiskers.

As his eye fell upon the two little girls, he called
them to him, and kissing them affectionately, lifted
Florence upon his knee. She colored violently, and
immediately made an effort to get down; but her
uncle detained her, saying very pleasantly, —

"I have quite forgotten — haven't I, Florence? how
much older the little city ladies are than those I have
left at home? My Jennie sits on my knee every
chance she can get, and she is so much taller than
you," — measuring three or four inches above her
head.

Florence sat still, but looked so painfully ashamed that her uncle was as much relieved as herself, to allow her, in a short time, to resume the seat she had quitted when he came in.

Ida, after a few winks with her gray eyes, — every expression of which Florence now so well understood, — began to entertain the guest in a mature manner, which at first amused and then surprised Mr. Niles. In the end, he found himself talking to her as if she were in reality a grown-up woman, while the little shy southern girl sat watching them both.

Mr. Erwin's reception of his brother-in-law was open and friendly. Indeed he felt so sure of Florence's ultimate choice, that he was making it quite an object to soften it to his sister's husband in the pleasantest way he could.

When her father relieved Ida of her care as entertainer, she found herself at liberty to carry on the practice of laughing at every thing connected with Grafton.

Getting so far behind his chair as to be entirely out of his sight, she commenced a series of pantomimic acts designed to call Florence's attention to some country peculiarity of dress. His collar was not so high as her father's, who was the pink of propriety and taste in all matters of dress and personal appearance, while his broad white cravat, irresistibly, as Ida slowly wound her handkerchief about her own neck in ludicrous imitation, reminded Florence of the strolling Methodist preachers, who sometimes spent weeks at Myrtle Bush preaching to the negroes.

Not the slightest peculiarity of dress escaped Ida's

quick, true eye — even the few spots upon the well-kept black suit, which had grown threadbare, she saw, and made them pass before Florence's amused and wondrous gaze. But in spite of all, there was something about uncle Niles which commanded the child's respect. She felt ashamed of herself as she laughed, and wished Ida would stop.

As the two uncles stood up together, she could not help thinking, also, that uncle Niles was the handsomer. If he was not so well dressed, he bore himself in all respects like a gentleman; and this certain something — to define which has puzzled older and wiser heads than that of our little Florence — made her recognize through the country guise the true nobleman.

Would the formalities of her uncle Henry's somewhat formal dinner table annoy him? Ida had warned her to expect to see nothing left of the knife but the steel plate on the tip of its handle, when any of the Grafton people should commence the dangerous feat of eating at the table. With many and very grotesque grimaces she had imitated the whole operation of parsonage meals, and Florence had learned to regard them as promising sport for her three times every day. With downcast eyes as this first dinner approached, Florence began to dread it. She had laughed so often over its imitation, she certainly must be rude when the reality was before her. She wished she could be excused, and whispered so to Ida; but Ida gravely told her it was impossible, her father wouldn't allow it. So the child, actually trembling, went to the dinner table, never venturing to raise her eyes once while there, and wondering to herself how

it was her uncle could talk so pleasantly, while he
was so awkward. One thing startled her: before taking their seats her uncle Henry asked Mr. Niles to
invoke a blessing, which he did in a simple, earnest
way, carrying Florence back to the deserted room
at Myrtle Bush, and to the silent father.

After dinner, Rachel would be impatiently waiting
to hear all; this Florence did not forget, and gliding
softly out, without noticing that the eyes of the two
uncles were following her, the child ran up to the
expectant nurse.

"De good Lord be thanked, little missus," said
Rachel, the moment they were alone together. "I've
seen him; he looks like dat dare good Father Mason,
whom de Lord sends to Myrtle Bush to have dem
blessed meetings, which are meetings for true. Now
I know sure, he never broke his bread without saying, 'Forgive us our sins and bress dis bread, for
Jesus' sake.' What did he say, and what did he do,
little missus? Glory to God! give him thanks foreber
and eber."

Rachel's enthusiasm had a very quieting effect
upon Florence. She forgot the old coat, and the
collar, and the white cravat — even the knife at the
dinner table, while she narrated every little thing
which had been said or done, Rachel constantly inter-
rupting her with "De good Lord be thanked. Bress
her name. Glory forever! — glory. Amen! Amen!"

Florence was not altogether pleased with these
demonstrations on Rachel's part. She did not want to
go to Grafton, and had no fancy for any thing connected with it: so she slid away again as quickly as
she could, and went out with Ida for the last drive

together through those busy, pleasant streets, which Florence was beginning to love almost as well as the drives along the level, smooth roads of her rice plantation at home.

Hardly had the children gone, when the two uncles commenced a conversation with regard to Florence, which struck Mrs. Erwin, as she sat listlessly listening, to be one of the strangest she ever heard; and if any thing had been needed to complete her idea of the want of any kind of sense in the ministry in general, and in the country ministry in particular, this would certainly have done it.

"There is one thing which you will allow me to mention to you now," said Mr. Niles; "as Florence is away, and as I must return to-morrow morning, I may not have another opportunity. You wrote Jane that a large sum was allowed by Florence's father every year for her support. It amused us very much, for it happens to be more than three times the salary we receive, and upon which, in one way and another, we manage to live, we think, comfortably and happily. Jane says — and I agree with her — that this money we could not by any means expend for Florence; and after considering it week after week, we have both come to the conclusion that we should much prefer, for this year, not to touch a cent of it."

Mr. Erwin looked at his brother-in-law with a cold, slightly contemptuous smile; no words could have said more plainly, "how very foolish he thought him." Indeed, Mr. Erwin had no idea that he really meant what he said, but immediately put down the conversation as a short sermon from the minister, intended to point out the Christian virtue of disinterestedness; so he only answered, —

"Indeed, that is rather singular, and I can't imagine how Jane can manage to live on such an income. To be sure, though we were all brought up to be economical, one of my good father's earliest lessons, and one to which, in my business, I owe a great deal, was, "never to spend more than you had."

"A rule to which Jane, too, has rigidly adhered," said Mr. Niles, laughing; "but the mystery of the thing to me always has been, how she contrives to make so little do so much. We all seem to have what we want, though not much that we could do without."

"For that reason you will find Florence's income will make you quite independent for the year. Buy a good many little family comforts which you have needed."

"That is precisely what my wife does not wish. She says her brother sent her at his death more money than his child can possibly cost us, and she very much prefers introducing no comforts or luxuries into our family which we should miss if they were taken away."

Mr. Erwin immediately thought of the new carriage — how different his sister was from his wife; but he merely said, —

The child and her servant made more difference in a family than any one could know until they had made the experiment; that he was sure his brother would not, on any account, have Mr. Niles incur a cent of extra expense for his child. The responsibility, even, he wished they should be well paid for. Then there were the teachers, if they intended her to have any.

She would share with their own children the
home instruction, Mr. Niles said. They intended
not to make the slightest difference in any family
arrangements while Florence was with them. They
were conducting every thing now as they considered
best for themselves, and if Florence should choose to
remain with them, she must find them as they were —
live with them so — choose them so — or not at all.

There was something so decisive in the tones in
which these last words were uttered, that, in spite of
his knowledge of the world, Mr. Erwin began to
wonder if it could be that Mr. Niles really was
meaning what he said, and not preaching a sermon;
and his answer therefore was, bluntly, "You surely
do not mean what you are saying?"

"I surely do," said the minister, smiling, without
taking the least offence. "Jane charged me not
even to receive money for the child's expenses to
Grafton. She says she has never had an opportunity
before of returning any of her brother's never-ending
kindness to her; and, indeed," said Mr. Niles, with a
slight tremor in his voice, "we have seen times since
we were married when his thoughtfulness has seemed
almost like a special providence from the hand of God."

"But this about the money, is — excuse me — extremely foolish," quickly returned Mr. Erwin. "I
cannot possibly consent to it. The child will really
require it for the many comforts she has always
been accustomed to."

"Rest assured she shall never want any thing
which her health or happiness requires," said Mr.
Niles, a little sternly; "if any affliction should be
sent upon us, so that we are unable to give her what

is best for her, we shall immediately draw upon you for whatever she may require; and now let it pass without any further notice."

"It is impossible — entirely out of the question — as foolish as it is unjust in you," said Mr. Erwin, warmly. "My conscience would not let me rest a moment if I should allow it. It can't be."

"Well, then," said Mr. Niles, smiling, "settle it with Jane. You both have the same traits, I see, and will readily understand each other; but as in this matter I act now under strict orders, you will forgive my obeying them until I receive new."

Mrs. Erwin gave a little cough; her husband knew it was to call his attention to the doctrine of "husband, obey your wife," contained in this new sermon. He felt excessively annoyed, particularly as he saw the eye of his brother-in-law glance with some sly humor towards the recumbent lady. He was glad to put an immediate end to the conversation, by declaring that nothing would induce him to retain the money, and that it should be ready for an order any time they chose to draw.

Perhaps there is nothing in this world more really annoying to a thoroughly worldly man, than to come actually in contact with what he considers the simplicity of unworldliness. He thought Jane had lost in her still country life what common sense she used to have; and as for Mr. Niles, he was an extreme type of an extreme class — really not worth a consideration, if he had not come actually in contact with him.

Mr. Erwin felt no pleasure at the additional security this gave him of Florence's return. He was sure of that before; he had all the compunctions of a strictly honorable man, who finds a trust committed to him suddenly embarrassed, and cannot see any way of extricating himself from it. He was only the more attentive to his minister-brother. In spite of his business and worldly turn of mind, he found himself respecting him more than he had ever done before in his life.

There was no end to the last things which Florence and Ida found must be done that night. Both were unhappy at the idea of the speedy parting. Ida tried to cover her grief by every odd, funny story which she could recall of country life; but Florence shed tears plentifully between her fits of laughter, and declared, over and over again, "she never was more unhappy in her life."

Indeed, the child fairly tired herself out with her emotions; so that when it came time for her to go to bed, she sank to sleep, much to Rachel's relief, as quickly and quietly as baby Grace herself.

They must take a very early start on the next morning. The children had all promised to be up and say "good-by;" but when Florence went down, no one was there but her uncle Henry. He thought it best not to waken the children, and Florence found herself quitting her uncle's house without any one but himself to part from.

Mr. Niles had not seen Rachel before, though she had had many a sly peep at him. There was something in the imposing appearance of the negro which troubled him; and, in fact, if he had owned the truth to any one, he must have said, that the presence of a slave in his own family was likely to be attended by more annoying consequences than any other part of his southern brother's request. He had, therefore, this morning a slight misgiving of evil, as, dressed so faultlessly neat, she stood bowing and smiling, and ready to grasp the hand which he cordially held out to her.

Was she to ride with them in the same carriage? Mr. Niles was as much troubled as Mr. Erwin had been on the morning of leaving Myrtle Bush. He, too, had never sat so near a colored person in his life.

Mr. Erwin saw and amused himself at his perplexity. "It is a wonder," he said, as the carriage rolled slowly away, "if that negro don't bring trouble in his parish to my worthy brother-in-law. Unless I am mistaken, he don't take to her any more than I did."

The journey was not to be a long one. If the cars met punctually, they would reach Grafton at twilight. Florence rode tearfully along, looking out at every familiar city sight as they passed it, as if she were taking leave of a friend. Mr. Niles made three or four attempts to interest and amuse her; but finding her only inclined to answer in mono-syllables, he took her hand in his, and they drove silently to the station.

Mr. Niles was quite relieved when he had safely deposited his charge in the cars. It was so embarrassing, every way he turned, to have the imposing looking negro woman with them. If Florence were only younger, so that people could see she needed a nurse; but such a great girl, why, it was making a baby of her in earnest.

Would she dream of sitting with Florence and himself in the same seat in the cars?

Rachel's place was with "little missus," and, without a question, she took it.

Hardly, however, was she seated, when the conductor approached them, and said, politely, to Mr. Niles, —

"There is a car for colored persons attached in the rear. Will you be kind enough to send your servant there?"

"I see," said Mr. Niles, glancing around the car, "many Irish nurses here. There is no reason why mine should leave."

"The only reason, sir," said the conductor, decidedly, "is, that she is black, and they are white. Our regulations are peremptory; if you wish this negro to ride at all, she must go where she belongs."

"I question such authority," said Mr. Niles, "and shall resist it. If my servant goes there it will be because she is forced to do it."

The conductor bit his lip angrily, and hesitated for a moment. The truth was, almost every day brought to him a recurrence of this same trouble. A negro with a white baby in her arms, if she would sit in the saloon and keep the door shut, was allowed to remain; but if one was seen in any place but that rear car, there was mutiny on board the train at once. Some numbers of persons, whose business was always every body's but their own, would enter a protest, and insist that the very letter of the regulation with regard to colored people should be obeyed. The conductors dreaded an obstinate negro almost as much as they did a collision; and next to one, they dreaded a neat, nice servant, with a gentlemanly-looking minister to protect her. Now, this conductor glanced from this party around on his half-filled car; he saw many eyes fixed upon them, and he knew very well all kind of temporizing was out of the question; so he said, authoritatively, and in a raised voice, "Well, sir, if you are wise, you will send her quietly, yourself; the car is very comfortable; she will ride as well there as here. If you refuse, she must leave the train at the next stopping place." He then moved away.

Florence and Rachel had both been most intently listening to what was going on, perfectly unable to comprehend it; but seeing that there was some trouble in which Rachel was concerned, —

"What dis? massa," said Rachel, as soon as the conductor had moved a few feet from her. "What dat man say I *must* do?"

There was a flash to Rachel's eye, beneath which Mr. Niles sank. He hesitated for a moment, then said, —

"This railroad, he tells me, has a law prohibiting persons of color from riding in the same car with whites." Mr. Niles did not even now raise his eyes; he felt, with a keen sense of inconsistencies, that it would be impossible to make a stranger comprehend how the north, with all that they said about the freedom and equality of the negro with themselves, should, in their practical treatment, place them so far in the scale of human beings below that which they occupied even in the slaveholding south.

Rachel immediately rose, and Florence too. She said, in a cold, cutting tone, —

"Dis, den, is dat happy land of freedom — dis dat great, glorious north — dis where the shackles fall

from every slave — dis where they say, "dear sister,"
and press the black woman's hand — dis dat place
dat Rachel think of and pray to live to see! Eh,
eh! De Lord forgive 'em all, and bless my good, old
South Carlinny."

Rachel took up the bundles slowly and carefully.
Indeed, the negro's heart was filled more with sorrow
than with anger. Every contact with the north dis-
solved some of those beautiful day-dreams which had
filled so many of the happy hours at Myrtle Bush.
The dearly-coveted boon of freedom, could it be
like every thing else in this world — not worth pos-
sessing here?

If Rachel preferred herself to go, Mr. Niles would
do nothing to prevent. Indeed, he knew from the
very first, that opposition would be useless; but he
was vexed and annoyed so as to lose the complai-
sance, which — if the truth must be told — was a part
of his nature. He was, therefore, now proceeding to
the door with Rachel and Florence, when he was
stopped by the loud voice of a man from the other
side of the car, —

"Hallo, there, mister!" it said. "If you have a
mind to stick to it, that ere nigger of yours shall
ride here, if you say so. I'll stand by you. We
don't let the conductors knock us round this way,
down by Boston. If we pay for a seat, we pay for
it; and it is ours as long as the money holds good.
We put into it black or white, and if any one has
any thing to say agin it, why, we just knock them
down directly."

All the passengers laughed, but Mr. Niles said,
pleasantly, —

" Thank you, friend. This woman would much prefer going quietly out to having any trouble made on her account; but I protest against this distinction as being against the laws of God and man."

"Amen!" said several voices; and as the party disappeared from the car, there commenced within it a vigorous anti-slavery discussion, which it was well for Rachel that she did not hear.

When they reached the small back car designated by the conductor, they found it as he said — neat and comfortable, and occupied by only two nice-looking, old black women.

Mr. Niles helped Rachel in, much more carefully and attentively than was at all necessary. His kind heart longed to make what amends it could; but he was not prepared to see Florence spring in after her, and take her seat close by her side.

"You will ride with me, Florence?" said her uncle, coaxingly.

"I shall stay with Rachel, please, uncle," said Florence, with an expression of the eye which Mr. Niles at once recognized as belonging to her father's family.

"It is not a proper place," said he, addressing himself directly to Rachel, whose good sense had thus quickly made itself known to him.

Rachel hesitated. It was the first time in their lives they had ever been separated, excepting from their own free choice. At last she said, glancing at her companions, —

"Go with your uncle, Miss Flossy."

"No," said Florence, angrily; "I shall not. I shall stay just where you do — I don't care where it is."

The whistle of the train sounded; and, without time for any further expostulations, Mr. Niles was obliged to hurry back to his former seat, leaving Florence with Rachel in the negro car.

How comfortable the minister's reflections were, as they flew along, may easily be imagined. He occupied, with regard to the subject of slavery, the common, sensible, northern ground — that it was a great evil, and would, in God's own good time, be wholly done away with. He felt grateful that he was born in a land free from this curse, and felt that for the wealth of California he would not own a slave. He had been, now, twenty-two years settled over this same parish of Grafton, and had mainly educated his people to hold the same views he did upon almost every subject; but of late anti-slavery notions were beginning to creep in. He heard them expressed more and more openly every month; and it was even beginning to be rumored that the young deacon, Benjamin Dean, was affected with the Garrison principles.

Mr. Niles was perfectly adapted to conduct the affairs of the church in a most thorough and efficient manner, so long as the waters were smooth; but a trouble, a difficulty, no matter how slight, seemed to disturb his judgment and his reason in exact proportion as they disturbed his heart.

Quiet and happy, he was a strong, very consistent man. Worried or perplexed, he seemed to drift about with as little purpose or meaning as a straw upon a swift-moving current.

Now, as he rode along, no one can tell how anxious he was — anxious about Florence and Rachel, home and the parish. Every mile that brought him nearer the end of his journey became a sensible relief to him. He began to dread even the change of cars, and really longed to reach the quiet, unfrequented railroad which, at last, would end his troubles. On the next railroad, however, there was no car for the colored; nor, indeed, did he have any more perplexity for the day.

People stared at them as they met them, and some few whispered to ask of Mr. Niles if Rachel were not a southern negro; but they came to the small station four miles from Mr. Niles's door, at last, without any further molestation; and, dearly as Mr. Niles loved his home, it seemed to him that its surroundings never looked half so pleasantly before.

The station was a queer little octagonal building, looking, Florence thought, as she first saw it, like the pictures she had seen, in English story books, of summer houses. As they went towards its door, a boy's head, in a close, blue cloth cap, pushed itself up over the top of a high bank, and a voice called out, —

" I'm here, father! "

" Ah, Frank! always on hand," said Mr. Niles, going to the edge of the bank. " What have you to take us home in ? "

" Deacon Dexter's team," answered the boy. " Mother thought the wagon was bigger than ours, and there might be a lot of luggage. I've tied them down here, 'cause Katy, you know, don't like the cars."

" All right, my boy; now, can you lend a hand to get these trunks round ? "

12

"I'll drive them up; the cars won't be back again."

So saying, the head disappeared; and soon Florence heard such a whoa-ing and backing from under the hill, that any one would have thought a coach and six had become involved in inextricable difficulties.

In a very short time, driving right up what seemed to be an almost perpendicular bank, came, first, a white horse's nose, then a bay one's, then two horses' heads, and so, by degrees, the whole establishment, consisting of a large, rough wagon, with two seats, and a small boy sitting on the front, looking, Florence thought, as her eye first fell upon him, like one of the monkeys hopping out of toy boxes, of which she had seen so many in New York.

Kate, the colt, being disappointed in not having found the cars to be frightened at, seemed determined to make what amends she could now. She shied away, first, from Rachel; but this the nurse was fast becoming accustomed to at the north; then she planted her two front feet very firmly, and declared, as plainly as a horse could, that nothing should tempt her to approach the pile of trunks.

"Steady, Frank!" said his father, standing by, without moving to arrest the plunging animal. "Rein her right up to them! She won't go? Well, give her some smart cuts with the whip. There, now. Once more, and you have her."

Kate reared, and dashed forward past the trunks, but was immediately drawn back; and old Billy, the bay horse, behaving in a most exemplary manner, as a minister's horse should, the contest ended, as it had so many times before, in Kate's giving up, and becoming at once docile and quiet.

Florence had passed through the respective stages of astonishment, fright, and admiration, as she witnessed the contest; but when it ended, she was standing with a face as full of life, almost, as if she had been an actor. Rachel had her hands raised. She never saw so little a boy placed, as she thought, in circumstances of such peril before; and a man standing by, and looking on, too! She was very indignant. It was much worse than the car for colored persons.

As the wagon came exactly into its right position, Mr. Niles said, —

"Well done, my boy! You have hit the nail right on the head."

The boy sprang out of the wagon, and, as he did so, looked to his father for an introduction.

"It hardly seems as if I need tell you, Frank," said his father, "that this is your cousin Florence."

The boy raised his cap with his red hand, and looked steadily in Florence's face. They both smiled; and this was their first and only greeting.

Frank now ran his eye curiously over Rachel, into whose head was slowly coming the idea that this boy, driver, servant, and every thing else, as he seemed to be, was in truth and reality a cousin of Florence — how very strange!

"Shake hands with Rachel," said Mr. Niles, remembering the morning affront.

Frank did so very cordially, saying at the same time, —

"I have heard my mother speak so often of Ra-

chel, it seems to me as if I had always known her.
This is uncle George's 'mauma,' I suppose."

"She is my mauma," said Florence, bursting out
into a very merry laugh. "My father was a northerner; besides, men don't have a mauma."

Frank blushed a little, but said, promptly, —

"Well, whosever mauma she is, my mother will
be very glad to see her, uncle George has written us
so often about her."

"Thank you — thank you," said Rachel, bowing
and smiling in a very pleased way. "Massa George
was always so good — always thought more of dis
ole mauma dan she deserve."

But Florence, while this conversation was going
on, had not allowed Frank to do all the looking.
She had found out that he was not a large boy —
indeed, she doubted if he was much taller than she
was herself — that he looked very much like his
father, only the white hair on the one head was exchanged for close brown curls on the other; and the
round, swelling outlines of the child's face bore no
trace of a care or a grief.

He was oddly dressed, or at least he looked so to
Florence; for his pants were short, showing a pair
of large, clumsy boots; and his jacket, instead of
being buttoned up to the chin, was open, displaying
shirt bosom, stock, and a collar turned over within
his coat. He had the corner of a red silk pocket-
handkerchief peeping ostentatiously out of the jacket
pocket, and his hands did not look as if they had
ever worn a glove. Still, the whole appearance of
the boy was — and so it struck Florence — not only
manly, but gentlemanly. She felt drawn towards

him, as if she had always — as he said of Rachel —
" known " him.

Every thing was expeditiously adjusted for the
four-mile drive which yet remained to them. Florence was very weary. It seemed to her as if she could
never ride that distance, particularly in such a looking vehicle. She had seen some as shabby at Myrtle
Bush, but they were only for plantation purposes;
no white person ever thought of riding in them.
However, she clambered in, making such very awkward work of it that Frank laughed several times so
merrily that she could not help joining with him.
Rachel was more clumsy still, but Frank's intuitive
good nature told him to be very silent and sober
during her speedy entrances and as speedy returns.

At last they were fairly in. Could it be that Mr.
Niles would trust that little boy again with those
horses? Such was certainly his intention; for he
never even touched the reins, or gave the slightest
direction for the backing and turning which immediately followed. Twilight was fast settling down
upon every object as they reached the road, and
started away on a brisk trot.

Early spring in the country is, to one unaccus-
tomed to it, a very dreary season. The brown
ground, parched and shrunk by the long, hard, winter frosts, with its deep mud ruts and its sluggish
pools, its old, gray stones lying upon its hard surface,
as if no sun or warmth could ever thaw off the clinging dampness; the poor, leafless, lifeless-looking
shrubs; the great, bare, desolate trees, with their
black, swinging branches, and their naked, pendent
birds' nests; the very walls, and fences, and houses,

have an ill-used look, as if they had been in the service of a hard master, and had not spirit enough left ever to start into cheerful existence again. Added to this natural and inevitable aspect, to-night, was the deepening twilight, wrapping every object in its mantle of gray — dark, sombre, almost funereal. Florence, weary as she was, was keenly alive to it all. The horses jogged along, now up hill, now down; the wagon rolled noisily and roughly over the uneven road. There was not a single living object in sight. Here and there, a brown farm house, without a piazza or a blind, — without a yard, garden, and, very often, without even a bare tree, — was all that she saw, as she strained her tired eyes, and peered out into the shadowed landscape.

Her uncle was silent; in truth, he himself was weary, too, and was thinking, just now, much more of the pleasant home to which he was going than of his companions.

Florence thought over all Ida's stories. It was far more dreary and desolate than even she had described; so Florence dropped her head, and was ready to cry.

Frank had been too busy with his horses to show any interest in his cousin; but just as the blue eyes were adding their own mist to the darkness, a pair of very bright, laughing, hazel ones peeped under her bonnet; and though not a word was said, she found herself smiling back.

"Get up there, Kate!" said Frank, glancing back over his shoulder at Florence. "Show yourself off a little! You've jogged on long enough minister fashion."

"Don't hurry them too fast, my son," said Mr. Niles, waking up at the sound of the word "minister."

"No, sir," said Frank, snapping his whip in true driver style. "We'll just show them they can go 'two-forty,' if they have a mind."

Away flew the horses like the wind; now drawing the wagon down, with a sudden jerk, into some deep mud hole, and now nearly tossing out the trembling negro, by striking the centre of some rock, lying by the road, in order to avoid a rut.

Mr. Niles was evidently used both to the roads and the driver. He relapsed into his former quiet; but Florence was entering most completely into the spirit of the scene. Naturally very fearless, it became at once, to her, sport; and instead of tears, Frank heard low but very musical bursts of laughter, as they dashed along.

"Halloo!" said he, suddenly checking his horses, "mother's is all lighted up now — see there!" He pointed to a small white house which lay about a quarter of a mile before them, on the side of a hill. It stood quite alone; Florence, as she looked eagerly at it, could see no other house.

"Why," said she, "is that the house? I thought we were going to Grafton."

Frank laughed; and, standing up in the wagon, pointed below them, in another direction. Florence jumped up to see what was there; and though Rachel held her very tight, she tossed to and fro like a ball, with every jostle of the wagon.

"I like that," said Frank, enthusiastically, as he sat watching her instead of the horses. "Not a bit

afraid of tumbling out, any more than I am, are
you? Can you see it?"

It! Florence wondered if he meant Grafton, and
answered, —

"No; all I see is a church and a few white
houses."

"Well, what more would you have? That is the
beautiful, picturesque town of Grafton — the residence
of the Rev. Edward Niles and his illustrious family."

"That!" and Florence's voice expressed such
undisguised astonishment, that again Frank laughed
heartily.

"Yes, *that.* It is a town of about twenty-five
hundred inhabitants — has two stores, a post office, a
tavern, two factories, and four doctors, three lawyers,
and one parson, not counting the Methodist, who
comes here to gather the lambs of his flock once in
four weeks."

"Frank!" said his father, authoritatively, "don't
be so trifling!"

"No, sir," said Frank, drawing down his face into a
mock expression of gravity, and turning it full upon
Florence; but at this instant his father caught the
reins from his hands.

"Whoa! there — whoa!" he called suddenly, and
very energetically.

"Ah, Jennie, is that you? and Totty too?"

"Papa! Papa!" called a very sweet child voice.
"Please, papa, take me in!" and Florence saw, as she
jumped up on her feet, a girl taller than herself,
leading a little child, coming directly towards them.
Totty was lifted into her father's arms; and then the
girl came round, and reaching over the high, muddy
wagon wheel, said, —

"Cousin Florence, I know! We are very glad to see you safe in Grafton, and Rachel too;" and the little nimble figure leaped over the muddy tracks, and offered both hands to the surprised negro. "Mother speaks very often of you."

"Jump in, puss; don't you want to?" said her father.

Jennie glanced at the thick cakes of mud which were rolling off from the wheels, and at her own clean dress, then said, "No, sir, thank you; I will be at home as soon as you are."

"Get out of the way, or I shall splash you all over," said Frank, resuming the reins, and starting. "You do well to get there as soon as we do, I tell you. Kate won't stand that."

Snap went the whip; but his father interfered, and Jennie answered by a laugh, which both Florence and Frank echoed.

"There's mother, I declare!" and Frank did not need his father now, either to see the figure which was slowly approaching, or to check the horses.

Totty clapped her hands, and shouted as if she had been just coming, as well as the others. "There's mamma, there's mamma!"

"Totty is always the noisy one," said the mother, coming now up to the wagon; "but where is my little Flossy?"

Florence rose slowly and shyly from her seat, but two strong, loving arms were thrown right about her, and without another word she was lifted from the wagon.

"Welcome home, my darling!" and warm, motherly kisses made the young orphan's heart throb quickly with a sensation both old and new.

Jennie caught Florence's hand as her mother dropped it; and while she turned to welcome Rachel, in the same true, earnest way, the two children walked on towards the house, which lay but a few rods before them.

What a small thing it was!

Florence thought, as they opened the front gate and we.it up through the long yard, that it must be the kitchen, and that the house lay in some other direction, as they build their houses at the south ; but Jennie walked straight up to the door, and as she opened it the pleasant home light streamed out from the parlor, and fell upon the tiny hall, with its small winding staircase, and its bit of a table, with the brown linen cover. Then Florence knew that this was her home.

What a cheerful parlor! Though Florence had never in her life seen one so small and low, still there was an air of taste, refinement, and cultivation, which, child as she was, impressed her immediately. The wagon drove up to the back door; and as the lights flitted back and forth through the different rooms, they had very much the appearance to Florence of the fireflies on the southern plantation. She had of late only been used to the gas-fixed lights; and these, with their changing light and shade, were very pretty to her now.

Where was the man servant ? He did not come, and her uncle was lifting out and bringing in the luggage. Every body was helping him, too; even Totty had come pulling in a large carpet bag, almost as big again as herself. But the whole operation was finished without a servant of any kind making their appearance; and no sooner was it done, than her aunt came to her and took her in her lap, pushing her curls off from her face, and turning it up towards her own, while she looked into it with the memories of the long past and the dead dimming her eye and quivering on her trembling lip.

Florence was awed by the emotion which she could not understand; she stole her hand softly into her aunt's, and sinking her head gradually on her shoulder, nestled down, as if at last she had found a rest.

And there the two sat, while the bustle of the arrival went on in the adjoining rooms; and by and by Totty came in and sidled along close to her mother, while she caught hold of Florence's dress and gave it pulls, to tell her in that silent way that she had taken a place which belonged only to herself. But this not being attended to, she clambered resolutely up, and seated herself without ceremony in Florence's lap. Her mother smiled, and putting them both down, left the room.

A few minutes alone — for Totty soon followed her mother — rested Florence, though she was so tired; every sense was on the alert, doing, for this night, at least, double duty.

Then came a bell — soft, musical — saying, as plainly as if its brass tongue were human, that it was used to call the family to a pleasant, social meal.

Totty made her appearance as it ceased.

"Come, come!" she said, quickly; "tea is all ready,

and we have some tarts;" and she held out her hand,
fat and soft as a cotton ball, and about as round.

Florence took it, and she pulled her along through
a narrow entry into a dining room, which was even
smaller than the parlor itself. But what a tea table!
There was a large, bright lamp burning upon its centre, and such a pile of snow-white bread, cake, tarts,
preserves, and delicate broiled ham; such shining
white dishes and glistening silver! It really looked
as if there was a little miniature lamp burning by
every plate. As they took their seats, Totty folded
up her hands, and glanced from under her eyes at
the plate of tarts which stood close by her.

Florence had almost forgotten a blessing would be
asked; but she listened eagerly as the solemn words
were uttered, and she was sure, as her uncle finished,
that she heard, through the open door of the next
room, Rachel's voice, saying, "Bress de Lord!"

There were so many questions to be asked and
answered, that the pleasant tea-table seemed likely
to last until bed time; and perhaps it might have,
but Totty gave unmistakable evidence, that having
had her tarts she now wanted her bed. So thanks
were returned, and as they rose Florence saw, for the
first time, an Irish girl, who, she thought, must be a
servant, enter the room.

"Rachel is in the kitchen close by you if you
would like to go and see her," said her aunt; and
Totty, having forgotten the nap, was clamorous to
show her the way.

The kitchen was the largest room Florence had
yet seen. Here stood a large cooking stove—an entirely new article to her. She had inquired what

they were of Ida as she passed the iron stores in New York, but had no idea how they would look in operation.

Sitting close by it, with the palms of both her hands extended, was Rachel.

Perhaps there was something in its warmth which called forth the pleased and grateful expression on the negro's face. Florence started as she saw it. Now, for the first time, she saw her mauma as she was at Myrtle Bush, without the heavy frown which was becoming the habitual expression of her troubled life in New York.

"Bress de Lord, little missus," she said, as Florence came close up to her; "dis, den, seem like home — eh, eh! even Rachel say *home*, now." And she pointed to the neat, plentiful supper which had been provided for her.

"White cloth, clean knives, all nice — Massa George sister, for true! Bress de Lord foreber and eber! Amen!"

But Florence had no great enthusiasm to waste to-night. She began to realize that she was very tired, and, like Totty, wanted her bed; and while she was whispering so to Rachel, her aunt opened the door, saw untold what she needed, and said she would have family prayers then, so that the travellers could go early to rest.

In a few minutes the same bell rang again. Florence thought to the end of her life she should never forget how it sounded; and then all, even to Ann, the Irish girl, began to move towards the dining room.

Rachel sat still, glancing longingly in at the open door; and as she looked, Mrs. Niles called, —

" Come, Rachel, here is a seat always for you."

"Thank you, missus. Bress de good Lord. He care for us now, for sure. I neber distrust him again, neber, neber!" So saying Rachel took the chair, and never for the whole year, at morning or evening prayers, was it vacant or tardily filled.

Rachel was not here to occupy the same room with Florence. She must go into her cousin Jennie's; but the nurse should not be far off; and Mrs. Niles, in her gentle, pleasant way, showed Florence the arrangement of the different sleeping rooms, kissed her fondly, and left her alone with her nurse.

Florence shut the door, and looking around the small, low room, felt quite disposed to cry; but she could not force a tear. After all, the same look of comfort and cheerfulness which spread itself over the house below was here too. The bed quilt was white as driven snow. The furniture was light, painted wood, with pretty bunches of flowers upon it, and the two windows had neat muslin curtains, with a cornice of bright crimson, and crimson bands to form the loops. The paper, too, held those tears back, for the ground was delicate straw-color, like the furniture, and trailing all over it were bright bunches of the radiant fuschia.

Florence never dreamed, as she sat there to-night, looking at these different things, that they had cost her uncle's family many an act of self-denial — more by far than she had ever performed during the whole of her short life.

Nothing was handsome, as it was in New York, but they were all so happy-looking! Aunt Niles would have felt well repaid for her planning if she

could have known precisely the effect it was produ-
cing upon this orphan niece to-night.

Florence went to sleep with Rachel sitting beside
her, and as she did so her mind was filled with a
crowding and jostling army of figures. Ida, and
George, and Grace, and the car full of strangers, and
the two negro women in the colored car — Frank
and the prancing horse, and Totty with her aunt and
Jennie — all chased each other before her half-shut
eyes, like the pictures of a magic lantern; but at last
she fell soundly asleep, and Rachel, kneeling beside
her, set apart and hallowed this first night in the new
home.

CHAPTER XII.

FLORENCE did not awake the next morning until a late hour, and when she first opened her eyes she recalled with difficulty where she was. The sun was shining in at her window, lighting up the pretty bunches of fuschia, painting the pleasant colored furniture with a bright, golden gleam, and then hiding itself in the long folds of the spotless curtains. All was so still, so very still, that the first intelligible thought Florence had was, that she was again at Myrtle Bush. Lying quietly, she watched the shadows on the walls, the shadows on the curtains, the shadows on the low ceiling. They seemed to be the only living things around her. Just so she had seen the sun glint in and the shadows dance to and fro, at Myrtle Bush.

She raised her head, almost expecting to hear the sound of negro voices in the yard below her window; but as she did so, she caught a view of the long, barren hill, the brawny, stiff trees, the brown, hard ground, and she needed nothing more to recall vividly enough where she was.

Her first impulse was to wish herself at the south, in New York, any where but there. She was still tired, and like all tired children, inclined to be fretful; but while she lay wondering whether it was best to cry or not, she heard a voice under her window, to which she raised herself again to listen.

"Harness Billy, and drive down to the deacon's for what, mother?" asked Frank.

His mother answered in a low voice, which Florence could not quite hear.

"Why can't I wait until Flossy is up? She will like to go too."

Still Florence could not hear.

"I don't believe in her being so very tired; she was as bright as a lark last night. I mean to throw a stick up to her window and wake her up. Why, it's most eight o'clock."

And now Florence heard a laugh which was evidently not a child's. She was very anxious to know whose it was, and who were out there; so she crept out of bed, and hiding herself under the window, carefully raised a curtain and peeped out.

There stood Frank, with a large stick raised in his hand, as if he meant to throw it; but he instantly saw her, and dropping it, touched his cap, and made a very low bow.

Florence dropped the curtain, but he shouted, —

"Come down, Flossy, and take a drive. I am going to Deacon Johnson's after some meat for dinner."

"Wait!" said she, peeping out again, and shaking her long, dark curls at him, as if they would take the sound up and carry it along.

"Yes, marm," said Frank; "only don't be forever. It's most noon now."

Florence thought the prolonged marm was very droll. She began to dress herself with all possible despatch, and forgot to cry. While she was busy with some refractory hooks, wondering all the time,

13

rather impatiently, where Rachel was, the door opened, and Jennie's pleasant face made its appearance.

Every one who has been to a strange place, filled
with strangers, knows by experience how differently
it appears in the morning from what it did on the
previous night. Now, Florence really did not know
whether this plain, pleasant-looking girl could be the
cousin Jennie she had previously seen. She looked
better, older, and more like a woman ; but a moment
longer brought out the same smile which had riveted
Florence's eyes upon her face, and her "good morning" sounded precisely like the "cousin Flossy" at
the road-side reception.

"May I go to ride?" asked Florence, yielding,
without knowing it, at once to the superiority which
every action and look of Jennie indicated. "I should
like to very much."

"O, yes, indeed," said Jennie; "but if you are not
careful, Frank will tease you half to death to go
every time he harnesses. He never wants to move
an inch alone; but you must have your breakfast first."

Florence heard Frank now calling to his horse, and
in a pretty, half-timid manner, asked if she might not
go without it? She should so much prefer the ride.

"Perhaps so," said Jennie, assisting her to manage
the refractory dress. "We will go down and ask
mother."

So down they went, hand in hand, and Florence
found a reception awaiting her hardly less cordial
than the one she received last night.

The family had been to breakfast an hour and a
half ago; but she had been allowed to sleep, hoping
a good morning nap would entirely remove the

fatigue of the day before. Her breakfast was waiting, and Ann, as soon as she heard that she had come down, made her appearance, bringing some smoking dishes with her.

Rachel, with her hands dripping with dish-water, stepped forward to see how " little missus " was looking, after having spent this first night of her life away from her.

" Frank shall wait," — so his mother said, — " until Florence has had something to eat ; " but when she saw how impatient she was, and how much more eager for the ride than the breakfast, she took off some slices of bread for her on her return, and told her to go. Wrapping her up warmly — for the morning air was still keen — she cautioned Frank to drive slowly and carefully, and return as soon as his errand was done.

Frank promised, and away they went, Rachel sending after them a troubled look, which amused the young driver.

It was not until they had ridden quite a distance that Florence remembered Ida's description of the family carriage.

Here in truth was the very same old Billy and open buggy wagon which had carried her over the hills four years ago; but when Florence looked at the large, bay horse, round and shining, with his arched neck, his long, flowing mane, and his proud way of throwing out his feet, she thought him as handsome as her uncle's carriage horses. The wagon was roomy, and it was easy enough. She could not have told, if she had been asked that moment, whether it was red or white, black or yellow; she only knew she was enjoying every step of the ride.

Frank had, of course, always lived in the country, and was a regular country boy. To him every fence every tree, every rock, all the turns and twists in the road, had their separate, living interest. Not a knoll, but it had some story connected with it; not a brook, but it babbled to him of some sweet memory. The very hazelnut bushes, growing rank around the road-side, or the drooping, pretty barberries, were hung to him with the ripe, tempting fruit, which he had so often gathered. All children are social, if left to follow out the dictates of their nature; but Frank was especially so, as Jennie had said; he disliked being alone as much as nature abhors a vacuum, and never was, if he could help it.

To have a new companion was a treat he had been looking forward to every day of the past year; but even in his pleasantest dreams he had hardly pictured her so pretty, so brave, and so willing to be amused.

One would have thought, to have heard these children talk, as they rode along, that they had always been together.

Florence was not as new to country sights as she had been to those of the city. To be sure, she had never seen the diversified scenery which was now before her; but the country is the country, with the same broad, bending, blue sky, be it north or south, and the feeling of freshness and freeness came back to the child, as the sharp northern breeze lifted up her hair, and twisted it round the small, flat hood with which her aunt had carefully covered her; or, creeping under the well-pinned shawl, made her shiver with a new sensation.

All at once the contrast between this ride and those she must have taken in the city seemed to occur to Frank.

"I declare, Flossy," said he, "how glad you must be to get off from those noisy stones in New York streets, and out of one of those miserable covered carriages! Why, I would as soon ride in a hearse as in them."

Florence laughed. She could not help wondering why she had never thought so, when she used to ride so much. So she said, —

"Uncle Henry's carriage is a very easy one. You lean back — back — as if you were going to lie down on something that was all velvet, or down, Ida says. I don't know what down is."

"Why, down is goose — you goose!" said Frank, unable to resist the comparison so naturally suggested.

Florence colored. She was not pleased; and Frank, seeing it, said quickly, —

"Don't be vexed, Flossy; I only meant just nothing at all, as mother says I do, half the time when I talk; but the carriage — tell me all about uncle's horses."

Here Florence was entirely in doubt. She had only noticed that they were handsome and black, and could tell nothing more.

"Was Henry ever allowed to drive them?"

He often sat on the driver's seat, but Florence thought never held the reins.

"I'll bet you a fourpence," said Frank, slapping the reins down emphatically on Billy's back, "that this horse will beat them both — long trot or short, I don't care which, only let me have hold of the reins."

What would Ida say to that, Florence wondered, but wisely made no further remark.

How short the ride was to Deacon Johnson's! and yet they had not met even a dog by the wayside.

Frank wanted Florence to come into the butcher's shop with him. She had no idea what kind of a place it was, and eagerly jumped out; but when Frank opened the door of a small room, and she passed in, she saw only quarters of beef hanging up, she drew back; but Frank seized her hand.

"Come," said he, "he is one of the people, and it won't do not to come in and say a word." So he really forced Florence within the door, and she found herself surrounded by the odd medley of a country butcher's shop.

On a small shelf, close beside her, were three or four glass jars of colored sticks of candy; an earthen mug held some clay pipes; cakes of soap were standing on end, like police men, to guard the treasure; and removed a short distance, as if not so tempting to light fingers, were a box of threads and tape, three small, undressed dolls, a box of cigars, and some papers of tobacco. Within and around, above and below, were hung festoons of colored paper, cut in fashion of honeycombs, soiled and torn now, but in the day of their pristine beauty, the pride and delight of Miss Angelina Maria Johnson, the eldest and most tasteful of the worthy deacon's family. Upon the counter, with great bloody knives, and saws close by them, lay pieces of raw meat, soiled brown paper, and rolls of untidy-looking twine; while half-cut cheeses, balls of white butter, strings of onions, and piles of potatoes filled up, it seemed to Florence's confused vision, every imaginable place.

"Deacon Johnson," said Frank, addressing an elderly, pleasant-looking man, behind the counter, "this is my cousin Florence, from South Carolina — uncle George's daughter. She has come to spend the year with us, and mother would like three pounds of your best surloin steak."

The deacon bowed stiffly to Florence, as if he thought she was a very small child to take notice of, and besides that, was — what was just about the same as being no one at all — a southerner. He certainly was not disposed to take half as much notice of her as he would have of a sheep or a nice, plump calf.

"Is your marm particular about its being surloin?" asked the deacon, deliberately turning over a large piece of the round.

"I think she is, deacon," said Frank; "she says she won't buy meat any oftener than she can afford to have it good."

"The round comes two cents cheaper on a pound," said the man, balancing his knife over it; "guess it will do, won't it?"

"I am afraid not, deacon," said Frank, turning round, as if he was going away; "I will tell her you haven't any thing but round."

"Well, I don't know," said the butcher, turning slowly to another piece; "I suppose I might cut her off three pounds of surloin, if she is very particular; but we always eat the round at home."

The deacon's knife came down now in good earnest; and as he weighed the meat, he said, —

"Three pounds and a half. You may tell your marm I shan't charge her nothing for the half."

"Thank you," said Frank, a comical smile creeping

over his face; "I have no doubt it is all very nice.
It looks good enough to eat raw;" and Frank made
a snapping motion with his jaws, which made Florence jump. She thought it was a great dog come in
behind her.

As the children drove away from the shop, the
deacon followed them with his eyes, and made this
remark, —

"That ere fellow is as full of the rogue as he can
hold. If his father don't look out for him, he will come
to the gallows, for all that I know ; and that ere little
gal is mere milk and water. I don't see what upon
'arth she wants to come here, a-sponging on our
minister, for. It is as much as we can do to support
him, any how."

Florence kept watching the piece of meat, which
lay in the bottom of a basket between them, as if she
was afraid of it ; and it may be questioned whether
the child had ever come so near a raw piece before
in her life.

The ride home was quite as pleasant as the ride
out. Once or twice she thought of Frank's calling a
covered carriage a hearse, as the wind, still continuing to play with her, blew her shawl over her head,
and turned the hood for a covering to her face.

Rachel was standing at the gate, looking up and
down the street, as they came home. She had not
forgotten Kate, nor the mud holes, of the night before; and though she had too much good sense to
interfere with what Mrs. Niles allowed, she had
passed a very anxious two hours, and now was as
demonstrative in her joy as she had been quiet
before.

"Dare dat Rachel," said Frank, imitating exactly the tone and manner of the negro; "she come to hunt up dat little missus, that 'lope with her cousin. For true, she glad to see her home gin. Eh, eh!"

Florence had never heard a negro word from any one but herself and Rachel before, since she came north; so she was laughing merrily, and a little noisily, as the wagon drove past Rachel into the back yard.

"Eh, eh!" said Rachel, as if continuing Frank's last words. "Little missus, don't be noisy in the street; dat not lady-like, for true!" and Rachel's white turban shook back and forth, "like a white day-lily in the wind," Frank whispered.

When Florence went into the house, she found that two little girls, daughters of Mr. Jones, the farmer, who lived next door, had come in "to see her." They were small, dumpy girls, with very brown faces, red cheeks, and short, light hair, cut off round in their necks. They wore two red hoods, lined with blue cambric; large blanket shawls, and brown calico dresses, with pantalets of the same material. Their thick, muddy boots Mrs. Niles had placed upon a braided rug-mat; and there they sat, with their feet wide apart, their hands covered with blue yarn mittens, crossed in their laps, and their great, expressionless eyes fixed upon Florence the moment she came within the door. She stopped and looked at them as if they were natural curiosities; and, indeed, it would be difficult to describe how different they were from any who had ever entered her child's world before.

The southern children are, as every body knows,

precocious; not so much in mental development as in the ways and usages of society : so are those who reside in the city; but for those who have always lived in a country town, it seems as if it took ten years longer to wake them up to any idea of the courtesies, almost the decencies, of life. "Green!" has passed into an extensive and vulgar use; but one is irresistibly reminded of it among the country little folks. It seems as if the verdantness of their fields became an intrinsic part of their being—as if every awkwardness of mind and manner sprouted upon them as luxuriantly as the weeds in their native soil. Nothing now could be more entirely ludicrous to a child bred in good society, than these two children, with their half-open mouths and their dumb silence. Florence did not know what to say to them, as her aunt told her who they were, and for what object they had come; but Jenny, who had been watching them in much amusement, now came forward, to their mutual relief. She asked questions for Florence, and answered them for the children, until they both began to fancy they were talking themselves, and pretty soon actually to do so.

"Myrtilda Jane" and "Sarah Louisa Maria Bates." Florence caught their names, and by and by began to have a feeling that they were actually living children, and not wooden images sitting up in the chairs. She remembered how Grace had put her fingers into Rachel's eyes, to see if they were glass, and she felt strangely inclined to put hers into these four pale-blue ones that stared at her, or to pull a wire, and see if they would not shut, as her wax dolls did at Myrtle Bush.

"Let's go out in the yard and play 'catcher,'" said Myrtilda at last, rather suddenly.

"Catcher!" Florence had never heard of such a play for large children. She had had it played with her when she was a baby, and had in turn chased babies round the room; but for such great girls, how strange!

Jennie had to explain to the visitors that Florence was not used to such hard plays, but would like to go out with them when the ground was settled, and run round their father's farm.

Emboldened by this, Sarah Louisa ventured the following request to Mrs. Niles, who at this moment came into the room:—

"Marm says she should like to have her"—pointing to Florence with her blue mitten—"come down and take tea with us this afternoon, if you ain't no objections."

Mrs. Niles saw, by Florence's face, that the request was an unwelcome one, and said,—

"Thank your mother, and tell her some time soon, Florence will be very happy to come; but she is rather tired to-day; and, besides,"—here her aunt drew Florence close to her,—"we can't spare her quite so soon."

"Yes, marm," said Sarah. "She may come Saturday, mayn't she? Mr. Jones said he wouldn't have no school then."

"Perhaps so. We will see when Saturday comes."

So the children tied their hoods, and as their errand was done, began to give unequivocal signs of being prepared to go. Mrs. Niles helped them off as expeditiously as she could, and Florence stood watching their little square figures as they disappeared down the hill.

"What language do they talk?" said she, turning to her aunt. "I couldn't understand hardly a word they said."

"Yankee English, my little Flossy; you will learn it very quickly — quite as soon as they will what you say."

"Ma'am!" asked Florence, as if the appellation contained a whole world of questions, doubts, and uncertainties.

"You never thought, Florence, that you speak English differently from us at the north."

"No, ma'am," said Florence, with the same expression of wonder.

"You watch then, darling, and see if you can't detect in what manner, for yourself."

"Yes, ma'am;" and Florence's soft voice had in it a shade of trouble, as if she had been accused of doing something wrong; so her aunt sent her away to forget all about it, in "helping Rachel to unpack and put away her clothes."

"*Help* Rachel!" why, such a thought had never occurred to her in the whole of her life, and it struck her now as something vastly amusing. She was busy and happy until the dinner bell rang.

"What is that?" she said, dropping an armful of clothes, and looking as surprised as if she had never heard one before.

"Eh! how your mauma know ebery ting? for sure, you *are* a little missus."

"Dinner!" said Totty, pushing her two round cheeks inside the door.

"Dinner!" repeated Florence; "why, the morning hasn't begun yet!"

"Dinner's come," persisted Totty, "and we got some beefsteak and a mince pie — come!"

Florence was not dressed for dinner, and Rachel was hurrying to perform her toilet, when Totty stopped her.

"Mamma don't put on her clean frock until after dinner, nor Jennie either — nobody does;" and she shook her little head very wisely.

"Come, Flossy!" called her aunt, from the foot of the stairs. "Never mind changing your dress until by and by."

Florence ran down so fast that Totty, not able to keep up with her, set up a shrill scream, which called her mother again to the stairs, and arrested Florence's steps very quickly.

"Hush!" said Mrs. Niles, in a tone which had much more of entreaty than authority; but Totty only screamed the louder.

"She wants to take hold of your hand," said her mother. "Totty is very affectionate, and loves cousin Flossy dearly."

Florence looked as if the affection was not so warmly returned, but waited for the cross face, which came pouting up to her.

As she entered the dining room, she glanced up at the clock. Half past twelve — just lunch time at Myrtle Bush and in New York. How very droll it was!

Mr. Niles's table was always a social place. He was occupied away from his family most of the day, and he felt very desirous to make this short time of meeting them a source of profit and pleasure to them all. They had to-day so many pleasant things to tell and to hear, that it was not until the meal was nearly ended, that Florence remembered Ida's description of the dinner table at Grafton. She glanced cautiously around to see how true it was, and was immediately struck with the ease and propriety of every person there ; even Totty divided her attempts to feed herself between a small silver fork and her fingers, using sometimes one and sometimes the other, with about equal dexterity. She felt her cheeks color with shame, as she remembered how she had feared to look up when her uncle first dined with them in New York.

After dinner, she must go with Frank all over the garden, yards, and fields, which were attached to the parsonage.

" Only a general voyage of discovery," Frank said — "touching at every port, on some future occasion."

Time, this day, was certainly winged. Tea came, then a short cheerful evening, and once more Florence went to her pretty painted bedstead, lying still in the soft lamp light, and twining and intertwining the bunches of curious flowers.

The next morning the first movement of Jennie awakened her. She opened her eyes, and found the room full of dim, gray light. She had not seen it before since she left Myrtle Bush, and it laid itself over every object in the room, like the familiar mantle of a friend.

" It is very early," said Jennie, softly, " but mother likes to have me get up and do my reading before breakfast, when I can."

"May I, too?" said Florence, rubbing her eyes violently.

"I should love dearly to have you," whispered Jennie. "I am reading Ruth, now, and it is very interesting."

Florence made an effort to waken thoroughly; Jennie stood by, helping her, with very merry bursts of laughter, until at last she was on her feet, yawning and stretching like a baby.

When the two girls sat down with their Bibles, together, the clear daylight came cheerfully in. Away in the far east Florence saw small rosy clouds, waking up like red-cheeked children; and there, with Ruth, and Jennie, and the beautiful early morning time, Florence began her second day.

When Rachel opened the door very softly, to see if "little missus" were still asleep, she found the children hand in hand, on their knees together; and hurrying away, she said, half aloud, —

"Bress de good Lord! bress his great and holy name! Rachel no trust him. She say, I must care for dis orphan: de great God has well nigh forgotten her; and de bressed Saviour say, 'O ye of little faith, shall I care for dem dare lillies, dat neider toil nor spin; for dem fowls dat neber sow and neber reap, for de very grass in de field, which to-day is, and to-morrow be burned all up in dat oven — and shall dat heavenly Massa forget dat little missus have need of all dese tings? Shame on dis ole mauma — she live till now, and not truss him. Isn't little missus much better dan dey — dese fowls, and grass, and lily? Neber fail to trust him again — neber, neber."

CHAPTER XIII.

WHILE Florence is becoming slowly acquainted
with her aunt's family, it will help forward the progress of our story, if we give the reader a little quicker
insight into its details.

With Mrs. Niles's early history they are already
acquainted. She was married very soon after her
brother George, Florence's father, had entered college; and from that time he made his home with
her, until his health obliged him to leave for the
south. To exchange the care of her father's family
for one of her own, and for that of the parish, was
not so great a change as it is to many persons. Accustomed to responsibility from her youth, it seemed
to become almost a second nature; and she brought
now into the difficult and sometimes arduous life of
a minister's wife, sound judgment, strong common
sense, — which indeed is often only another name for
sound judgment, — warm piety, and active, earnest
habits of thought and feeling. With the singularity
which seems so often to attend the choice of a
partner for life of such natures, she selected from
among many, who thought the "virtuous woman
above rubies," a man in some respects decidedly
her inferior, or, at least, her opposite.

Edward Niles was handsome, agreeable, a leading
scholar both in college and the theological seminary,
and devotedly religious. He loved his profession

with a warmth and sincerity which was in itself one of the best recommendations. To serve his Master — serve him simply and faithfully — was his only ambition ; and none could have more effectually allured his wife to share his pathway with him.

Perhaps she did not see, through the glory of so much goodness, that somewhere — whether in his mental or moral faculties it would be difficult to determine — there was a certain vein of weakness, seldom apparent, but yet always there. It rarely, almost never, betrayed itself to the public ; no living being ever knew that Mrs. Niles was herself conscious of it. If it had any effect upon her, it was not to weaken in the least her attachment to her husband, but to make her a little stronger, a little more positive, a little more watchful.

Perhaps she would have evinced to an observing eye her consciousness of this defect in her husband's character by the over-careful training which she had bestowed upon her children as they advanced in life. We have before said that this weakness consisted in an inability to act with his usual energy and discretion whenever he met with any unpleasantness ; it mattered little of what nature it was ; a hard feeling, an unkind word, seemed to act upon him like the excessive chill of a polar climate upon the physical system of travellers. They benumbed, they induced a mental torpor, amounting sometimes to a seeming deprivation of his faculties. Mrs. Niles may have learned to know the drooping of the eyelid, and the dim, hazy expression of uncertainty which invariably on such occasions flitted across his

14

face ; certain it is, that she always managed to have the bold, ready answer in waiting, as it would have seemed, for the emergency ; and if he inclined to totter for an instant in his forward walk, her strong arm was ready for him to lean upon.

George, her eldest boy, — and another namesake of Florence's father, — was emphatically the mother boy. He seemed to inherit, *she* fondly thought, all that was valuable in the character of both parents. He grew up, too, quiet, gentlemanly, studious, and his whole character was deeply tinctured with the religious atmosphere which had been around him from his birth. He might have said, with some few other blessed ones, that he never knew a time when he did not love his Saviour.

He had been sent to college, and was now preparing himself for the ministry in a theological seminary. Into every year of his educational life his parents had woven a chain of self-denial, sacrifices, prayers, and anxieties. Many such had been woven by others — many such broken, and with it the hearts of those who had been forging it, link by link; but George Niles garlanded his with flowers, twining in sweet little forget-me-nots, heart's-ease, and the dear promising anemone.

Horace, the next boy, was his father's child, resembling him remarkably in personal appearance, but no more so physically than mentally. That blemish was there too, but unfortunately visited upon the next generation, with a want of power of resisting — yielding easily to temptation; falling to-day, and repenting and mourning over it to-morrow — wetting his mother's pillow with such tears as only an anxious mother can shed, to-night, and, with the first light of morning dawning in upon her, glad and bright as the sunlight, full of fresh hopes, new resolves, and strong intentions.

He was now just entered upon his college life. The boy was not contented with any thing short of what George had received; and as he was intelligent and "took to learning" with more fondness and tenacity than to any thing else, his parents reluctantly allowed him his choice.

Perhaps it was the uneasinesses and troubles into which Horace was constantly plunging that gave to Jennie a sedate womanliness far beyond her years. She was too old — far too care-taking; premature responsibility chilled the young life-blood, sent the pulses with too slow a beat, and drew already the very faintest shadow of a crowfoot around the corner of the eyes, which should have been clear and smooth as a summer sky.

Consequently Jennie was seldom free and joyous as other children. If she played, it was for others; if her amusements were not those of a grave, advanced character, it was because she must suit them to some less precocious child. Her mother saw the evil, but could not remedy it. Upon the eldest daughter in the family of a country minister, with the multiplicity of demands and the failure of supplies, always rests an amount of thinking and planning which surely may excuse their becoming prematurely old. It was a great comfort in one way to Mrs. Niles to have a competent, willing child to depend upon; in another, it gave her many hours of troubled thought for the child's future; but Jennie was so

gentle, so tender, so loving, if she was not sunshine
in the family, she was the sweet, soft moonlight, and
in spite of her fears, her mother rested in this child
as she did in the solemn, quiet night.

Frank was, as we know, boisterous, full of joy and
life, all unformed, quick in his better, quick also in his
more faulty, nature, good-natured, obliging, but imperious and demanding. Underlying the whole character was a vein of wit, of strong Yankee humor,
which bubbled up to the surface in all times and
places, with a great want of reverence to control it,
and with not too sensitive an appreciation of the
feelings and character of those by whom he was surrounded.

Next to him came Totty. The child was baptized
for her father's mother, Eunice. It was not a pretty
name for a baby, and in a warm-hearted, demonstrative family, one would think there was a conspiracy
to banish the baptismal name. Indeed, the children
here had become quite large before they felt sure
what they were to be called; so it came naturally to
pass, that Totty had always been Totty since she
had been any thing at all.

Every body that saw her said Totty was spoiled;
and as she belonged to that spoiled class, the babies
of a family, there is very much probability that she was.
Mrs. Niles had been so strict and exemplary a mother
with the other four, perhaps she thought she would
assert her right with this last one to follow in the
track worn by the feet of so many repentant parents.
So far, she had managed Totty always to be in every
body's way, always out of her place, — if a child like
her can be said to have any place, — always crying

when she should be still, and still when she should
be noisy. In short, Totty was now, and promised to
be in the future, the family mistake.

When Mrs. Niles received from her brother
George, some weeks previous to his death, a letter,
requesting her to take charge of this orphan child,
she had not for a moment a doubt or misgiving. If
her own family and parish cares were already quite
as much as she could well attend to, she very well
knew nothing in a woman's nature is so elastic as
her heart, and that if hers once took the child in, it
would give to her power to perform the additional
cares.

Florence's coming was almost like receiving a
grandchild, for the two Georges, her own and her
brother, were strangely mingled in her affections.
Her son was now just what the brother was when
she parted from him, and she had met him so seldom
since that she retained him in her memory in all
the freshness and gentleness of his early manhood.
She regretted his residence at the south; his southern marriage was a constant source of uneasiness to
her until she had seen and loved the fair young bride.
Then came troubled thoughts when she knew he
must be a slaveholder, for every throb of her good,
strong, honest heart was in favor of freedom. He
was a kind master; she heard he was reforming his
slaves; he was doing at the south an extensive and
thorough missionary work among the negroes; God
was signally blessing him. What right had she to
mete or measure out to him the where or how of his
life? Was he not in other and far better hands?

Now and then there came a present from him. At

first she had many thoughts of the way in which the
money had been earned. That slave labor — it clung
in its curse to every comfort it brought into the parsonage. It could not take from the love and remem-
brance of the giver, but it made itself felt and acknowledged by the conscientious minister's wife,
though it never found an utterance in a word of chid-
ing from her lips. If she could have dissevered herself from circumstances, she would have perished
rather than lived by what cost the happiness and
lives of so many immortal souls; but she knew that
deep and heinous as the sin of slavery is, those are
not to blame upon whom the evils of the system
have now fallen. Revolting from slavery, she made
the nice and just distinction between the slaveholder
and the slave trafficker; between the masters who
" were worthy of all honor " and those masters who
refused to give unto their servant that which was
just and equal, forgetting that they also have a Master in heaven.

She had inclined to ask of her brother that Florence might come to her without the slave; but a
little mature deliberation made her feel how hard it
would be for the child to be separated at once from
parents and from home, and come to a life so entirely
different from her own. She knew too well of Rachel, and her long-sustained and faithful character,
of her exemplary and devoted piety; and if a negro
must come north, she had often rejoiced in the good
judgment of her brother in choosing such a one.

Still no one can tell, but those who have lived in a
quiet New England family, what a change the admission of two such members would be likely to make.

Mrs. Niles foresaw, and though her heart longed for and clung to this only child of the dear dead brother, she was by no means ignorant of the days and weeks of trouble which she must necessarily bring to her. Florence must be, in every sense, one of them — her own child — with northern habits, prompt, efficient, learning at once to depend upon, and only upon, herself. It was a task, indeed; and so Mrs. Niles found it before the second day of Florence's stay with them had ended.

If Florence had been called upon to characterize the days of the week which intervened between her coming and the Sabbath, she would have used for them all, the one epithet of *busy* — doing what she could not have told, but always occupied, always happy. "She had not," as she said to Rachel, when they sat down for the home review of Saturday night, "had a moment in which she could be homesick." This she said apologetically, for it seemed to her hardly pretty or proper to be so contented when she had dreaded Grafton so much, and when Ida thought it was such a poor place in which to live. Rachel had been busy too; but to-night this was not her reason for being happy. The "bressed privileges little missus," she would say; "prayers in de morning and prayers in de evening; and de good Lord keeping watch over all. Who can say but his Sabbath may be a Sabbath for true, here? His great name be thanked foreber and eber! Amen!"

The coming, looked-for Sabbath proved to be a cold, gusty day — such a one as often returns to freshen our memory of the winter which has but just passed. Dark gray clouds rolled up in heavy

masses from the brown horizon; little patches of
blue sky fled away from them, as if they were pursu-
ing enemies; and even the glad, warm sun hid itself
in their sombre folds.

Through the creaking trees the wind whistled clear
and shrill, like a host of early magpies; and the
bunches of dead leaves, which had valiantly with-
stood the storms and fury of winter, now dropped
resistless, as though this last were "the unkindest
cut of all."

The very mud pools had a thin covering of ice,
and broke in under the horses' feet with that peculiar
sound so suggestive.

It was the first day since they had been at Grafton in which the sun had not shone. Florence was
very susceptible to all such external influences, and
as she rose early to finish the history of Ruth with
Jennie, before breakfast, the chill of the morning
spread itself over her, as gloomily as it did over the
landscape. Indeed, it was a very chilled little girl,
with numbed fingers and chattering teeth, that came
down to breakfast, and had the chill warmed off in
that way so familiar to every northern child, but so
strange to her, by having her hands held still in
Ann's warmed apron.

And then there followed — what child is proof
against such sensuous motives for loving? — a much
nicer breakfast than those of the week.

Mrs. Niles, like a woman of sterling good sense as
she was, thought much more of adapting her ways
and means to human nature as she found it, than of
turning the great stream to meet and be acted upon
by her plans. Nothing that God had implanted did

she knowingly neglect; and reasoning that the sense of taste was a gift of his, as much as the other senses, she often endeavored to turn it to a good account.

Sunday, of all the days in the week, *must* be — Mrs. Niles's *must* was always imperative — the pleasantest. Among the smaller means of rendering it so, was to provide some agreeable change for their table. This she did simply, but unfailingly; and the appeal to the appetite, which so many would have thought beneath the dignity and solemnity of the day, came regularly with every returning Sabbath, and with the happiest effect. No remark was ever made upon it, but the children soon learned to regard it as a holiday — a special time, even by this little mark, set apart and made an occasion of additional happiness to them.

Then followed prayers, differing only from those of every day, by each child's reciting the fourth commandment, and the singing of a hymn. The hymn chosen on this morning was one very familiar to Rachel. It had always been sung in the Erwin family before it was broken up, and George had carried it gratefully with him to his new home, waking, far away, the strains of that old melody — a link binding the past, present, and future; for those who had sung it, and those who were now singing it, should one day chant the same, mingling it forever with the new glad song.

The first line came to Rachel like the voice of a dead friend. She caught it up, faltered out a few broken words, then burst into a flood of tears. Mrs. Niles understood at once what it meant, and

motioning to her husband to proceed, no notice
was taken of the negro, excepting by Florence, who,
leaving her seat by Jennie's side, walked softly across
the room, and put her hand in the trembling one of
Rachel.

There seemed to be something soothing in the light
touch, for Rachel immediately commanded herself, and
before the second verse was ended, her clear, sweet
voice rose above the others, and gave a depth and
earnestness to the worship which it had never possessed before.

All the children looked wonderingly at Rachel;
they had not heard such singing before; and, indeed,
it was almost as new to Florence now as to them, for
the last time she could remember that Rachel had
sung was on board the steamer, as they came north.

We cannot pause to follow the family through
their pleasant Sabbath arrangement, though, as afford-
ing a striking contrast to the manner of passing the
Sabbath in New York, it would not be unprofitable,
but must pass over the Sabbath school lesson, so
carefully prepared under Mrs. Niles's supervision, to
the starting for church as the tinkling bell began to
summon them.

Rachel had been early informed by Mrs. Niles that
there was a seat in the front gallery reserved for
colored persons; but there was only one in the village besides herself — that was old Rose, who lived a
mile or more away, and seldom came to church.

So, after little missus was ready, the very first person that appeared with her bonnet on was Rachel.
How surprised she would have been if she could have
known how much anxiety this first appearance of a

negro, and a slave, at church, had cost the worthy minister, and that even Mrs. Niles was not without some fears on the subject!

Mr. Niles had suggested a few of the points which troubled him to his wife, and found her, as usual, prepared to meet them. "How could they get Rachel to church? Surely it would not do for her to walk along side by side with them. The warmest abolitionist in the state couldn't do more."

"She should lead Totty," Mrs. Niles answered, "and then it wouldn't matter where she was."

"Would she be willing to sit up stairs alone — and if she was, would not the people think they were making a great difference between themselves and a negro? Where in reality was the difference between the negro car and the negro pew?"

"There was no occasion," Mrs. Niles said, "to settle all these questions to-day. Rachel was told she was to occupy the front gallery pew, and had shown more interest in learning of Old Rose than in objecting to that. And for the people, it had been the custom, from time immemorial, for this seat to be so occupied when there were persons of that class to fill it. Any one who would find fault now must be censorious indeed."

"She would attract the eyes of the whole congregation. Preaching to such an audience would be a difficult and unpleasant matter."

"If the people looked thoroughly to-day, they would be through with it at once; at least, this national curiosity was something over which they had no control, and the less they thought about it the better." So the bell kept on tolling, tolling, until it came to the stroke upon which Mr. Niles generally left home, and they all started.

Totty was very proud to be Rachel's guide. The good nurse had already won the child's heart by her kind, motherly ways; and if Totty was missed from her mother's side, she was almost sure to be found by Rachel's.

Rachel fell back a step or two from the rest, and drew from Totty full accounts of every thing they passed. Indeed, she was so occupied and so respectful in her position, that Mr. Niles found this fear giving way to his "first, and secondly," as he approached the church.

This day there was to be no service among the Methodists; so his church would be unusually well filled. As a common thing, these were the pleasantest Sabbaths to him; but to-day he could not entirely lose the feeling that there would be just so many more eyes to look at Rachel.

He could not help seeing, as they came to the porch door, that Deacon Benjamin Dean was on the steps in the position of a sentinel, and that he looked curiously at Rachel; or that Mrs. Johnson, the butcher deacon's wife, drew the skirt of her new black silk a little closer around her as the negro passed; but Frank, with admirable presence of mind, just at this juncture, took Totty's hand from Rachel's, and, sliding his own in its place, went up stairs, along the whole length of the church, and into the front slip, leading her, as he was fond of leading his mother.

Mrs. Niles glanced up at him with a world of mother's pride and affection; and, peeping down at her from over the tops of the high pews, the brown head shook its close curls, and the bright, hazel eyes shone with the purest of all lights — the consciousness of doing what was kind, bravely, with no fear of being laughed at.

Having seen her seated, he put down his own Bible and hymn book for her, and had some vague idea of hunting up a footstool; but his father was already in the pulpit, and he knew service would soon begin.

As he came down, a group of boys were waiting for him at the foot of the stairs.

"By George!" said one of them; "she is as black as the ace of spades! Is she a real slave, Frank?"

"About as much of a one as you are, Bill," answered Frank, laughing.

"Did she ever get whipped, I wonder?" asked another.

"Not half as often as you have, Sam, I am not afraid to venture a dollar," said Frank.

"Was she ever sold?" asked a big, red-headed boy.

"No," said Frank, decidedly.

"Nor bought?" asked the same boy.

"If she wasn't sold, I don't know how she could have been bought," said Frank.

"Now, none of your gammon!" answered the same boy. "Deacon Ben says they are all bought, and sold, and chained, and whipped to death, and a great deal more."

"More than whipped to death?" asked Frank, contemptuously. "What came next?"

"Buried alive," answered the boy.

"Good! Buried alive after they are dead — a very likely story! But there is Mr. Stone."

Mr. Stone, the sexton, and the terror of all small boys found lingering around the porch, now made his appearance, cane in hand. The boys quickly disappeared to the right and left, most of them going where they could stare at the negro to their hearts' content.

It was as Mr. Niles had foreseen — all eyes were turned towards the side of the gallery occupied by Rachel. Through the first singing, if the negro had once turned her eyes from Mr. Niles, she would have encountered such an array of "black, blue, and gray" fixed intently upon her, that it must have made her, at least, very uncomfortable; but there she sat now, as perfectly unconscious as if Mr. Niles and herself were alone in the house. If her gaze ever, for an instant, wandered from him, it was only to take in "little missus," who, among the group in the minister's pew, was about as conspicuous as the slave above.

Gradually, by the time Mr. Niles had well entered upon his sermon, the eyes, having become familiar with the black face, sought the new white one; and as only those in the side slips could get a view of it in full, those behind were obliged to content themselves with the small city bonnet, — one of Mrs. Erwin's last purchases, and very pretty, with its white and purple wreath of flowers, — and with the janty cloak, of a pattern so new and peculiar that half the mothers in church, if they had been self-watchful, would have caught themselves in plans as to how they could alter over Betsy's, Jane's, or Susan's cloak in the same manner, for the next winter.

Though Mr. Niles had striven to fortify himself

for precisely what he found, he was evidently discomposed; and it was not until he saw how fixed
Rachel's attention was upon him, that he was able
to enter fully on the duties of the occasion.

If there was no one else in that whole audience
listening to him to-day, there sat one, with such an
earnest, asking face, that it suggested to him the
verse, "If he ask bread, will he give him a stone?"
There should be nothing cold, nothing stony, in this
sermon of to-day, if God would help him; so Mr.
Niles, with his own eye often wandering to Rachel,
began to grow interested in his discourse, and to
command, in spite almost of themselves, the wandering thoughts of his congregation.

Mrs. Niles watched the conflict and the victory
with much anxiety, from the minister's cushioned
pew, just beneath the old-fashioned pulpit.

At noon, no one returned to the parsonage but
Mr. Niles. The Sabbath school followed the morning services immediately. In this Mrs. Niles had a
large class of old ladies; and all her children, even
down to Totty, were members of other classes.

Florence was to go with Jennie into that corner
where, as she approached, she saw the two little girls,
Sarah Jane and Myrtilda Bates. They began to smile,
and beckon her to come and sit between them; but
Florence, with a shyness amounting almost to fright,
clung to Jennie, and tried to look away, as if she did
not see them. This was the first time in her life that
she had ever been in a class, or a member of a school,
of any kind; and it was not agreeable to her to be
surrounded by so many unknown white faces. She
had come to-day only as a spectator, and had no les-

son: this she heard Jennie whisper to her teacher, and therefore felt at liberty to observe as much as she pleased.

Mrs. Niles had taken Rachel into her own class, and also into the seat which she occupied as teacher; thus adroitly silencing every objection as to " sitting in the same seat with a colored person" from the various members of her class.

After Sabbath school came the eating of the lunches which the country folks had brought in to stay their somewhat clamorous appetites; and this part of the occasion, to say the least, was very amusing to Florence.

Their own had not been forgotten; but it was slight, by no means comprehending the very hearty meal which made its appearance, by degrees, from the multitude of tin pails and small, covered baskets which so quickly took the place of the hymn and question books, when the Sabbath school was over, upon the great table in front of the superintendent's desk.

Frank was the master of ceremonies now — here, there, and every where; picking up old Mrs. Tompkins's basket when it fell, and catching the red, rosy apples which came tumbling, one after another, from many a hidden receptacle, many of them well dinted by the little thumb which had strayed into them, "just to try and see if they were mellow," during the solemn hours of divine service.

A chatty time this was, too — literally the meeting place of the village; for here many met who never met elsewhere; and precious little bits of news were passed about, which had been in keeping for the occasion during the previous week.

Young as Florence was, she noticed, and was attracted by, the special marks of deference which were paid to her aunt. Around her were gathered the oldest and the poorest, but none of the eager questioning, none of the whispers, or the suppressed laughter, which were every where else. If the child had only known that Rachel and herself were the occasion of an unusual excitement to-day, she would hardly have been more surprised than she was; for, in truth, the whole scene was a very novel one to her.

Rachel had been trying to coax Totty to come and sit upon her lap, by way of having something to do for her own relief. She had no idea, before, how very embarrassing it would be to be the only black person in a room. To be sure, she had enjoyed Mr. Niles's sermon; "it was gospel truth for true;" and she was contented, so far, in the quiet, cheerful parsonage life; but this being in God's house, and among God's people, and finding herself *alone*, was a life so inexplicable to her, that she had no power of defining how she felt, as she looked through the small panes of glass out into the chill, gray day, with a longing for Myrtle Bush. Perhaps, as the sadness crept over her heart, it crept also over her face; for as, unable to get Totty nearer to her than a smile brought her, she walked to the less frequented part of the house, a queer little figure slipped along after her; and hardly had she turned her back to the assembly, before she felt some one softly touch her arm.

"You feel kind of lonesome, don't ye?" said the woman, or girl, or whatever she was — no stranger would have been able to decide which; for upon a child's body she carried' a face so old and wrinkled

15

that the first glance of it made Rachel start as if she
saw a ghost. " You're kind of lonesome now, ain't
ye ? " repeated the woman ; " I think ye look as if ye
were. It's pokerish here, with only that little white
gal — now, ain't it ? " And the small, shrivelled face
relaxed into a smile so hearty and cheerful that it
reminded Rachel at once of the bright flame bursting out of an ugly, twisted pine knot.

" Its always lonesome away from my own home,
way down in South Carliny," said Rachel, drawing
herself up, and speaking slowly with the utmost
English propriety.

" South Carliny ? " said the woman ; " that is
where they have slaves, ain't it ? You didn't come
from way off there, now ? — du tell ! "

At this last injunction, understood literally by
Rachel as meaning, " Please to render me what information you can with respect to South Carolina,"
she was beginning to make another formal answer,
when she was interrupted by Jennie, who, without
wishing to be too forward, had kept her eye upon
Rachel, ready to come to her relief in a moment,
should she be needed.

" Rachel," she said, " this is Miss Mehitable Foster.
You will learn to know her very well, as every body
else does that lives long in Grafton, particularly if
they are in trouble."

" Hush you there, now, little pet ! " said Miss Mehitable, turning one of those ugly-sunny faces full
upon Jennie. " I jest saw her a standing here, you
know, as if she was feeling sort of bad ; and I
couldn't stand that, nohow. It must be awful
strange if there ain't nobody else jest ——— " Here

Miss Mehitable suddenly interrupted herself, and
gave a variety of little coughs; then, catching her
breath, as if she had with difficulty swallowed some
obstacle, she went on : "I mean, if I was the only
white person in South Carolina, I might jest like to
have it recognized that I was a human being, if I
wasn't a —— " Here came a very spasmodic cough,
at which Jennie heard Frank's smothered laugh from
a few pews back. Miss Mehitable heard it, too; for
she turned suddenly, and said, —

"You there, too, Franky boy? Well, well, look
out, or you won't git no extra pockets in that 'ere
next new jacket, when it comes."

"I only thought, Aunt Hitty," said Frank, jumping not very reverently over the tops of the separat-
ing pews, "that your words seemed to act like that
cayenne lozenge I gave you one Sabbath — made
you inclined to cough!"

Miss Mehitable held up two fingers in a very
threatening attitude, shook them at the boy, laughed
a little laugh, wonderfully musical and merry, considering what a very ugly mouth it came out of, and
slipped — it is the only word which exactly expresses
her motions — back to put on old Mrs. Mensen's
long, yarn socks, upon which the good lady had been
pulling in vain.

Rachel's eyes followed her with such an open expression of wonder, that Jennie said, softly, —

"She is a poor, deformed thing, Rachel, but, for
all that, one of the very kindest and best hearted
beings in all father's parish."

"De good Lord hab mercy on her!" whispered
Rachel back; "I tink for sure she be a ole woman.

Den I look down to see if she be a little child and
wear pantalets. Poor thing; poor thing!"

"She isn't a poor thing," said Jennie, smiling;
"there isn't a happier person in Grafton. She is
always doing something for somebody, and every
body seems to think so much of her. We all call
her, as Frank did, 'Aunt Hitty.'"

"How ole be she?" asked Rachel, still keeping
her eyes fixed upon her.

"Old? I don't know. I don't think any one
knows, exactly. That is the only thing she isn't
perfect about. She don't like to have questions as
to how old she is; it makes her angry."

"Eh, eh!" said Rachel, smiling. "She be woman
for true then. I almost tink little girl; but no,
no; woman for true. Neber have no husband.
Neber——"

"Aunt Hitty have a husband! What an idea,
Rachel!" and even our demure Jennie had to laugh
— if it was "between meetings on Sunday"—at
the droll thought.

Old Mrs. Mensen's socks being now adjusted to
her satisfaction, Aunt Hitty came back again, bringing a fried doughnut, turned and twisted in a very
remarkable manner.

She was swinging it on the edge of a small, shrivelled forefinger. It was a kind of cake Rachel had
never seen before; and take it now, with the peg
upon which it hung, it looked curiously enough; and
she held it out to the negro with another of those
smiles. Rachel took all the smile most gratefully,
but expressed her willingness to let the other remain
where it was. The finger then swung round to-

wards Jennie, and to Rachel's dismay, the child not only took it off, but actually commenced eating it, saying, as she did so, —

"You make the nicest doughnuts in Grafton, Aunt Hitty. Thank you. I love them dearly."

"Little pet always has something kind to say. Her mother's own child," said Aunt Hitty. "What's bred in the bone will out in the flesh. There ain't no helping on't."

And now the bell for afternoon service began to ring out, and there followed immediately such a stampede from the church that both Florence and Rachel thought service was to take place somewhere else; but by degrees the same people began to return, though Rachel, from her lookout in the gallery, noticed that it was those who went first who returned last.

Pretty soon Mr. Niles made his appearance; and then, as by general consent, the knots and groups which had remained fixed until this signal for disbanding, broke up, and by the time the minister had taken his seat in the pulpit, the congregation had assumed a quiet and orderly aspect.

It had seemed so impossible to Rachel, during the various processes of lunching, that the room could again be any thing but a dining room, that she looked with much surprise upon the regular congregation, wondering, as she ran her eye keenly over the pews below her, what had become of all the baskets, and pails, and apples which were so conspicuous a short time before.

The afternoon service presented its usual complement of sleepers; and though fewer eyes wandered for a long time to the negro in the gallery, so many more were closed in sound slumber, that, perhaps, if the worthy minister could have taken his choice, he would have preferred the task of withdrawing them from the gallery to opening them as they were fixed now.

This had not been an easy or a happy Sabbath to Mr. Niles. He offered thanks when it was past, and was so unusually fervent in his prayers for forgiveness on all wandering thoughts, that some of the more tender-hearted of his parishioners, feeling slightly troubled for their own share in them, lingered in their pews, hoping to get an encouraging smile from him as he passed out, which should say he did not mean them; but Mr. Niles saw no one before him but his wife. If he could only reach home, and be with her!

The sun had stolen out while service had been proceeding, and the children, as they sprang off the last of the high steps, and found themselves once more free, broke out into so many and so different ways of expressing their joy, that Florence could do nothing but watch them. In New York, Ida and herself had always been permitted a long walk after church; should they have one here in Grafton? If Frank and she only might go down in that grove back of the house, where they had been on Saturday, how delightful it would be! But she dared not ask. At Myrtle Bush her father had taken her with him to the negro yard, after they had returned from their long drive to church, but he had always gone to conduct a meeting for them there; and though the walks were the pleasantest part of the Sabbath to the child,

Florence could not now recall that her father had ever taken her out for the walk alone.

"Run along, little folks," said Mrs. Niles, dropping back among them almost as if she had divined about what Florence had been thinking; "you have been still in church all day, and I want you to get as much enjoyment and exercise as you can out of your walk home. See there, Frank; there is the first robin redbreast I have seen this year."

"I declare, mother, so it is," said Frank, catching up a pebble and hurling it at the bird, without a moment's thought.

"My son," said Mr. Niles, turning gravely round, "do you forget what day it is?"

"I only wanted to see, father," said Frank, "how much of Florence's rice she had brought from Myrtle Bush in her crop."

Rachel's eyes were immediately fixed upon the bird. Could it have been at Myrtle Bush? She wanted to take it in her hands; to hide it in her bosom; to coax from it some of the answers to the questions which her heart yearned so to ask, and which Cato's letters only imperfectly answered. Florence might learn to be happy north, for was she not among her own? but for herself, the thrill of heart, the bounding of the pulse, and the tear which would start to her eye as it followed the bird that might have been at Myrtle Bush, told her that the north was no home for the southern born and bred, if the skin was tinted by the warmer rays, and the eye had looked out for years upon its deep-blue sky, its coming and going, but never all gone flowers — if the ear had been tuned to the softer tones, and the kind-

er, or, perhaps, more readily kind words, which are
so necessary for the quick kindlings of the quick
hearts.

"Dis dat north!" Rachel sighed, as she looked
after the bird. "Poor little birdie, go back, go
back; dis no compare with dat beautiful old South
Carliny."

CHAPTER XIV.

THE changes of the seasons — spring, summer, autumn, and winter — are no more distinctly marked in the world's annals than are those of the days of the week in a small, well-regulated country family. Each day has its allotted tasks — its things to be done then, and then only. Its routine is as clearly and sharply defined as the budding and bursting of the leaves, their full-grown beauty, their decay, and their death.

If these had existed in the city, they had never come to Florence's knowledge. She herself had nothing to do with what was done for her daily comforts and necessities, any more than if she had been swung in a basket in the air and fed by birds. Indeed, she hardly knew there was a kitchen to her uncle's establishment. She never put her foot within it; and, excepting as she heard Rachel speak of the different servants, or met them around the house, she could hardly have told how many or whom her uncle employed. She never thought of her aunt as having any thing to do with the establishment but to sit at the head of the table. Her astonishment at the different way in which matters were conducted at the parsonage may well be imagined. She saw Jennie every day sweep and dust the parlor, dining room, and study. She had even had a peep at her, busy in Frank's room making his bed. Her aunt was often

busy for hours in the kitchen; and though she had
never felt that she could go in without an invitation;
yet once, when she had gone for Frank, she had found
a table full of unbaked pies, and her aunt with her
hands covered with flour.

But all this astonishment was nothing in comparison with what was in store for her when Monday
morning dawned, and the bustle of washing day
actually began.

There was no hurry at the breakfast table, no
omission of a single religious duty; but every body
and every thing had such an active, ready look, that
the unconscious influence was not long in making
itself felt by Florence.

Jennie was to wash the breakfast dishes; and as
she prepared them nicely for the operation, Florence
sat by watching her with much interest, but never
thought of offering to help her.

Jennie glanced up at her slyly as she sat indo-
lently looking on, wondering why a little girl, who
seemed so obliging and pleasant, never thought to
offer to do the slightest thing or take a step. At
length she said, laughing,—

"Come, Flossy, you have looked at me long
enough. Don't you want to take hold of this nice,
clean dish towel, and wipe my dishes for me?"

"Can I?" said Florence, jumping up with much
delight; "I should so love to!—only you must teach
me; I don't know any thing about it."

"See here," said Jennie, slowly and carefully going
through the feat. "It's as easy as easy can be."

And so Florence, to her delight, found it. When
Mrs. Niles, a few minutes after, passed through the

room, she had quite a pile of dishes spread out before her; and as her aunt laid her hand softly on her head, and said,—

"Now I have two little daughters to help me; have I not?" Florence felt both proud and happy.

While they were thus very busily engaged, the outer door opened softly — so softly that they did not hear it until a voice said close up to Jennie's elbow — so close that she came very near dropping a large dish she held from the start,—

"Busy, little pet, always busy, helping your mother, or somebody else. Sometimes I think I wonder how you can take the trouble to breathe, when it is only for yourself."

"Why, Aunt Hitty!" said Jennie, "how you scared me! I didn't hear you come in."

"But I did, pet; not down the chimney, nor in at the window, but lifted up the latch, which you know is not the 'other way.'"

Florence had stood as still looking at her as if she had turned her into stone; though she well remembered her talking to Rachel on the Sabbath; still, near to, she was smaller and more singular-looking than she had seemed even then.

"This," said Aunt Hitty, turning full upon her with her pleasant, small eyes, "is our little southern cousin — is it? Well, miss, hope I seed you well;" and she dropped a droll little courtesy.

Florence said, gravely, for want of knowing what else to say,—

"Yes, ma'am."

"Well, now, pet," continued Aunt Hitty, as if she thought she was rather too simple to be taken any

more notice of, "where is your marm? I am going
to Mr. Cass's, to make a pair of trousers to-day, and
can't stop a minute; a minute is an hour, you know,
where folks pay for't — some folks, I mean. Your
marm ain't one of that sort, but I knows them that
be. So where is your marm, pet?"

"Sit down, Aunt Hitty, and I will call her," said
Jennie, wiping her dripping hands.

"Call her — bless you! Why, pet, I couldn't wait
long enough to have her called, if it would not take
a jiffy. I will jist run up myself; she is putting the
chambers to rights, I suppose."

"Yes, up stairs, somewhere. You know the way."

"I should think I had been here as often as once,"
said Aunt Hitty, snapping her eyes and her fingers
at the same time, and disappearing.

"Who is she?" asked Florence, in a whisper, as
soon as she was fairly gone.

"A good little deformed tailoress, who goes
about sewing for boys. She comes here a great
deal, and we are all attached to her."

"Attached to her!" What could there be in her
to attach any one to her? Florence was too well
bred to ask the question with her lips, though her
face very openly expressed it.

Aunt Hitty went softly up stairs, opened all the
doors, as if she were most perfectly at home, — which
indeed she was, — until she found Mrs. Niles, as she
had expected, "putting things to rights."

"That 'are new jacket of Frank's," said she, putting her head into his room, and finding his mother
in the act of hanging it up, "I seed a button coming
off from it yesterday. I threaded my needle before I

came out, and thought I would jist whip in a moment and set it on tight; he is such a master fellow to lose every thing that ain't jist like iron. He would lose his head if it wasn't fastened on tight, I know."

Mrs. Niles, well knowing that this was only a preliminary to something of more importance, handed her the jacket, and sat down by her while she slipped on her headless thimble, pinned on the little square pin-ball, filled with pins, in front of her waist, tied her scissors into her apron string, and, to all outward appearances, prepared for a day's work.

"You have hearn, I suppose," she began, after a few jerks at the linen thread, to test its resemblance to the iron Frank required, — "you have hearn, I suppose, that down in Crane's deestrict we have a meeting reglar after we have all done our dinner — at early candle lighting, you know."

"Yes; I hope it is good," said Mrs. Niles.

"Well, I can't jistly tell," continued she. "It ain't neither here nor there, I suppose. Praying nor preaching can't save us, unless we have the believing heart; and perhaps there were a great many believing héarts there — no knowing. But this was what they call a 'sperence meeting;' every body, even the women folks, were to tell their own sperence."

"Did you go?" asked Mrs. Niles, smiling in spite of her efforts to keep sober.

"La, yes; of course I went. I hain't no sperence, you know, and nobody never expects none from me; so I could jist slip in, easy like, and it wouldn't make no difference to nobody. In fact, I didn't see as any body made a difference to any body else, or had

any sperence more than I did — any body but Deacon Ben; he always has a heap."

"Did he speak to your edification?" asked Mrs.
Niles.

"La, yes, I spose so; his own edication, if nobody else. The fact is, Miss Niles, he ain't got
nobody now in this ere world but himself and the
niggers, and when he don't talk of one of them
two, he don't say nothing; that is all. One would
think, to hear him talk, that the Lord Jesus Christ
didn't die for a single white person but Deacon Ben.
Even them thieves on the cross were as black as
Sambo, or he wouldn't have wanted them in Para-
dise with him. Now he is full" — and Aunt Hitty
came nearer to Mrs. Niles, so that she could finish
her sentence in a whisper — "of your black woman,
down stairs — choke full. Our meeting, sperences,
and all, was about her."

"Indeed! I didn't know that he knew her. Rachel hasn't been out at all."

"Never you mind that;" and Aunt Hitty's eyes
snapped like small coals. "He don't need to know
her. He says she is a poor, benighted slave; and
all through the sarmon yesterday, instead of listening to the minister, as the deacon ought, he was
a-looking at her, poor, injured body, with the marks
of chains upon her wrist, and the scars and unhealed
wounds which the driver's lash had left upon her.
He said he saw her holding up in her emaciated
hands the chains of three hundred thousand human
beings, and that their clink drownded the prayers
and praises in the house of the Lord. I teld Miss
Harmon" — and here Aunt Hitty laughed that soft,

peculiar laugh — " I didn't wonder the poor thing's
hands were thin, if she had such a lot of iron to hold
up. Why, even my iron thimble tires mine, sometimes, after I have been a-sewing on hard cloth all
day, where they have clocks with minute hands,
Miss Niles: you don't keep them things, you know.
But this ain't nothing to the pint. The pint simply
is, that Deacon Ben is a leetle too big for his place.
He wants to " — Miss Hitty stopped, searched for a
comparison, then said, laughing — "he wants to do as
I have seen an old rooster a great many times — get
up on a fence, and crow, crow, crow, until some one
takes notice of him. If he can't get the white hens,
why, it don't marter; he will be jist as content with
the black, only so some come. But, bless me, Mrs.
Cass has a minute clock, and a second one, too; so
I had better be off, or I shall hear something worse
than Deacon Ben."

She ran nimbly down stairs, but no sooner reached
the last stair than she turned and ran as nimbly
back. Putting her head once more inside the door,
she said, —

"Miss Niles, you won't worry now one bit about
Deacon Ben; now, will you? I have hearn a Shang-
hai crow fifty times without stopping, and all the
harm that came of it was, it seemed to hurt his own
throat — made him kind of hoarse, you know."

"I shall not worry, thank you, Hitty," said Mrs.
Niles; but the little tailoress saw a troubled look
which was not usual on the good wife's face. It fell
over her like a cloud; she paused many times on
her way to Mrs. Cass's, and wished she had left Deacon Ben to take care of himself.

But Mrs. Niles did not. To be forewarned was in this case most emphatically to be forearmed; and besides, it was not unexpected to her. The shadow which had fallen upon her husband had shown the coming trouble, and in all such cases it was a relief to her to have a little time beforehand for preparations. If she was not mistaken, the deacon would bring his own reports of the last evening meeting before night; and if — she must be forgiven for the plan — she could only find some needful way of occupying Mr. Niles from home, perhaps she should be able to answer the deacon's inquiries, at least to her own satisfaction; or, what was better, he might see Rachel, and do what he could with her.

Mrs. Niles appreciation of Rachel's good sense increased every day. She had, as we have before stated, as thorough a knowledge of her character as can be derived from another; but the way now in in which the nurse had adapted herself to the simple family arrangements, her willingness to make herself of use in any and every way she could, and the quickness with which she saw into her own plans for the growth and formation of Florence's character, gave her a high opinion of both her head and heart. Her principal doubt now was, whether it would not be better to call Rachel, and have an explanation with her, with regard to the way in which her having been a slave, and now an inmate in their family, might affect the parish generally; but after some reflection she decided to let matters take their own course, and if the deacon should come, to trust entirely to Rachel to manage as her own sense should dictate.

There was some important family shopping to be done in a large town six miles distant. The day was fine, the roads mending fast. All the children would enjoy the drive. Mr. Niles was very Monday-ish; and what wonder? the anxiety of the previous Sabbath had been worse than the preaching. He was all ready for the slight change and recreation which the drive seemed to promise; and Mrs. Niles watched the happy party with many fervent wishes, that the deacon's visit might be over before they should return.

In spite of her cool, calm judgment, she felt annoyed. Deacon Dean could be very troublesome if he would; and indeed, if the truth must be told, one great reason for inducting him into his sacred office was, that he found so much fault with the management of church affairs, it had been judged best to throw a little of the responsibility upon him, hoping in this way to keep him quiet; and it had thus far succeeded. He had, however, now been harmless quite as long as was in his nature; he must have an outlet. Perhaps it was well it had taken the course worn by the broad, deep channel of the great national sin.

Very busy Mrs. Niles and Totty were, when the rumbling of heavy wagon wheels warned them that somebody had come.

"Deacon Ben," said Mrs. Niles to herself, taking another stocking to darn off from her large pile; "now for it."

"The minister was not at home, but Mrs. Niles was; would she do as well?" Ann asked, as she opened the door.

16

The deacon cleared his throat, which meant, "No, not half; there is no talking with a woman." But he said he would come in, and accordingly did so.

Mrs. Niles had made up her mind that he was to have "up-hill work;" so she left him to fight his way over and under the obstacles which she so well knew how to put before him. And, indeed, the probability is, that she would have foiled him entirely, and sent him away as surcharged with philanthropy as he came, if she had not been afraid he would have spent it upon the first object he met, less able to bear it than she was herself.

Unfortunately for the deacon, he had stopped on his way to the parsonage, to talk with Mrs. Drummond, who was generally known to have power of language enough for all the other inhabitants of Grafton.

Of late she had become convinced that "God never intended any of his fellow-creatures to be held in slavery;" and this had formed a bond of union between herself and the deacon, which had been growing stronger and stronger every day since it was known Rachel and a southern child were to come to Grafton for a year.

During this morning's conversation, the worthy pair had worked themselves up to a perfect storm of holy indignation. So many severe things were to be said to the minister who could slumber in Zion when the enemies were pouring in, in such a destructive flood upon her, that, really, it hardly seemed to Deacon Ben "as the fire burned," that he could wait the slow motions of his horse to be conveyed to the parsonage.

Could he at once have annihilated time and space,

he might have said some very severe or impudent
things, as the hearer pleased to consider them; but a
good deal of Mrs. Drummond's froth had time to die
away as old Bob trotted leisurely along, and what remained, ceased bubbling the moment he encountered
Mrs. Niles's firm eye. He wished — moving uneasily
in his chair — Mrs. Drummond had come herself; it
was so much easier for women to talk to women.

At last Mrs. Niles opened the flood-gates, and after
a good deal of dashing back, then up and almost
over — but not quite — out it came.

The details of the conversation our limit will not
allow us to present to our readers; but the deacon
was always heard to aver afterwards, that "it was no
wonder poor Mr. Niles did not feel right and act
right on every occasion; no one could tell what effect
home had in knocking down the powers of a man's
mind. Even stone was worn away by continued
drippings."

Mrs. Niles listened until the last sound of the re-
treating wagon wheels had died away; then quieting
the somewhat quickened beatings of her heart, —
which the deacon would have been very happy could
he have discovered, — she sat down quietly to ascer-
tain, if possible, the real motive for the visit. Let it
suffice to say, she never suspected it. The deacon had
been so careful to wrap and re-wrap it up, under
words, admissions, and shadowy requirements, that
she could never have known it was all settled at
Mrs. Drummond's, that the minister was to be sum-
moned upon the moment to become an active, zealous abolitionist, or to leave his parish. Away jogged
old Bob, carrying all these "extra demonstrations"

as safely stowed away as he had brought them; and
Mrs. Niles had the satisfaction of hearing her husband drive into the yard, rested and refreshed by a
pleasant ride, and as unscathed by the deacon's visit, as if no deacon ever existed. The call, however,
had the effect of preparing her for much more trouble
with the parish than she had expected, and made her
determine, early in the impending conflict, to take her
stand, and keep it, let what might come.

Like a good general, she did not wait for the ene-
my to be at her gate before she began to organize
her own method of meeting and repelling; and her
first movement in this line was, to have both Florence and Rachel enter as quickly and as quietly as
possible upon a regular routine of home duties.

Rachel began to be seamstress, aiding Ann whenever needed, but generally occupying the low chair
by the back dining room window, with a large basket
of work close by her side, and a table which held,
with a precise neatness quite remarkable, every article needed for her sewing.

Florence, after a week's more vacation, as Frank
insisted upon her calling it, began to study regularly
with her cousins, reciting either to her uncle or aunt,
as the children had been for some time accustomed.

This was like Myrtle Bush, only now she had those
of the same age, and, as she found, of about the same
acquirements, to study with her. No more masters,
no careless, half-learned, sorry recitations, but the
same kind voice to lead her on, the same gentle, patient way of waiting until the crude thoughts took
shape and words.

Thorough and faithful! these were again the watchwords; and from over her pile of sewing, Rachel looked on with glistening eye, and an often half-breathed, " De good Lord be thanked!"

So passed away quickly the spring months, and summer came stealing on. Busy and joyful, Florence never asked herself whether she was happy or not.

Whatever sources of annoyance her residence in their family might be to her relations, no one of them all was apparent to her. The country was becoming every day more and more beautiful. Her life out of doors was scarcely less busy and happy than that within. Every morning Frank had some new place to which he must take her, every night some new thing which she must come " right off" to see; and even Jennie, in the delight of having a companion so full of freshness and life, was tempted away from the graver and more quiet in-door occupation, until her mother said, with a feeling of relief, " that Jennie was growing to be quite a child again."

Long letters, full of commiseration and sympathy, came quite frequently from Ida. Very remarkable letters they were too, as written by one so young; but they only drew from Florence, in return, a few commonplace lines. She felt ashamed to tell Ida how happy she was, hunting up birds' nests, and picking early summer flowers; going over to farmer Bates's to see Myrtilda and Sarah Ann, who, now they had got over their shyness and learned how to talk, proved very pleasant companions. Indeed, the whole routine of her daily life was in every respect so different from Ida's, that when she sat down to write her, she found, as she so often complained to Jennie, that she had not a word to say.

Three months thus passed by, and one would hardly have known the red-cheeked, rather noisy child, who was fast learning to climb fences and wade in brooks almost as well as Frank, for the pale, drooping, downcast child of her first three months in the city. Rachel, with her fond, watchful eyes, could not but acknowledge that she grew faster, and was a more perfect picture of health, than even when at Myrtle Bush; and with this improvement in her darling, her heart softened a little towards the hitherto uncongenial north. Fortunately for her, Mrs. Niles had not called her in to the conference with Deacon Ben Dean, and coming very little in contact with any one, black or white, she was beginning to forget that she was one of the "accursed race," particularly as she had not yet seen even old black Rose.

Three months! and during this time the philanthropists in Mr. Niles's society had been agitating, agitating, without so far being able to do any thing more. Mrs. Drummond had been attacked with a lung fever, which had confined her at home, and prevented her from doing her accustomed share of the talking. Perhaps it was owing to this that so much external quiet had been maintained.

But her health returned to her with the return of other of God's blessings, like the green springing grass and the flowers; and one of the first walks she took was down to the parsonage to unburden her heart.

Mrs. Drummond was not unlike the "dear sister" in New York, a woman full of natural kindly traits, warm-hearted, impulsive, lacking judgment, and reminding one, in her adventures "after the right," of Don Quixote. No mill wheel too stout with which to do battle, no broken head so severe, to leave a memory of itself one minute after the pain was gone.

Her very goodness and kindness made her the more dangerous, for she enforced an opinion with a present of some rich dainty, and nailed her arguments upon you by a pleasant act of attention and affection, which a heart must have been made of the hardest marble to withstand. Mrs. Niles for these reasons dreaded her more than all the deacons of the parish put together; and it had been an immense relief to her, if the good lady must be sick at all, that she should be so just at the time when a real weakness had made its way into her own domestic matters; for Mrs. Niles could not but feel and acknowledge that if you gave slavery no other name, you must at least call it a national weakness. With a woman who had passed a long life as an actual slave, and a live slaveholder, the owner of more than one hundred and fifty human beings, in the very bosom of her family, — the latter related to her by ties of nature and affection, — she must be considered now as coming in pretty close contact with the whole thing.

Her calls upon the sick Mrs. Drummond were always kindly, but brief. She took much pains to be attentive in the way of inquiries through her children, and by nice sick dishes prepared by her own hands, but sought no opportunity for a conversation. Mrs. Drummond, however, as we have said, came to have this interview as soon as she was able.

Florence was out working in the garden with Frank. As she passed through it, she stopped to inquire if this was the little southern cousin; and as

Florence turned her pretty face up to hers, and held out her hand all covered with the clinging black earth, Mrs. Drummond — who was naturally fond of children — could not help confessing that she was just as sweet and pretty as the roses on the bush by which she stood ; and that it was a sin and a shame to bring down God's curse upon such a little innocent thing by making her the owner of body and soul of so many of her helpless fellow-beings. Nor was her troubled feeling at all assuaged, when Florence, attracted readily by the kind eyes and kind smile which beamed upon her, broke off a bunch of opening rose buds, and with that ineffable grace of childhood, held them towards her.

"Kiss me, darling," said the good lady. "You are as sweet as the rose buds your very self."

Florence's rosy lips touched hers. Ah, Mrs. Drummond! are you going to be a Judas, and sell your Master for only a child's kiss?

Stately Rachel opens the front door, bowing and smiling; for she, too, feels and acknowledges the warm benevolence of the pale lady's heart, who stands there waiting for admission.

Mrs. Drummond recoiled a little as her eye rested on the slave. Much as she had read, thought, and prayed for them, she had never actually seen one before; and, imposing as this specimen was, she was impelled by an uncontrollable emotion to avoid her, as we should the actor in some very tragic scene, the bare recital of which had so often filled us with horror.

Mrs. Niles read, before the door had closed upon Rachel, however, that the lady was in part, at least, disarmed; and trusting to the kindly heart, she determined to make a direct appeal to that, throwing the guilt of the inherited sin upon it for forgiveness, sure that it would weep if it must cast it off.

Nor was she wrong. What she said met — thanks to the rose buds and the kiss! — first, a shower of tears, then a word of sympathy, and finally a sigh of sorrow over the poor, dear child, who "surely can't do any thing to help it until she has grown to man's estate."

She must stop, as she goes through the garden again, for another pleasant word with the little child. She must take one more pretty bunch of flowers, which Florence has been busy preparing for her while her heart has been warming towards her in her aunt's small parlor. She offers the kiss this time. It is the last part of the flower gift; and Mrs. Drummond bears them both away together — carries them home, to keep them in her room and in her heart, ready to help her through the evening when Deacon Ben is to drop in, to talk over the morning call.

"He has no more courage than my old Tabby, who grows to be afraid of a mouse," was Mrs. Drummond's soliloquy, when he told her the result of his call at the parsonage. "Now, he will go away and say, 'That poor woman has been sick so long that her mind has grown about as weak as her body. I don't think there ever was much to her, after all.'"

But Mrs. Niles, standing by her window, sees the little gift of flowers, sees the kiss, and, sitting down quietly again to her work, says, in a very composed tone, "'And a little child shall lead them.'"

Past those two rapids, now, in the stream of parish matters, and good Mr. Niles has written excellent sermons, and performed active, zealous pastoral work, with many secret thanksgivings to Him who numbereth the hairs of our heads, that he has guided them through what might have been the occasion of much trouble and discord.

Summer, passing on, brought with it not only the promise of quiet, but the glad vacation time. The children at the parsonage had passed through one term of good study; the college boy, Horace, had finished his second year, and would come home full of sophomoric greatness; George was also one year nearer his professional life, and he, too, would come, bringing his rich promise with him.

Home for the glad summer holidays! — home! home! The cry went out from the parsonage, and the children took it up, and repeated it over and over, until its echo seemed to grow into one continuous chain, binding the comers, and bringing them ever nearer, and yet nearer, as time drew noiselessly on.

Florence remembered Henry's arrival the last summer. How different it was! How different every thing was! And yet she had come to Grafton reluctantly, unhappily. Well, it could not be that she had made such a mistake. Horace would prove like Henry; and then she should wish — she knew she should — that she was back again in New York.

CHAPTER XV.

"THE boys"—so all the family liked to call them
—were both to arrive on the same night in the same
train of cars. Frank was once more in requisition
as charioteer, and so was Kate, who, seeming to know
what was required of her, made sundry demonstrations of unwillingness before leaving the yard, much
to Rachel's terror, as Frank had teased Florence,
who was a little timid about the new cousins, to go
with him, and who sat demurely perched up on the
high back seat, alone, and without exhibiting the
least symptom of fear.

Frank, when he saw it, paid her the greatest com-
pliment he could by telling her he "shouldn't be at
all afraid to leave the horses with her while he went
up to see the boys jump out when the cars stopped."
And he carried his admiration so far as actually to
offer her the reins as he drove again to the safe place
under the hill — a proof which Florence very wisely
declined, proposing, instead, to climb up herself, and
see if they were there. Accordingly, up she scram-
bled, as the train came thundering in; and when the
two young men alighted, they found no one there
but a blue-eyed child, with long, dark curls, and the
gladness of the sunny south stealing out from her
half-open, half-welcoming lips.

" There is Flossy, true as fate!" said Horace, who
first saw her, making a spring towards her; but Flor-

ence avoided him, and, running to the top of the
bank, called down it, —

"They've come! Drive up, Franky!"

As she came back again, her eye fell upon George,
and his striking resemblance to her father chained
her to the spot, without the power of removing her
eyes from him. He came to her, and took her gently
up, without the least resistance. She put her arm
about his neck, and said, —

"I almost thought you were my own father come
back again."

"Do I look so much like him? I am very glad.
You will love me, then, for his sake — will you
not?"

"Yes," said Florence, kissing him, and leaning her
cheek against his. The child had adopted him at
once in the place of the dead father, and George had
accepted the trust.

"You are partial, little cousin," said Horace, good-
naturedly; "but you will like me better when you
see what I have for you in my trunk."

Perhaps so; but Florence's instincts were strong,
and she drew away from him now.

And now came the horses clambering up the hill,
as they had a few months before for Florence, only
Frank was much more noisy — much more desirous
to show his elder brothers that, having held the reins
since they went away, he was equally capable of
doing so now they had returned.

It was a very merry ride home, much merrier than
on the night Florence came; and there were relays
of the family all along the road, beginning with the
father, and ending with the mother, near the cheerful, tree-hidden home.

Even Rachel had begun to feel as if she had part
and parcel in "the boys," and, standing near the
door, had her ready hand for the somewhat scant
luggage which the two students brought. She, too,
was impressed with George's resemblance to the
"good dead massa," and, taking up the corner of her
white apron, wiped away the tears which fell like
rain, as the slight but manly figure, the eyes clear,
and radiant with the same sweet look of inward
peace, and the same kind smile, looked once more
upon her. The resemblance in the tones of the voice,
even, were marvellously exact; and, instead of her
usual cheerful "How d'ye?" Rachel met the young
minister with a broken and indistinct —

"De Lord God ob Abram, and Isaac, and Jacob,
Massa George's God, bress you, foreber and eber.
Amen."

"Amen!" said George, solemnly.

There was something dirge-like in the words; and
they struck a chill to his heart, which even the happy
" coming home" could not at once dissipate.

And now, with only a few hours of rest, commenced a series of holiday pleasures, in which Horace, who had been making an extra attempt to be
industrious and quiet at college, seemed determined
to expend the animal spirits which he had bottled up.

All but the minister were pressed into active and
immediate service. To-day his mother, George, every
one, must go five miles out of town to the whortle-
berry field, taking dinners, shawls, lunch, and all the
pleasant et cæteras of picnicking with them; and to-
morrow George, and Jennie, and Florence — Frank
always had to fight his way in — must go to Snake

Mountain, and see if the view had grown any the less beautiful, now he had been so long amid the flat scenes of —————— College. Every day and every hour this strong, impetuous boy drove from pleasure to pleasure, dragging with him, in spite of pale cheeks and sleepy eyes, the two tired little girls. There seemed to be something about Horace which no one wished to resist. He was so generous, so unselfish, so merry-hearted, he could thaw, like a warm, spring sun, the very iciest resolves. If you knew he was doing wrong, and really blamed him, you could not help doing so with a gentle, loving voice, much more "in sorrow than in anger." There was not a dog, even, in all Grafton, that did not run up to him, and hold its head still to have it patted when it saw him; and for the children, he could have walked the streets like a militia captain, if he had seen fit.

In the midst of all this hilarity a letter came to Mrs. Niles from her brother Henry in New York, saying that George had been quite sick with the whooping cough, and was not now recovering as the physician thought he should. He needed change, country air, and nursing. Could not Mrs. Niles take him for a few months into her pleasant home? Mrs. Erwin did not feel that she could leave the city, and, indeed, was not much of a nurse if she could; but he knew how perfect Mrs. Niles was in this capacity; and Rachel, of whom George was very fond, would be willing, he did not doubt, to assist her.

Mrs. Niles hesitated; she had already a larger family than she well knew how to care for, and a sick child makes such an addition! Mr. Niles remembered the little boy as a very pleasing child, and

inclined to have him come; indeed, he felt as if his
wife's nursing could almost restore the dead to life.
But before they had had time to decide, another letter came from Mr. Erwin. George seemed to be
growing weaker every day. He should come with
him by the next train, without waiting to hear.

Mrs. Niles fervently wished it had been after the
boys' vacation; but as there was no help for it now,
she prepared to make the best of it, and despatched
Horace to the station for the unexpected visitors.

Poor little George! it only needed for his aunt to
have one glimpse of his poor, pale face, and she
opened her arms to receive him as if he had been
her own. But he was to be Rachel's boy. Hardly
noticing any one else, he tottered by them to her,
and holding up his hands, so thin that they looked
almost transparent, he said, —

"Mauma, I've come!"

"Bress de Lord, yes, I see!" said Rachel, staring
at him as if she was looking at a ghost; "you come
for true; but whar's my big, fat boy?"

"He coughed all away, mauma," said the child,
smiling, but, in doing so, stretching his white lips
until the action resembled a grin; "but he come
back again now."

"De good Lord grant it!" said Rachel, fervently,
holding him away from her, and testing his weight
as she would have done a firkin of butter. "Eh!
eh! he weigh no more dan a two weeks baby, poor
little fellow! There! mauma will."

And clasping him close to her warm, motherly
heart, Rachel rocked him to and fro, while he laid
his head upon her shoulder, and turned up his fear-

fully large, bright eyes as if he was unwilling for a
moment, even, to lose sight of her.

And so the debate was settled. And Mrs. Niles,
as she saw the meeting, felt that she could truthfully
assure her brother that George would add in no way
to her trouble, and he might leave him for the rest
of the summer.

It is singular how the presence of sickness immediately affects the spirits of a house. No sooner had
George been borne over the threshold of the door
than there seemed to enter with him a quieting influence. Mr. Erwin was impressed with the order
and stillness of the house. It was, to him, almost
like a church. The hushed tones of voice which all,
even down to Totty, adopted, for fear of disturbing
the sick child; the soft footsteps; the checked laughter; and the quiet tones of conversation, — all reminded him of the country meeting house between
service, to which he used to go when he was a boy.
He thought it exceedingly dull; indeed, even for the
day that he remained, the wonder was in his mind,
all the time, what could induce people to live in such
a place, when New York was in the same country!

He had never seen his sister's family all together
before; and though he could not but acknowledge
that they were good-looking and well-behaved, he
thought they must grow up to make a very tame
kind of men and women. For Florence, he was
pleased to see her looking in such excellent health,
and as if the *ennui* did not kill her; but he had less
doubt than ever that she would be in as great a
hurry to return to them as decency would permit;
and though he was kind to her, he paid her as little

attention as possible, in order not to make her discontented. Ida had sent her some little presents and a long letter. Florence had no time to answer the letter, but packed up in her uncle's valise a large bouquet of wild flowers, which she and Frank ran over the woods to gather, on the morning of his departure.

If she had seen Ida's face as she took in her hands the poor, withered things, she would have wished she had left them forever, " to blush unseen."

After his uncle's departure, Horace made every effort to have things resume their former attitude, but it seemed as if the spirit of fun stood silent and rebuked. All their amusements now assumed a graver, more quiet character, and the college boy began to look forward impatiently for the return to college life. Every one seemed to think more of " Georgy," as they called the new comer, to distinguish him from their own George, than they did of him. No excursion was received with much favor which was too far for Rachel, with her light burden; and in spite of his good heart, and superabundant good nature, Horace could not help, many times during the day, "voting the sick child a great bore."

It almost seemed as if " Georgy" was conscious of it, for he avoided Horace, and was in reality afraid of him; always taking refuge in his cousin George's arms, if he came suddenly into the room and Rachel was not there. Probably there was something about Horace which reminded him of his own brother Henry, yet Horace was always kind and gentle with him, if he did wish him back in New York.

17

Mrs. Niles, watchful mother as she was, saw, with a slight uneasiness, that Georgy's visit made more difference to him than to any one else, and by a little extra attention strove very wisely to make amends. She planned a hunting excursion for him, which would keep him active and happy; or she sent him to execute some social commissions, of which he was very fond. She even allowed him to take old Billy, and ask pretty Katy Drummond, with whom he had been in love ever since they two could walk alone, to take a drive with him to a neighboring town; and finally, as the last and greatest occasion of vacation, consented to a large and somewhat general picnic, in "Seymour's Grove," down by the gently running Lemon's Creek.

This was to be, in deed and in truth, an occasion. Horace was here, there, and every where. Not a brown house in all the parish into which he did not put his bright face, with the invitation, "to come and have a good time; if they could not contribute any thing else to the entertainment, they could bring cheerful words."

To be sure, occasionally he received a dash of cold water; but Horace was just the boy to bear a whole shower bath with only a laugh and a shrug of the shoulder, and as he generally took Florence with him, she had the full advantage of all his droll rencontres. There was one among them, however, which she could not understand, and which she reserved to talk over with her "minister cousin," the first time they should be alone together.

It was the visit to the farm of Deacon Ben Dean. He lived two miles out of the village, and Horace

had teased her, with Frank's assistance, to walk out
there with them; for, although Florence was so
many years younger than himself, she was pretty
and lively—so different from the northern girls, that
he always enjoyed having her with him almost as
much as Frank did himself.

On they went, up hill and down, now stopping to
sit down on a large stone to rest, and now jumping
over the stile into a field full of the most tempting
berries; picking bunches of wild flowers, wreath-
ing them into all manner of fantastic shapes, then
tossing them away, as if the very fulness of their
own young life and joy required a prodigality of
nature's.

Horace forgot by the wayside his sophomorical
dignity, but began slowly to resume it as they came
in sight of the brown house in which the deacon
lived.

"Now behave," said he, throwing as far as he
could a bunch of violets which Florence had
pinned on the front of his felt hat. "The deacon,
like England, 'expects every man to do his duty,'
and if we don't take him 'this side up, with care,'
farewell to any hope of some of those delicious cream
cakes for the picnic. Come, Flossy, tie your hat on
and step up as demurely as if you were two hundred."

"Yes, sir," said Florence, dropping a courtesy, and
drawing down her face.

"Walk like Aunt Hitty," whispered Frank.
"There, now, straighter, and come down heavy
like, first on one foot, and then on the other."

"I don't like to," said Florence, after taking a step

or two, much to the boy's amusement. "Aunt Hitty can't help it."

"She is right," said Horace. "You know, Frank, mother says never mimic a deformity. It is mean."

"I am sorry," said Florence, the tears starting into her eyes.

"Poh! little puss, don't be silly," said Horace; "you didn't mean any thing wrong."

"But you said it was *mean*," sobbed Florence.

"True, South Carolinian," laughed Horace; "but there comes Deacon Ben's dog, and his master isn't far away."

Following close upon his dog, there was the deacon, who stopped as soon as he saw the children, and sat down upon a log which happened to lie by the wayside. His house was never visited by a chance passer, for the road stopped at its door, and whoever came up must have come "on purpose."

He had been a little shy of the minister's family since his call on Mrs. Niles; and though he was far from quiet, what he did was done in secret. His first thought now was, therefore, which of his actions had come to Mrs. Niles's ear, for which she had sent to request a little private conversation. He assumed a dogged look as the children came nearer, and was preparing himself evidently for a rencontre. There was the "southern gal, too; what on airth could have tempted them to bring her."

Ministers' children, if at all bright, soon learn to adapt themselves to their father's parishioners. They have extra advantages for the study of human nature, and really may carry with themselves into life an aptitude to see into motives, and to handle them, which belongs to no other class of children. So, now, Horace saw the winter of the deacon's discontent, and suited himself wonderfully to it.

Sitting down on the log, and whittling away with his penknife, in exact time with the whittling of the farmer, he entered into a dissertation on crops and cattle, which would have given rise to the opinion that he had made them his study in college.

"He hadn't come on no errand for his marm;" such was the deacon's conclusion, after a few minutes; "and if the little gal did own slaves, it wasn't any more than manners to ask her into the house." So he proffered the invitation, which was readily accepted. Florence had been often now at farmer Bates's, but never within an "out-of-town" farm house like this; so she looked about her with very wondering but well-bred eyes, and had altogether a modest, inquiring look, which, as the deacon had no daughters — only three great rough boys, — struck him, in spite of his antipathy against her, as something very pretty. He opened the door for her, and ushering her into the kitchen, said to his wife, a tall, thin woman, hard at work, —

"Mother, here is the minister's children, and that ere cousin of theirn."

Mrs. Dean was not overflowing with the milk of human kindness, and she was busy too, and ill-pleased at being interrupted: so she said, —

"The gal from the south, what owns slaves, eh! Well, I have no desire to see her coming inside of my door, for one. She don't bring a blessing with her, I guess."

Florence heard her without comprehending what she

meant; and as Horace drew her in, she sat down in a wooden chair, which the woman pushed towards her.

"She hasn't come to ask you to buy her slaves, Mrs. Dean!" said Horace, pleasantly. "I don't think she would sell one if you would give her their weight in gold; so don't be afraid."

"I don't know about that," said Mrs. Dean, shaking her cross head. "I never heard of any on um who didn't love money better nor the body or soul of their fellow-beings; and such a chit as she is, to have that big black woman tagging round arter her! We should call it pretty shiftless up here."

"Well, well, Mrs. Dean," said Frank, who had been watching her with a flashing eye through this last speech, "we didn't come here this morning to talk about slavery, but about a picnic. Suppose we change the subject."

"Yes, that is always the way! change the subject. Frank Niles, do you suppose you will be able to change the subject at the day of judgment? I jist want to know, now, — and I ain't afraid to ask it, nuther, — what right a little pale-faced thing like that has to own a hundred and fifty — I dare say, babies and all, there is twice that number — of immortal souls. Answer me that, will ye?" said Mrs. Dean, approaching Florence, and putting her arms a-kimbo, as if she was prepared for a fight.

"Ma'am?" said the frightened child, looking in her face.

"Ma'am!" reëchoed Mrs. Dean; "yes, you may ma'am as much as you please, but that is no answer to my question! What right have you to own human beings? Did God give them to you?"

"Yes, ma'am," said Florence, simply.

"Yes, ma'am! how dare you?" It was evident that Mrs. Dean's temper was now getting the better of her. "How dare you say that wicked, awful lie? Suppose I should seize you and sell you; would it be any excuse for me to say that God gave you to me?"

"What does she mean?" asked Florence, looking round at Horace with a wondering expression. "I don't understand her."

"Don't pretend any such thing. You speak English — don't you?" said Mrs. Dean, without giving Horace time to answer.

"Yes, ma'am," said Florence, but at the same time rising and going towards the door.

"Well, then, here I enter my protest"—and Mrs. Dean held up her great red hands—"against the entire sin of slavery, whether it is found at the south or the north, in our minister's family or in my own."

"Dorothy," said Mr. Dean, interfering, but in a very mild tone, "this little gal isn't the only one in the world to blame. Perhaps, arter all, as Mrs. Niles says, the sin ain't as much hern as those who brought it upon her."

"Not hern! no, never hern, nor his, nor yourn, nor mine; always just nobody's, where there is wrong!" sharply rejoined Mrs. Dean; "but I'll raise my voice until it can be heard like a trumpet, from one end of this mighty land to another."

"You won't have to exert yourself much more, I am thinking, Mrs. Dean," said Horace, in whose eye a twinkle of fun showed he was more appreciative of the mirth than of the impropriety of the scene.

"No, I will speak so that the very dead shall hear in their graves," went on Mrs. Dean.

"The dead in sin and misery you mean, my dear," mildly interpolated the deacon.

"The dead in chains! those who are wearing out the life of their souls in everlasting slavery," chimed in his wife. "Those for whom you," approaching Florence, and shaking her hand in her face, "are accountable to the great Judge. Go home with you, and put every slave at liberty, before the setting of to-day's sun, or God's curse rest forever upon you."

"Come, come, Mrs. Dean!" said Horace, now beginning to lose his own temper; "this is a little too bad, and not at all what I brought Florence down here for to-day. I hope you will take breath long enough to consider the picnic, and some fresh cream cakes, which I came to beg from you for it."

Mrs. Dean gave two or three snorts, very much like those an impatient animal gives when it is first conscious of restraint, then went to the opposite side of the room, and sat down.

Horace followed her with his eye, keeping it steadily fixed upon her, as if he saw the resemblance to the animal, and was endeavoring to subdue her by the same means he should use with one; and boy as he was, she was soon conscious of being under his power.

Whether owing to the weakness in her husband's character, which she was afraid it would tend to increase, or whether owing to her own natural love of independence Mrs. Niles, had always been careful to maintain for her family, in very many respects, an entire independence. She never encouraged the system of gifts any farther than it was in her power to return them. Managing to live entirely upon their salary by various devices, all of which she kept rigorously to herself, she openly expressed the belief that the workman was worthy of his hire, and that the salary which Mr. Niles received was not one whit or tittle more a gift, or a personal favor, than the money which she paid in fair exchange for any commodities she might purchase in the village. Whenever Mr. Niles's services as preacher and pastor were not valuable to the amount of money received, the people could say so, and they would leave the place open to another.

While, therefore, she struggled to make her children examples in every good word and work, she never had either their life or their spirits hampered out of them by the dread that they should do or say something which some one might not approve. There was no such bugbear as "the people" in her home; and the consequence was, that her children could hold up their heads and feel and act like other children.

Now, Horace had only the feeling that Mrs. Dean was an ill-tempered, ill-mannered woman — one to whom he could say a number of very cutting things, if it was gentlemanly, which it certainly was not. He had, moreover, that quicker insight into human nature which I have said belongs to the children of a minister's family; and this led him to see that the end of an anti-slavery discussion certainly was not cream cakes: so he changed the subject with much adroitness, and was, in a few minutes, as deep in dairies and cream with Mrs. Dean as he had been, a few minutes before, in farming matters with her husband.

Slowly he worked his way around to the desired object, and had the satisfaction not only to have the promise of a basket full for the picnic, but to see a tin pail make its appearance, loaded with them, "to take home to his marm for tea."

Florence had two angry spots burning on her cheeks. She had not left the door, or taken one step back, when Horace was proceeding with his manœuvres; but there she stood, looking anxiously at him, and feeling as if his conversation would never end.

As soon as they were out of sight of the house, Horace burst into a long, loud laugh.

"I declare, Flossy," he said, "if that wasn't as good as a farce. Why, you little tragedy queen, one would think you were called upon to resent every insult offered to the south, to see how soberly you took Madam Dean's denunciations. That is small talk in comparison to some I have heard. Here, try her cream cakes, and see if they won't smooth out the remaining front of the trouble."

"I would not eat a mouthful of her cake if I knew I should starve," said Florence, pushing back the tempting morsel. "What right has she to talk to me about my own property? One would think she owned my slaves, and not I myself. I never heard any thing so impudent."

"But, my fair cousin," said Horace, assuming a very gallant air, "if you live long at the north, you will be very apt to hear a great deal of just such impudence. You know, we northerners do not believe, as Mrs. Dean says, in buying and selling human beings. We hold that all men are born free and equal, and that, in matter of fact, you have no more right to hold Rachel, for instance, in bondage, than she has you."

"Rachel is free — papa made her so;" said Florence, eagerly; "but for Juno, and Cato, and John, and Maum Sylvia, and Hannah, and Bet, and all the rest of them, they belong to me."

"That is the very thing Madam Dean and some others of us good northerners complain of — that they should belong to any body but their own individual selves."

"I don't see how they could belong to themselves," said Florence, innocently. "They are none of them white."

Horace and Frank both laughed; and as they did not like to see their little cousin's face wear the troubled look it now did, they changed the subject. But nothing could restore Florence's cheerfulness to her. She walked silently and sadly home, and as soon as she saw her cousin George, ran to him, and whispered she had something she would like to talk with him about when they were alone together.

George noticed that she had such an anxious, eager expression every time their eyes met, that he took the earliest opportunity to lead her away alone, and inquire what had gone wrong; and as she eagerly detailed to him what Mrs. Dean had said, and Horace too, she was not at all comforted by seeing as troubled looks come over his face, and to hear him say, simply, —

"My dear little Flossy, you are at present quite too young to worry about this matter. You cannot do any thing to help those poor creatures if you would. All you can do now is, to pray to God to convert them, and prepare them for the great gift of freedom, when, in his own good time, he shall send it to them."

Florence looked at him with such an expression of blank astonishment that he felt compelled to say, —

"You cannot understand, now, Flossy, all the relations of owner and slave, nor why we, who live at the north, all feel such an abhorrence of slavery; but the older you grow, the better you will comprehend it. Be content, now, to wait five years."

"Mrs. Dean said I must free them all before the sun sets," said Florence, eagerly, "or God would be very angry at me. What do they want to be free for? I am sure they may, if they wish to. Only, who will take care of Myrtle Bush?"

"And who will take care of them, Flossy?"

"I am sure I don't know. I suppose, Mr. Jones, the overseer, will."

"But not if they are free. Mr. Jones is your overseer, not theirs. And what will become of those who are very, very old? I suppose there are a great many such there."

"O, yes, indeed!" said Florence, eagerly—Maum Jenny, and Dinah, and—and ever, ever so many more."

"Then we will leave them to Mr. Jones, to take the best care in the world of them while they live, and we will fit those who are young to be free as soon as their little missis is old enough to make them so. Will we not?"

"Will that do? Will that be right? Will God love me, and take care of me, if I can't do any more now?" asked Florence, eagerly.

"He certainly will," said George, a solemn, sad look gathering over his face. "Ask him to make you a good, conscientious little missis, and lead you, as you grow older, in the right way. To such a prayer he never turns a deaf ear."

"I will love to ask," said Florence, contentedly; "and will not forget it to-night."

When George Niles repeated the above conversation to his mother, she expressed much regret that Florence's mind had become troubled upon the subject of slavery. She had hoped she could pass this year without its being agitated. Then, if she returned to her uncle's family in New York, there would be very little probability of its coming before her for years, at least. Indeed, before she should be of age, Mrs. Niles hoped it might become a question of politics, and be decided by other and wiser heads. Now, however, while she fully approved of what George had done and said, she felt that Florence must receive from her the north side view of the matter, even at the risk of its implanting thus early the seeds of uneasiness, which might eventually produce trouble. The picnic came quickly on. For a wonder, the day proved auspicious, and not a single cloud arose over the social any more than it did over the earthly horizon.

Seymour's wood was made — so every body said — for a picnic; and certainly, if not made, it was hallowed to the usages of one from time immemorial. It would be difficult to say what makes a picnic such a popular festival in the country. Perhaps it is that there is a freeness and freshness under the blue sky, which the stiffness and regularity of country life prevent being felt where the quiet home people are shut in by four square walls; but whatever the reason, it certainly is the only gathering place where every body feels really and truly at liberty to do as he pleases.

Florence's visits among the parishioners had heretofore been very limited, and it must be acknowledged her call upon Mrs. Dean had not made her very desirous of a nearer or more intimate acquaintance. Much as she had heard and thought of this time, its approach filled her with a species of dread; and if she might have been allowed, she would willingly have remained at home.

Not so Rachel. She had had her share in the preparations which were made at the parsonage; had made peanut candy, and even ventured to prepare a plate of wafers so exquisitely thin, and so gracefully rolled, that Horace declared they looked like the scrolls upon which the fabled gods might be expected to send down their decrees to poor mortals.

Little George, carefully wrapped up, went to the grove in Rachel's arms. Perhaps it was the contrast between the two which excited so much attention — Georgy, white as a lily, with his large blue eyes and soft brown hair, laying his transparent cheek so often and so wearily against the black face, that always wore, as he did so, a look of such troubled love. Indeed, if Mrs. Niles could have chosen a way in which to present Rachel to her parishioners that would most nearly touch and interest them, she could not have selected one which would make the appeal more directly.

"They are a real picter," said Aunt Hitty, moving round from one gazing group to another; "and the poor little fellow looks as if he loved her jist as well as if she was his own marm. Any body can see, too, with half an eye, that if she's black she's got a heart white enough. It is as much as I can do to keep from crying right out, it is such a picter. I never seed the like in all my life afore, and I hain't got the heart even to offer to take him half a minute while she rests her arms. He looks so contented like, I shouldn't wonder if God made those black arms a chariot for taking him right up to heaven."

Aunt Hitty soon made her way towards them, and was, in spite of her peculiar personal appearance, which at first almost frightened the sick child, in a few minutes amusing him with the wreaths of oak leaves which she twined and plaited with a peculiar ingenuity almost amounting to taste.

Indeed, the most gleeful laugh which the boy had uttered since he had been at Grafton burst from him, when, fastening a brilliant display of the red fox berries in among the leaves, Aunt Hitty, standing on the tips of her little feet, put it on Rachel's head.

Aunt Hitty's success drew towards them first one and then another of those who had gazed on at a respectful distance, until Rachel found herself hemmed in by a circle of strange white faces, but all wearing a pleased, cordial look.

Florence, too, avoiding Mrs. Dean, soon began to

make acquaintances, and with her pretty, winning
ways, opened the hearts of those upon whose finer
feelings the deacon had been working out his aboli-
tion schemes.

"It's a pity! God forgive her! I don't see how
she can help it." Such became the common senti-
ment of the occasion; and if the picnic did no other
good, it certainly had the effect of bringing the people into closer and more forgiving contact with the
blot which rested for the time upon their good
minister's family.

Horace voted it "an entire success;" and every
body else regarding it in the same light, they were
ready, at a late hour, to unite in "prayer and praise,"
which went up — who can doubt it? — most ac-
ceptably, on this festive night, from those grand
old woods.

A day or two only remained of Horace's vacation.
These were spent with the holiday spirit which
George's arrival had interrupted, in full force again.
So much life and pleasure were compressed into the
waking hours, that Florence began to droop and look
heavy-eyed, as she had for the want of some of this
same thing in her quiet New York life.

"You must be still again, and shall, as soon as
Horace goes," said the watchful aunt.

CHAPTER XVI.

Home life at the parsonage immediately after Horace Niles's departure assumed its old phases. The children's vacation was over, and they returned to their tasks, if with some reluctance, with really fresh vigor. Florence, during these happy, busy weeks, was becoming thoroughly acquainted with all the varieties and enjoyments of New England country life, and she had entered into them with an ardor and interest which conferred upon those to whom they were " a twice-told tale," much of the freshness and vivacity of her own feelings.

Her letters to Ida grew every time shorter and shorter, and brought at last from the sensitive cousin the abrupt question, " Was it possible that she could find sufficient enjoyment in the tediousness and monotony of country life to forget her ? "

Florence had found neither tediousness nor monotony; so she tried to explain to Ida, but could do so only imperfectly, and received in reply a few cold, contemptuous lines, which did not tend to warm her heart very much towards the distant city cousin. She was silent to her aunt and Jennie about the letters which were passing between them, but with true childish simplicity made Rachel her confidant, and was, perhaps, rather encouraged in her growing coldness by the negro's oft-repeated —

" Miss Ida ! Miss Ida ! eh ! eh ! For true what she

18

know about Grafton? She just wait, be sure, until
little Georgy go home; he tell her. De boy more
sense, sartin now, dan dat big gal! eh! eh!"

There was another event, which, though to a certain extent it threw a gloom over all the rest of
the family, had a most happy effect upon Florence.

George Niles had for the last year evinced many
of the consumptive tendencies, which, at nearly his
own age, had made themselves apparent in Florence's father.

It is not at all improbable that, with the hereditary tendency lying dormant within them, the very
same sacrifices and self-denials had led to the same
result. No one can tell how many young men break
down in the midst of their preparatory course for the
ministry, for the want of a little more of those means
which they cannot earn, and which they cannot
accept.

God in his own mysterious way orders these events
we know, but it is one of the saddest of all those
hidden decrees that pales the cheek, and dims the eye
and lays the strength of the young man low, just
when he is bringing into that whitened harvest field
the one high purpose of gathering in those sheaves
to his Father's garner.

Mysterious way! hidden decrees! so we call them
as we watch, with fainting hearts, one after another, —

"By the road-side fall and perish,
Weary with the march of life."

Weary indeed, for all along that march, that road-side
has been thickly strown with obstacles to combat

wants, privations, debts, weariness — weariness such
as no words can ever describe; discouragement, not
mental, but purely physical; gazing out eagerly from
the small, dim window of his close study, into that
broad harvest field, and seeing drop slowly, slowly,
between him and it, that dark, heavy curtain which
no mortal hand can ever raise; conscious of powers
which could do God good service; eagerly, anxiously
making the one talent ten, and then wrapping them
all up, not in the napkin for the purpose of hiding
them from their master, but in that shroud over
which is rolled the stone of the sepulchre.

It may be that the church has no responsibility
here, but if they have, there will arise, to bear testi-
mony against them in that last day, many young
men, who, like George Niles, might have lived long,
useful lives, doing the work which the church is left
to accomplish, with a little delicate, timely assistance.

Perhaps, in that day when we shall know as we
are known, all that is mysterious and hidden will be
shown to be only that secrecy into which we ourselves throw those events which we dare not in our
selfish short-sightedness investigate.

If over the early graves of so many of our young
clergy we should inscribe an epitaph which should
at once convey the cause and nature of their death,
we must write, —

"Died from over-exertion, caused by the neglect
of God's people."

George Erwin had borne cheerfully, and without
one word of complaint, many privations which even
the commonest mechanic would have shrunk from.

These had all been unknown to his parents, and when sometimes they wondered that the bills which they paid so cheerfully for him were so small, they did not suspect that they had been made so by self-denials, whose severity they could hardly have imagined.

At present all unfavorable symptoms were slight. If Rachel saw the shadow when she first saw George, it was only because she had watched the same stealing so silently over her young master; and when now she fixed her eye with such a soft expression of pity upon him, no human being but a mother would have noticed and divined what she meant.

And to Mrs. Niles the fear was so indistinct, so kept back by that reluctance to allow its possibility, that while she guarded with such jealous care every avenue by which the destroyer might approach, she turned a deaf ear to the echo of those footsteps ever approaching nearer and yet nearer.

Marking the slightest change, the least unfavorable symptom, she was ready to assign any and every reason for it, but what in the depth of heart she knew was the true one. She felt almost impatient with Rachel when she heard her draw a deep sigh, as the slight sound of a cough came from the adjoining room, and wanted to quarrel with the kindness which stood ready to close a door or a window, if a draft, however slight, blew over the shoulders of the half invalid.

Once she heard Rachel saying, in reply to some inquiries for little Georgy, —

"De *leetle* Georgy bery well, tank you, but I hear de sound ob de angel's wings in dis dere house."

Angels' wings! — were they waiting for that first born, that "summer child"?

George must have occupation away from his books and usual professional studies. He must not return to the theological seminary for the present, and while summer was fading, and his life's young blossoms were fading too, he must be made to feel that he was wearing out the remnant of those fleeting days in his Master's work.

To keep him pleasantly occupied, without fatigue, was the end and aim now of all Mrs. Niles's plans; and among those most readily adopted was the one of teaching the children — a great relief to both Mr. Niles and herself, and of equal benefit to the children, as giving them a young, fresh teacher. Florence, growing more and more fond of her cousin, became at once a docile and delighted pupil; and day by day the young minister might be seen with little Georgy in his lap, and the other children gathered closely around him, conveying to them not only those lessons of earthly knowledge, but those more important ones which should be remembered long after he had gone to his reward.

As the leaves began to tinge with the early autumn hues, Mrs. Niles made every day, or George found for himself, some missionary work to be done in the well-cared-for parish. On most of these excursions he took the little girls, or, if Jennie thought herself of too much importance at home, went with Florence alone. One visit there was in which he found her a most useful auxiliary; that was to old black Rose.

Rose Cooley had come to Grafton before Mr. and

Mrs. Niles, and had purchased or taken possession — it was never known which — of a small shed, which, just outside of the village, had been used by the earliest settlers as a place for sleeping, while they were at work upon the surrounding woods.

She had put on here a board, and there a patch of twigs, until the shanty was safe from rain and not very cold. By degrees she had made a small yard, a bit of a garden, a hen-coop, and various other necessities of life. No one ever questioned her right to the spot; and whether it was legally hers or not, possession was emphatically nine points in *her* law. Surmises with regard to her early history had long since been given up. Nothing ever had been learned of her, and nothing, every body felt sure, ever could. There had been — so the shrewdest thought — some tale of sin and shame, perhaps of positive crime, connected with her; but whatever it was, she was a harmless member of the community now, making her scanty living by the sale of herbs, sage, summer savory, and the like, which she cultivated in her small garden.

She attended Mr. Niles's church not oftener than once in two or three years, and showed no disposition to receive or encourage the minister's calls whenever he passed her way.

As she grew older, and the day came hastening on when the account for that past life must surely be rendered, her situation weighed heavily upon him who felt that he had the care of souls, and representing her situation to George, his father begged him to leave no means untried to reach and benefit her.

George's first visits were as ungraciously received as his father's had been, old Rose only lifting her head with a careless nod as he came in, but expressing her joy at his departure in a much less ambiguous way. She had no reply to his remarks but the briefest, and but for a natural tenacity of purpose, George would have allowed her to travel for the rest of her life her own way, unmolested.

Walking one day in the direction of her house with Florence, it occurred to him as a possibility, that the child, always accustomed to the negro race, might be able to do what every one else had so signally failed in ; nor was he less sanguine, when, coming in sight of the shanty, she clapped her hands with joy to see a building which reminded her of the negro houses at Myrtle Bush.

Giving her no idea of the character of the woman she was to see, he tapped softly, and saw Florence start with delight as the negro tones said gruffly, " Come in."

" It is old Rose's house," said George, as he slowly pushed back the door. " I want you to see her and talk with her."

Rose's small, twinkling eye glanced quickly over the new comer, but instead of meeting the ordinary look of wonder and fear with which the children of Grafton regarded her, she met a smiling face and a look of recognition, which, as if by magic, kindled one in her own.

" How d'ye, Aunt Rose," said Florence, walking straight up to her, and holding out her hand.

Rose got up from her chair, and taking the little white hand between both of hers, gave it the first cordial shake she had given for years.

"Hud d'ye, little missus," she said pleasantly; "where in de world did you come from? Did ye drop down from there?" pointing to the sky from out her small window.

"O, no, Aunt Rose," said Florence; "I came straight from South Carolina."

"I tink so; I know so for sartin," said Rose, snapping her eyes; "no north to dat ere." And she looked over Florence from head to foot, as if she was measuring every particular of her personal appearance.

"And my mauma is here too," continued Florence, drawing out a large block which served for a footstool, and moving it close to Rose's chair; "shouldn't you like to see her?"

Rose gave two or three expressive shrugs, and said, "Radder see you, little missus; don't care much for de niggers."

"Where did you come from, Aunt Rose?" continued Florence, without taking any notice of the slight put upon Rachel.

Rose glanced up at George, and shaking her head, said, "Can't tell; don't know; neber knew. Guess didn't come at all."

George suddenly thought it might be well to leave Florence for a little while alone with the negro. She was evidently not inclined to make any remarks before him, and was beginning to be, he thought, a little ashamed of the cordiality into which she had been betrayed. So, saying he would walk on a quarter of a mile, and leave Florence to rest until he returned, he went quickly away.

No sooner had the sound of his footsteps died in the distance, than Rose, turning to Florence, said, —

"Little missus, you keep de secret de ole nigger tell you."

"Yes, Aunt Rose," said Florence. And then followed a communication more confidential than Rose had ever made before. Perhaps it was true, perhaps it was not; but it answered the purpose of interesting the southern child in the old deserted negro. When, after an hour's absence, George returned, he heard Rose laugh before he reached the house, and found Florence in no hurry to leave; and when she did so, promising the negro, with much earnestness, to come again soon.

Now, as they walked slowly home, George told Florence all that had ever been known of Rose in Grafton; also of the fears which the good people entertained that she was wholly unprepared to meet that change which must, in the order of nature, soon come upon her.

"But my mauma must come to her, then," said Florence, eagerly; "mauma is good, and talks so beautifully of Christ and heaven, she makes every one wish to go there."

"You shall bring Rachel here soon with you, then, Florence," said George. "I wonder I had not thought of that before."

Not many days elapsed before George, accompanied by Florence and Rachel, made another visit; but this time not with very good success.

Rachel had no fancy for the free negroes of the north, and old Rose — as she emphatically said — "did not like niggers;" so Florence must, after all, be left to do whatever of this good work God designed to have done. She was a ready and willing

coadjutor with George, and at last became so fond
of these visits that she often went alone. Occasionally she met another visitor there, the only one, before Florence, who had ever been at all welcome.
This was Aunt Hitty; and the bond of union may
have been, that being deformed and odd, old Rose
considered her as in some measure cast out from the
human race, as she was herself.

When Florence first found her there, she was
half inclined to make a speedy retreat; for, kind as
Aunt Hitty was, the child was more afraid of her
than of the negro; but Rose, as if divining her fear,
and unwilling to lose the visit, drew the block, now
sacred to Florence's use, close up to her, and put
her arm around the child, as if offering her protection.

Aunt Hitty gave a great many little starts as she
saw the familiarity, and as she said, in repeating the
occurrence to Mrs. Niles, "couldn't help wondering,
to save her life, how such a delicate, pretty creature
could bear that black thing so near her. For her
part, she felt as if, like, a shudder went all over her,
jist to sit and look at her. If Deacon Ben only could
have seen it," she thought, "they wouldn't hear any
more about abolitionism this five year."

About this time Rose began to give indications of
failing health, which called for much sympathy from
the kind-hearted Aunt Hitty. With the peculiar
obstinacy of some natures, the more sure the negro
became that she was passing beyond the power of
her own herbs to help her, the more determined she
seemed to be that nothing else should. She resolutely withheld all complaints; and when the village

doctor, sent by Mr. Niles, dropped in to see her, she threw his saddle bags out of the door, and told him that, if she were only able, he should follow them. But, in spite of her resolution, the disease — dropsy in the limbs — gained with fearful rapidity. Aunt Hitty, as she came to the cottage, used to hear, with horror, the groans which seemed constantly to escape her, when she thought no one was near; but the good woman carried into the hut a cheerful face, and performed her many little acts of kindness, as if they were a part of her regular every-day life.

By degrees Rose became accustomed to her, and would ask her to do things which she was entirely incapable of performing for herself. Aunt Hitty, therefore, came and went at all hours, and with her little brown basket on her arm, seemed to pass through the town of Grafton like a collecting agent, picking up tumblers of jelly, warm rusks, fresh biscuits, or whatever delicacies the people thought would be acceptable to the sick woman. Rose never thanked Aunt Hitty. Indeed, it may be questioned whether she ever felt an emotion of gratitude towards her or any one else.

On a cold, bleak day, towards the last of October, Aunt Hitty, wrapped up in her blanket shawl, walked quickly towards old Rose's house. The nearer she approached, the more noticeable it was that the more quickly she walked; and if any one had watched her closely, they would have seen that she cast many timid glances around her as she proceeded. She never approached a thicket of bushes without running by them, and when she came to the large trees which skirted the road along at a short distance before reaching Rose's house, she dropped her thick veil over her face, and with very evident tremor proceeded. Even the old gray rock, so near the hut that Rose had always called it her barn, seemed to have a terror for her to-day; for she kept as far away from it as the opposite fence would allow, and stopped if as much as a falling leaf rattled on her way.

But whatever cause of affright Aunt Hitty may have had before reaching the hut, it was not until she opened the door that it fairly overcame her. Starting back then, she uttered a series of screams which might have been easily heard by any one passing by on the high road. They were, however, suddenly stopped by the loud, stern voice of Rose.

"Come in," it said, "and don't make a fool of yourself."

Aunt Hitty glanced quickly up and down the dark, lonely woods; not a human being was in sight; no help near. The leaves continued to fall, as if making sport of her fears; and in her very eye a gray squirrel leaped out, and tossed towards her the shell of the nut he had just been nibbling.

"Come in!" called Rose again, seeing that Aunt Hitty stood as if petrified. "If you must be always putting your nose into oder people's business, what de name of sense gwine to turn and run tuder way for? Come in, dere, I say."

It was a very blanched face which poor Aunt Hitty turned towards Rose now; so pale that the old negro laughed — a shrill, discordant sound it was — as she said again, —

"Name of sense, what now? Neber see a nigger

boy afore? One tink you see de ghost ob some ob de speerits. Haugh, haugh ! "

Whatever Aunt Hitty may have felt, the object which had occasioned her fright seemed to be quite as much a partaker of it as if she brought an occasion in herself. His first movement was to dash through the small window near which he was standing when Aunt Hitty entered; the next was to push by her, overthrowing her as he rushed out of the door.

Rose caught his arm and held him from the first; and as at last he fairly confronted Aunt Hitty, there was something in the kind expression of her face, frightened as she was, which arrested him.

"Dere now, stop dat," said Rose, authoritatively; "you Pomp, come back, and don't make no more fool ob yourself dan de good Lord has made ob you; and you, Hitty Foster, name ob sense, can't you see dat are noting but a big nigger boy? Flesh and blood, what he got ob it. Haugh, haugh!" and again came the unpleasant laugh.

Aunt Hitty now deliberately stood still and faced the object of her alarm.

He was a black boy, tall, and so thin, so fright-fully emaciated, that she might be forgiven her feeling of fear. His skin was of the darkest hue, and the long, woolly hair looked like a fantastic wreath of black dandelions, when they are ready to hold under the chin to show their New England use of telling whether the "mother wants you." His eyes seemed by far the larger part of his face. The great, white balls looked unnaturally dilated, and as he rolled them round with that quick, frightened look, they were absolutely ghastly. His cheek bones protruded

from his face, and the skin was drawn so tightly over
them, that it almost seemed as if a touch would
break it. Then the mouth, with its thick, white
lips, and the nervous way in which it was constantly
opened and shut, revealing teeth like ivory, only
added to the death-like aspect.

A living skeleton! hung about with a few torn
clothes, so peculiar in their texture and fashion, that,
as Aunt Hitty's tailoress eye took them in at a glance,
they only served to make the figure more weird and
unnatural.

Like many other frightened women, Aunt Hitty's
first impulse was to directly address the object of her
terror, and she faltered out, —

"Who are you, and where did you come from?"

"You never mind now," interposed old Rose.
"Name ob sense, what you care? It's Pomp, my
grandson, for all eber you know, gwine to make me
a visit."

She laughed, and the boy distended that unnatural
mouth as if he meant the distortion for a laugh too.

"Your grandson, going to make you a visit,"
repeated Aunt Hitty, slowly. "Can't say rightly
that I see any remarkable family resemblance."

"Not see! He favors me mighty much," said Rose.
"Making me a visit, sure. Why not? Come to
take care ob de ole black woman; make her garden
when de snow comes. Haugh, haugh!"

"Where did you come from?" asked Hitty, still
addressing her remarks to the boy.

"Neber you mind, tell you. He come; dat's all.
Let him alone, can't you? He not gwine to speak.
Get along, Pomp. Name ob sense, why don't you
move?"

Pomp, staring first at Hitty and then at her, moved towards the door, and was darting out, when Hitty stopped him.

"Here," said she, holding out the brown basket of biscuit she had brought with her, "take them. You look — why, you look most starved."

The hand that was extended for the basket was so like a bird's claw, that Aunt Hitty drew back as it approached her, and Rose said, —

"De boy starved, sure enough. Look dat hand! Neber see de like. Eat 'um up, Pomp," she called after him, "but don't tief de basket. Bring it back, for sure."

Pomp's great, hungry eyes had already devoured its contents; but, taking the biscuits out one by one, and piling them up, he put the basket carefully down on the table, and rising on his bare toes, as if he must move stealthily, he went softly out.

"Dare he goes," said Rose, as he shut the door. "Now, for mercy sake, Hitty Foster, bite out dat dere tongue ob yours fore you dare to say what you seed here to-day."

"Has he run away from jail?" asked Aunt Hitty —this being the probability which his personal appearance made seem the greatest.

"Jail bird!" said Rose, chuckling. "He run away, may be, and may be he didn't run away. Neber you mind. You gwine to keep dis ting to your own self, Hitty Foster. Dat all you hab to do."

"Of course; yes; most certainly," said poor Aunt Hitty, hardly knowing what she was saying. "Keep it to myself — of course."

"Neber tell nobody; Miss Niles, nor nobody," said Rose, snapping her eyes very emphatically.

"No, no, of course not; but why not tell? Where did your grandson come from? He looks starved. Give him some tea. This ere ain't the way to treat folks."

"You let me alone for dat, Hitty Foster! Prehaps I know, prehaps I don't know; none of your business, neder."

"I wonder," said Aunt Hitty, seating herself, and speaking slowly, as if something had taken away her breath, — "I wonder now if this ere is *he?*"

"Name ob sense, it ain't a gal — is it?" asked Rose, laughing.

"A gal! O, sartin not; but I wonder if it is he that has been a dodging behind the things when I came along lately? As sure as I am alive," — and Aunt Hitty drew her chair a little nearer to Rose, — "I have seen those very eyes peeping out at me as I came here. Sometimes it was right from the middle of a clump of bushes, sometimes it was out from the branches of a tree; once it was behind the great gray stone. I thought," — aunt Hitty's voice sank to a whisper, — "I thought it was a wicked sperit of some kind, or I was growing crazy, I couldn't tell which."

"Dat dere head of yours go mad," said Rose, with much contempt in her tone. "'Tain't big enough here;" and she touched her forehead with her forefinger. "Berry like you see him; member him always, see him once, no mistake. Hunger dig deep, paint black picters, not berry handsome eder."

"Yes, as true as I am alive," said Aunt Hitty, "it must have been he, and no one else; and I am justly glad to think it is flesh and blood."

"Skin and bone, radder; but neber you mind, you let dat boy alone, dat's all."

Aunt Hitty hurried through her call, and with many injunctions of secrecy from old Rose, took her departure. Not daring to look at the right or left, she moved swiftly away, and hardly drew a long breath until she had left the hut, and the woods, and the high stone fences behind her, and began to come near the more thickly settled part of Grafton.

As she came opposite the parsonage, she happened to remember how often Florence went alone to the negro's hut.

She was immediately filled with so many troubled forebodings, that she was obliged to cling to the gate in order to prevent her falling. Go in and warn Mrs. Niles she could not, for she had bound herself by a promise to the most perfect secrecy; and yet, if any thing should happen, who would be so much to blame as herself?

She walked up to the door of the parsonage, and then ran back, as if the promise were the angel with the sword of flame, guarding it from her entrance. She tried to quiet herself by saying that she had received no harm, and certainly a child would not; but the great rolling eyes stared constantly in her face, and those long, lean fingers were clutching at the empty basket which swung on her arm.

Frightened afresh at these vivid recollections, she rushed into the house, opened the door of the room in which the family were sitting at tea, and said, abruptly, —

"Little Pet, go with Florence every time she goes to old Rose's; or, no, no, you ain't much larger and stronger than a bird. Frank, be a bold boy, and don't see your cousin walking off down to them ere

19

woods, where the lions, and the tigers, and all them ere things be, alone. Do you hear now? — don't be lazy, but play the beau for once."

"Now, Aunt Hitty, if that don't beat the Dutch! What in the world are you talking about?" said Frank, always the first to speak.

"Well, well," said Aunt Hitty, hurriedly, "you just look arter her, some on you — that's all;" and she shut the door as suddenly as she had opened it, and disappeared.

Many comments this singular behavior of Aunt Hitty drew from those assembled around the tea table, but none were so expressive as the one she made upon herself as she went quickly home.

"I told her, and I didn't tell her, nary; and so, let come what may, Aunt Hitty hain't no blame to rest on her shoulders, as far as I can see."

Then the good creature drew a sigh, which was an immense relief, and tripped along.

At any other time, Aunt Hitty's singular behavior might have dwelt upon Mrs. Niles's mind; but at present all thought of it was soon chased away by other and more serious matters, which fully occupied her. The coming on of this fall time was peculiarly dreary and dreaded by her. Every falling leaf, every withered flower, every mark of early decay and death, had to her a sad and solemn import, such as they had never had before. In vain she strove against these influences, in vain she endeavored to consider them all foolish, visionary, weak. Not a tender twig drooped its head, not a dry leaf rustled to her feet, but it whispered to her, O, how sadly! of the last dread doom. And yet not one of all these anxieties must be known; with the weight pressing ever heavier and yet heavier upon her heart, she must move around in the regular routine of every-day duties, cheerful, hopeful, smiling. There is no nobler sight, in all God's world, than a mother with a deep sorrow always present, and the outward calm, the strict and unyielding self-control, which carries into all the minor duties of life the careful attention, the minute watchfulness, which characterize her happier and freer days. Even to her husband Mrs. Niles could not speak; to allow the anxiety seemed almost to insure its fulfilment. Besides, Mr. Niles would not have recognized the necessity for these feelings. If any thing, George seemed to him to grow better as the cold weather came on. He had no doubt the sharp autumn frosts would entirely restore him, and was talking and planning for his return to his studies. Even George himself was, so far, almost entirely unconscious of the strides the disease was making. He could not see that month by month he grew weaker; that his cough slowly but steadily increased; that his breathing, after a slight exertion, became difficult; and that the pains in his lungs and sides, which at first only came and went, were now almost constant. That white harvest field was ever before him; and gazing out into it, he never saw the curtain dropping, dropping, before him. His mother had always been his confidant, his dearest friend. To her he loved to talk of that busy future, of his parish, his sermons, the crowns of his rejoicing which he hoped one day to bear with him to that other, better land.

There they sat, hour after hour, day after day, and

as he talked, his mother seemed to hear only the
quickened breathing, and the soft rustle of the coming angels' wings. Yet she spoke cheerfully to him
of life, and of what he — alas! it was to her *might*
have done, if God, in his great love, had spared him.
All unconsciously, in the mean time, the children of
the family went happily on. George's pale cheek became to them an incentive for far more perfect lessons
and more quiet behavior. "Hush, children; George
has fallen asleep," was sufficient to still them in their
freest, happiest times. Florence and Jennie rode
with him every day, and as this was the first time in
her life Florence had ever seen the brilliant northern
autumn, she was as glad and happy a child as ever
danced among the yellow leaves, or wreathed them
into bunches of brilliant flowers.

The sadness was not all the mother's in the family,
for even Rachel was not without her heavy heart.
Her letters from Cato, though coming with marvellous punctuality, had of late seemed to occasion her
many sad thoughts.

Even if she had been inclined, there was no one
to whom she could tell her trouble but "little missus," and of course Florence was too young to render her sympathy of much real value.

The source of Rachel's trouble was the absence of
any mention in Cato's letters of their fourth son,
Dick. This boy, now about sixteen years of age, had
always been most especially the mother's boy. More
delicate than was common for a negro child, he had
required and received, through the kindness of his
master, special indulgences. He had been much with
Rachel at the house, and had been allowed to play

round in the room which Florence, as a child, occupied. In this way he had grown up more attached to his mother and to "little missus" than any other negro on the plantation. Nor was this all; he had early imbibed from his mother, and from the reading to which he occasionally listened, a strong desire for freedom. It was not enough for him, when he was talking alone with his mother, to be told that some day he should be free. He was determined that he would not grow up to manhood a slave, and while his earnest protestations to that effect were too much in accordance with his mother's feelings to meet with any reproof, she tried to regulate them to such an extent as was compatible with her own burning sense of the wrong and injustice done to the black race by keeping them *slaves.*

Dick had begged and prayed her to bring him north when she came, but of course she could not, and the most troubled feeling which she brought away with her from Myrtle Bush was the one occasioned by leaving that boy. For the first year of her absence he seemed to be doing unusually well. Cato wrote of him as the "smartest ob de six, and so like his moder;" and even Mr. Jones, the overseer, in his letters to Mr. Erwin, had spoken of him as one of the most promising hands on the place. But for the last four months no word had Cato written of him, and though Rachel's own letters reiterated the anxious inquiries, still there came no reply.

Had he been doing some grievous wrong? Had he run away? Was he sick? Was he dead? Early in the morning, and late at night, over and over again, Rachel asked, and the ominous silence was the only reply.

Now, indeed, the sick but slowly convalescent child proved a blessing to the nurse.

She had early adopted Mrs. Niles's policy to make Florence depend more upon herself — to leave her to think and do without finding some one always ready to prompt or relieve her; and little Georgy had proved of much assistance in carrying this out. Really needing the very care she had so long bestowed upon Florence, she had naturally given it to him, and had the satisfaction of feeling that she was, under the kind care of his heavenly Father, instrumental in saving his life. Mrs. Niles, too, was in reality relieved of what would otherwise have been an impossible burden, and so she frequently comforted Rachel by telling her. Although it was now late in the season for Georgy to remain in the country, he was still so feeble that Mrs. Niles wrote to his father her fear that the city air and manner of life might, with the absence of his excellent nurse, protract the already slow recovery, and therefore she offered, in a manner which left no doubt of its sincerity, to have Georgy remain with them through the winter. In doing this Mrs. Niles did not forget the good which was constantly accruing to Florence by having Rachel otherwise occupied than for her, and it gave her much pleasure, and raised Florence's character in her estimation, to find that however much loved and petted the sick child was, she never exhibited any jealousy, or the slightest wish to have him return home.

Not so Totty. The first thing which opened her mother's eyes to the defects of her education was the ill temper which she constantly evinced, whenever Georgy happened to be any more petted or favored than she was herself.

Mrs. Niles had also noticed, perhaps with the true mother's sympathy, the cloud which hung over Rachel, and gently, after months of secret uneasiness, drew the confession from her; and there was something in Rachel's last remark, which rang over and over again in Mrs. Niles's heart, as she sat watching her own failing boy.

"Cato write too much ob submission to de good Lord. No one always say, he do right, he do right, unless their heart keep saying, he do wrong. He no reconciled to let him do as he has done; he want him do some oder way. He gwine to trust him cause he must, and it's something berry hard he not leave to dat Massa in heaven. It's Dick, I know — dat boy close his heart."

And so fell the dark fall shadows around the parsonage; but they fell like the shadows on the mountains, with bright glances of sunshine defining and finishing their outlines, and in these golden spots walked happily the young, fresh hearts.

CHAPTER XVI.

FLORENCE was not deterred for a single day from visiting old Rose by Aunt Hitty's warnings. Indeed, every body at the parsonage had forgotten them. The good woman was so accustomed to doing queer things, that if they had thought of this at all, it would have been only as a freak which was not worth a moment's sober consideration. To carry some little nice thing to Rose was as much a part of the week's employment to Florence as it was to attend to her other regular duties; and her aunt allowed her always to purchase something from the large sum of spending money which her uncle weekly sent her.

Whether incited to new attention by the suggestion of Aunt Hitty, or because George was now unable to take so long a walk, Frank generally considered himself bound to accompany her, and carry her basket; and though old Rose at first showed him plainly enough that she considered the whole race of white boys as great vexations, yet, as Frank often said, as he went laughing away, "None were so blind as those who would not see, and he had determined not to see any thing after he went into the hut but her handsome black face." So by degrees, his pertinacious good humor wore away the negro's dislike, and he put the crowning glory to his success by his care and skill in gathering in her precious supply of garden herbs. She began to be glad to see him, and to tell him stories of those wild woods upon whose borders she lived, which, if they were true, were very wonderful indeed.

Of late Frank had noticed a peculiarity in old Rose's treatment of them, of which he strove in vain to convince Florence. Frank, for his age, was a quick and acute observer; and the more he failed to convince Florence, the more watchful he himself became.

She seemed always on the alert when they were there — asked, frequently, what the noise she heard was — and if but a dried limb fell from the woods, or a chance nut dropped on the rocks near by, looked wistfully towards the door as if she expected something. She also made particular inquiries with regard to what they saw or heard as they came along, and questioned Frank in such a sharp, stern manner, that he often wondered whether she were not angry with him.

One day, as they were leaving her, she said to him, —

"Now, none ob your hunting up all dem dar tings, dat hab de breath ob life in dem as you go long with you. Lebe um for company to de ole black woman. Hear, boy?"

"Neber touch um, Rose," said Frank, with a slight imitation of her manner. "Lebe um all for company, raccoons and all."

"Mind you, dere, and do it, den; neber stone away my squirrels, or wildcats, or any ob dem tings you hear running along mong de bushes. Gwine to mind?"

"Sartain," said Frank, "always gwine to mind, for true."

"Name of sense, dat's a boy!" said Rose, laughing, in spite of herself, and the children went out.

Whether roused to more notice by the negro's injunction, or whether there actually were more noises in the wood than common, Frank was attentive to every thing that went on around him. He called Florence's notice to the different song of the late fall birds, and the low, monotonous chirping which the insects made, as if deprecating the effects of the cold which was fast ending their short life.

Suddenly he seized a small stone, and hurled it with violence into a thicket of bushes; and the instant it struck, there issued from the spot the short, quick cry of human pain. The children stopped as if a hand had arrested them. Then there was a rustle in the bushes as of some one breaking them down, in a rapid retreat; and Frank, leaving Florence alone in the path, dashed into the woods, in the direction of the sound.

It retreated for a moment, then, making a sudden stop, came back; and, as Frank threw himself across the path to intercept it, a black boy came directly towards him, pushed him out of the way, and made for the spot where Florence was still standing.

"Little missus," said the boy, catching her hand, and kissing it over and over, "I couldn't help it; I must come, or I die."

The suddenness of the action brought from Florence a loud scream, and Frank was in a moment at her side again, but, more astonished even than she was at the appearance and behavior of the boy, could not utter a word.

The boy, looking up in Florence's face, seemed to hear and see nothing else; but after the first few words, though his lips kept moving, he did not articulate a single word.

"Who are you?" at length asked Florence.

But his only reply was the same inarticulate motion of the parched lips.

"Where did you come from, and what do you take hold of this girl's hand for? Let it alone, I tell you;" and Frank's courage gained strength every moment, as he saw how powerless the boy was. "Move out of the way, I say."

"He is hurt," said Florence, now noticing blood, which was streaming from his temple.

"He throw de stone," said the boy, finding his voice faintly.

"I throw the stone!" said Frank; "why, I thought it was a wildcat, or some animal. What terrible eyes you have got! Was it you hid behind the bushes?"

"Go see little missus," said the boy; "I die if I no see her now."

"Who are you?" asked Florence, looking keenly at him. "Get up! Here is my handkerchief; wipe off that blood. Where did you come from?"

"From Myrtle Bush;" and the boy stole a quick frightened look at Frank.

"He is a fugitive slave, as true as I live," said Frank, returning the look: "but get up, can't you? and speak for yourself."

The boy raised himself with a slow, tottering motion, upon his feet, and as he did so, Florence unconsciously helped him. When he stood up he proved much taller than Frank, but so thin as to look more like a black shadow thrown upon the wall at sunset, than like a living boy.

"You came from Myrtle Bush," repeated Florence. "You are not Dick, are you?"

"Yes, missus," said the boy, dropping again on his knee. "I rudder die dan stay dere widout you and my mudder; so I come."

Such a beautiful welcoming smile stole over Florence's face that the many doubts and forebodings which had filled the young slave's heart vanished in a moment; and to Frank's utter astonishment and dismay Florence threw her white arms around Dick's neck, and half smiling, half crying, poured out such a string of questions as he had never listened to before.

The boy's face, too, lighted up with such an expression that it almost seemed as if another new life were born there. He made no attempt to answer them, but only looked at her, as if in so doing she might read them all.

"Let us go home to mauma," said Florence; but, stopping, as if the thought had just struck her, "Dick's trunk, who will carry that?"

"I will come for it with Betty," said Frank. "Where is it? here or at the station?"

Dick laughed; it was frightful to see what a contortion it was. "Dis my trunk," he said, shaking the few rags on his back; "I got no udder — been so long coming — so long;" and his face twitched as if the very thought gave him a spasm of pain. "Tink

Dick neber, neber get here. Tink he die on de road, and neber see little missus nor dat mudder."

"Come," said Florence, taking hold of his hand and drawing him along. "Come; it's only a short walk; not so far as from the oaks to the back water at Myrtle Bush. Mauma will be so glad. Do you know, Dick, she has been very much troubled about you?"

Dick shook his head; made no reply, but after walking a few steps stopped short.

"Me no go to see her," he said, trembling, "she neber forgive me — neber, neber!"

"O, yes, she will," said Florence, coaxingly; "I'll tease her till she does."

"Little missus for true," said Dick, with so much fondness in his tone that it made the tears come into Frank's eyes; "but mudder, when she know all, neber forgive poor Dick!"

"She shall!" and Florence's foot came down imperatively upon the ground.

"O missus, you don't know!" and a shudder ran all over Dick's thin frame. "I berry bad, I tief, missus — I tief!" and his voice broke into a long, loud wail.

"You tief, Dick!" said Florence, dropping his hand, and drawing herself up, as if on the instant she became the condemning judge.

"Yes, missus, I tief all fader had; but it wasn't much; I neber spent, neber, unless I most starve;" and here he drew from the bottom of his pocket three silver dollars; "here dis to go back; I'll earn it all; Rose says I can; and I must come, little missus, or I die."

"Come to mauma!" said Florence; "she will understand; I don't."

"Neber," said Dick; and again the heart-breaking cry. "She say me no boy ob hern — her boy neber tief — her boy neber run away — her boy neber break his fader's heart — no boy of hern — go away, Dick — go back — go back."

"Come, Dick!" it was all Florence seemed to have the power of saying. "Come to mauma!"

"He don't look as if he was strong enough to walk half that distance," said Frank, with a little anxiety as to the sensation that a fresh addition, in such a plight, might make in passing through the village. "He had better go into Rose's house, and wait until his mother — if Rachel is his mother — comes out here to him. It might frighten her to have him come in upon her so suddenly. We had better go home and tell her first."

"Dick's a tief," repeated the boy. "Mudder say neber had sich a boy. He plantation nigger, not hern. Go back, go back!"

Florence glanced from Frank to Dick in much uncertainty; but Frank saved her the trouble of any decision. "Come," he said, "it will be dark now before we can get home, and Rachel can come. We mustn't lose a moment. Dick, — if that is your name, — go into old Rose's house, and wait there until we come. We shan't be gone much more than an hour. And tell her," he said, as Dick turned to obey, "to give you the best she has in her house to eat; we will return it with interest by and by."

Florence waited until she saw Dick enter Rose's door, which he did without once looking behind him; then the children ran quickly, hardly stopping to take breath, until they came in sight of the parsonage.

Frank was the first one to attempt to form a plan for communicating the intelligence, with some caution, to Rachel. Florence was too much excited to have any thought of the kind; and she impatiently interrupted Frank's wise suggestion by saying, —

"Mauma couldn't stop to hear it slow; she must come right off;" and so she opened the door of the house, and finding Rachel in the dining room, with Georgy in her arms, singing to him, said, abruptly, "Dick has come!"

"De bressed Lord!" ejaculated Rachel; but with such a strange, wild look, that Florence was alarmed. "What dat you say?"

"Dick has come!" repeated Florence; "I just saw him down in old Rose's woods."

"Down in ole Rose's woods? Dick come — Dick — de Lord forgive me, a· poor miserable sinner. Dick — Dick — hab mercy upon me — Dick?" and Rachel put Georgy down upon the floor; and seizing hold of Florence's arm, said, so sternly that the child trembled, —

"What dat you say? De Lord have mercy on me — what? what?"

"Why, mauma, don't!" said Florence, pulling away her arm, with some impatience. "I told you Dick has come — now he is waiting for you; come!"

Then out into the gathering twilight walked Rachel, accompanied by the children, without another word. The cold, keen fall air, sent through her frame sharp, icy shivers; but she felt them not. It almost seemed as if she was changed to stone, and had no power left her but the one of moving forward in the direction towards which Florence was leading her. Silently and softly, as if the very ground bore evidence to the emotion which was too strong for utterance, they passed along. The children—awestruck by the solemn, speechless negro—did not, by word or sound, break the stillness until they came in sight of Rose's hut, and saw a dim light streaming from the small window.

"Dick is there," said Florence, pointing to it. "Frank told him to wait quietly until you came; but you will be glad to see him, and forgive him for all that he has done wrong—won't you, mauma?"

"De bressed Lord have mercy on us both!" said Rachel; and the tremor of her voice told that the torpor of the first shock was passing away.

"Perhaps you wouldn't like to go in," said Frank. "I will just open the door and call him out here. Old Rose can be as cross as a bear when she don't just fancy a thing."

Rachel stopped, and Frank, opening the door of Rose's house, found Dick crouched on the wooden block, looking more like an animal than like a living human being. Old Rose, a few feet from him, seemed endeavoring to give him courage; but Frank heard him say,—

"No boy of hern—a tief—go back, go back!"

"Come, Dick," said Frank, "your mother is here waiting for you."

The boy writhed back and forth as if some one were torturing him.

"Name of sense!" said Rose, sharply, "why you

set dere making a fool ob yourself? Up and be off,
or I will help dat dere, pretty soon, too!"

Striking at him with a cane which she kept near
her only made Dick shrink lower and lower; but at
last Frank approached him, and, for the second time
in his life, — the first was when he led Rachel into
church, — laid his hand gently on the bowed, quivering head.

"Come," he said; and the gentle kindness of his
tone reached the boy's heart. "Your mother will
be glad to see you. I am glad you ran away. I
wouldn't have staid there, and been a slave, if I were
you, and had two feet to run away with. Be a man
about it! You have as good a right to be free as I
have. Now, stand it out!"

The look of gratitude and joy which shot from
those great, glassy eyes Frank never, to his dying
day, forgot.

"Dat's de boy!" said old Rose, rubbing her hands
until every bone cracked in the intensity of her delight. "Go long, Pomp! Neber you fear; he'll take
care ob you. Hear dat, now! No slave in Frank
Niles. Dat's de boy! Run away himself for true."

"He no tief," said Dick, who had partly risen, falling back upon the block.

"I should steal too," said Frank, enthusiastically,
"and murder, for all that I know, if I couldn't get
my freedom without. If all you stole was money to
come north with, you are no worse fellow, in my way
of thinking; and we will take up a subscription, and
send every cent back."

"Name ob sense, hear de boy! — good!" ejaculated Rose; and Dick once more yielded to the kind

20

boy, and went with him to the door. But Rachel
had become too impatient to brook this long delay.
As they opened it, there she stood; and, forgetful of
the theft, of the running away, of every thing but
that he saw her, Dick, with a wild scream, but now
of joy, threw himself into her arms.

We cannot any further describe the meeting.
Poor Dick, amidst all his joy, kept up the unceasing
plaint, "Me tief — me tief!" And Rachel, while
she wept and smiled by turns, chided and blessed.

The arrival of such an unexpected visitor at the
parsonage, it may be supposed, produced quite a
sensation. Mrs. Niles would not allow the boy to be
questioned until she made sure that he had had a
plentiful supper. So wan and hunger-stricken an
object she had never seen before; and though he
seemed to turn with loathing from the food before
him, she only saw in this an evidence of the extremi-
ties to which he had been reduced.

It was not until the next morning that she would
allow him to tell his story, and we lay it before our
readers in its simplest and briefest form.

Ever since his mother's and Florence's departure
from Myrtle Bush, he had been determined, if possible, to join them at the north. He did not dare to
hint this determination to a living being at Myrtle
Bush, but, keeping it constantly in view, began, very
soon after their departure, to make his plans. He
worked with a faithfulness and assiduity which he
hoped would attract his overseer's attention, and
bring him a reward. But Mr. Jones, while, as we
have already said, he was aware how good he had
become, had no thought of giving him any thing

more than praise in return. When Dick became sure of this, he turned his attention to the secreting, from time to time, such of his allowance of food as he could spare from the appetite of a hard-worked, growing boy. This was a slow accumulation; and his clothes, too, every new suit of which he guarded with so much care, became quickly worn, and unfit for travelling. But, not discouraged by these obstacles, he went patiently on, hoping with that cheerful, elastic, young heart, and never giving up for an instant the one sole object of his life.

Dick might have gone on so for years, but a temptation was put in his way which he could not resist. Rachel was in the habit of sending Cato, from time to time, the wages which, as a free negro, she now punctually received from Mr. Erwin. The money, in Cato's careful hands, grew fast, and was becoming enough to be an important aid, some day, in purchasing his own freedom, or — if little missus, as Rachel felt sure she would, should give it to him — that of one of his boys. Dick saw the pile of money, and in a moment the Tempter had him for his own. He would take enough of it to go north, and, when once there, he would work, and return every cent. It was not stealing — it was only borrowing; and he must be *free*. Through the long summer day, when he was working away so diligently in the rank rice field, the very birds seemed to sing but one note as they flew over him. In the dark, still night he heard it in his dreams, always the same. It called to him when he opened his eyes in the soft, morning light; it whispered to him, always, always the same — "*Free! free!*"

To secrete his father's money was not difficult. Cato would as soon have doubted himself as his boys; and what Dick took was a very small part of the whole. But no sooner was it in his possession than he bound up his hidden stores, and in the night, when the whole plantation was asleep, took his way stealthily from Myrtle Bush. All night long he hurried on without daring to look behind him, endeavoring to benumb his senses so that a sound should not reach him that might render him timid.

He had spent too much time in studying the points of the compass to be easily bewildered. On, straight on, where that north star led! Poor, ignorant, frightened boy, he had yet fresh within him his mother's teachings; and under that star-lit sky, in the hush and solemn night stillness, he fancied the bright, moving guide the hallowed star in the east; and confusedly through his mind ran a wonder if the child and the mother he was seeking were not one and the same with those towards whom the wise men hastened.

Day came all too soon. There was neither weariness nor hunger to retard him. *On — on!* It seemed as if his whole being was concentrated into the meaning of this one word; and when the cars came thundering by him, sudden and new as the phenomenon was, it left no impression upon him but the one of longing for their speed. He knew that no negro could travel on southern cars without a permit from his master, so that he had little hope of availing himself of their aid; and now, as, guided by the smoke, he stumbled on to the track, daylight was gray and sombre in the east, and there must come hours of laying by; no one whom he had ever known must see and recognize him: indeed, it were safer far to remain entirely hidden, that no clew could be offered to any inquiries which might be made; so Dick chose for himself a safe hiding place beneath a thicket of bushes, where he might sleep away the day, and be refreshed. to resume his travels with the friendly darkness.

For days and weeks Dick pursued the same plan. He had no means of judging where he was, and how far behind him lay his home. There still was the north star; and, fortunately for him, not a stormy or an entirely cloudy night had come since he had started. At length, even with the help of the wild fruits and roots which he found by the way, his stock of provisions became exhausted; and with many misgivings he yielded to the stern necessity, and, approaching a negro cabin, after watching until he made sure that no one remained but an old negro woman, ventured to enter, and solicited food.

"Run away?" said the woman; "gwine to de north? Well, de good Lord bress you! I hab neber set eyes on you — neber seed you, no more nor if you neber was born; so help yourself, and start on."

Dick ate like a famished animal, and, with a nice bundle of provisions for the swift-coming need, and many blessings, started again on his way. Encouraged by this success, he went for a shorter time without refreshment, and for weeks found both food and shelter, kindly granted whenever he asked. Sometimes now, too, he began to get short rides, which saved his bruised and tired feet; and occasionally he rested for days in some lonely negro house, working in the mean time for those who kindly sheltered him; always keeping, however, the secret of whence he came inviolate.

But he found, unexpectedly, that the nearer he approached to the north, the greater his difficulties became. People were more inquisitive, and, if they aided him at all, did so grumblingly. Often faint and exhausted, he was denied both food and shelter by the whites, and, alas for him! every weary day's journey brought him where there were fewer of his own color. He learned, very soon after passing Mason and Dixon's line, that new hardships must mark each step of his farther progress. But, in contrast to the negro race generally, these obstacles only served to increase his power of endurance, and his determination to accomplish the end of his journey. Never was he more resolute than when his feet were bleeding, every muscle strained and sore, and his appetite clamorous for food. "My mother!" — even the wish for freedom, as he grew weaker and weaker, lost itself in a child's longing for her. He used to feel, sometimes, that, one step back, death was awaiting him, and that his only chance of life was in reaching her.

So far, Dick's money had been nearly untouched, hoarded carefully with the hope that when he should reach Grafton he might be able, with only a slight addition, to return it to his father; but to travel now, all inexperienced as he was, without it, was only a waste of time and life; so he unwillingly used it as his greatest emergencies required; and worse than the pain and fatigue, to the right-minded boy, was the sight of its gradual decrease.

It often seemed to him that, in exact proportion as his clothes became worn and travel-stained, and the privations which he was enduring made him thin and ghastly, more money was demanded for the most trifling aid.

Three dreary months passed in this way slowly along, and Dick found himself at the north, but not near Grafton; nor could he make any of the many people of whom he inquired understand where the place was to which he was going. Vermont was the nearest point towards which he could receive satisfactory direction; and one young girl of whom he asked his way — and whom, for some reason or other, he never forgot — advised him to take the cars for the next two hundred miles, and explained to him, quite at length, how he could make the ride not a luxury only, but an economy; and, so encouraged and directed, he got on board a train, paid what seemed to him a ruinous amount of money, and found himself in a few hours, as if by magic, carried over what would have been an almost impossible distance to him on foot, all exhausted as he was. It was too costly a luxury for a second trial, however; and Dick resumed his foot travels, but with more elasticity and hope, if hope can be said ever to have left him.

The nearer he approached to Grafton, — and now he was so near that his eager inquiries with regard to its distance were correctly answered, — the more heavily began to weigh upon his conscience the fear of his mother's anger when she should know of his theft. So occupied had he been, during the early part of his journey, with the one idea of reaching her, that, excepting as a motive for bearing hunger, the money had not troubled him ; but as one obstacle after another was overcome, it seemed as if the treasured gold grew heavier in proportion as it actually became lighter; and when he began to read that name for which he had so longed upon the guide boards placed at the dividing of the road, he wished himself back at Myrtle Bush — dead — every where or any where but going to face that mother to whom he knew the spotless integrity of her boys was dearer even than their lives.   Every mile of that long, pain-paved road seemed to rise up before him in judgment.   As he laid himself down at night under a stone wall, behind a barn, in an outhouse, any where that he could be at all protected from the cold, northern air, chillier than the night breeze, curdling his blood, and freezing up every warm emotion, came the memory of his theft.   His father looking for his lost son was lost in that father looking for his lost gold ; and pointing back to ask his forgiveness, and to make restitution, was the sad, angry face of his mother.

When the church and town of Grafton came actually in sight, so worried and conscience-stricken had Dick become, that they almost seemed to him like the judgment seat ; and he felt that, instead of his mother, an inexorable Judge was there awaiting him. He approached the town in the direction of the wood in which dwelt old Rose, and, after haunting the woods like a ghost for days, driven by the sharpest pangs of hunger, he ventured to approach her door, and knock.

Rose's astonishment at his appearance may be

easily imagined; but his very forlornness, for once, addressed itself to such of her better feelings as remained; and when she heard his story, her fondness for Florence made her desirous to give him protection, and bring about their meeting as soon as possible. But Dick's conscience growing every day more and more sensitive as his stolen glimpses of "little missus" made him more anxious to speak with her, constantly defeated every plan Rose made; and the negro would probably have soon forced him to a disclosure, if it had not come about in the way already described.

This story Dick was weeks in narrating; indeed, it was years before he exhausted the wonderful events which, from time to time, had happened to him.

With this singular addition to her family, Mrs. Niles, as might have been expected, found much more trouble than with any of the others. The cold weather came rapidly on; and though Dick had been warmly clothed directly, yet, so emaciated had he become, and his young blood was so poor and weak, that no external warmth seemed to produce the slightest effect. It was as if he had a fever with one continuous chill; and both Mrs. Niles and Rachel began to feel that, if relief could not be obtained for him soon, he must die.

Quite a family of invalids the parsonage had now become; but the hush and gloom which so often attend sickness were not there. The children knew nothing of all the anxieties which were weighing down the hearts of the elder portion of the family; and Jennie grew even more and more elastic, more light-hearted, as if God were already lighting up the star which should shine in the night of her parents' darkness.

Florence sang and danced in and out of the sick rooms like a ray of sunshine. Her heart was so full of its own exuberant happiness, that no cloud could rest for a moment near her. With Frank she kept up an unceasing round of cheerful child-pleasures, never, apparently, more contented or merrier than when they were making for themselves some trifle into a world of amusement.

Georgie was growing slowly better, and added his own share to the happiness which was resting upon this family side by side with the long, dark shadow of death.

Fall in the country is, to most people, a dreary season. It requires stout, young hearts, with life all before them, to see the yellow leaf and the withering grass unmoved; and who can estimate the fountain of joy when it gushes up so pure and fresh that it gives back the faded hues to nature, and brightens up the dead or dying landscape with its own living green!

Nutting, for a season, took the place of every vanishing pleasure with the children. Even Dick, wrapped up in the warmest covering that ingenuity could devise, would grow warm, as the brown nuts came pelting down upon him from the high trees; and George, driven now by his mother, would sit in the carriage, in the midst of the sport, receiving and emptying the laden baskets, while his boyhood seemed to come back, with its innocent pleasures, into his heart; and as his heavy eye lighted, and his pale cheek flushed with a color so like and yet so unlike that which had mantled it in his own nutting days, his mother looked at him through tear-dimmed eyes, and thought how soon he would enter upon the "eternal youth."

How fast one holiday succeeded another! Scarcely had nutting gone before Thanksgiving came; and Mrs. Niles made it Thanksgiving, with all its beautiful and true New England meaning; never, however, for an instant forgetting that one who sat at their festive board, before the next falling leaf should be drinking "new wine in his Father's kingdom."

"Almost as good as Christmas," said Florence, wild with excitement and pleasure. "When you are a minister, and settled over a parish, Cousin George, I will come every year north from Myrtle Bush to spend it with you."

"Not with me, my little Flossy," George said many times, in a whisper, to her that day; "but at the good old parsonage."

"And you will come, too?" Florence invariably asked.

And then George would draw the sunny face close to his, and kiss her instead of answering, with which response Florence was well satisfied; but the mother, with her watchful eye, saw and understood it all; and as the hours of the day drew one after the other so quickly to their close, her compressed lips, and the sharp lines which deepened round her temples, told to no one — to no one but God — the agony with which she marked the desolation which was coming upon this dear home holiday.

Towards night the snow began to fall — the first

of the season. To Mrs. Niles's tired nerves it seemed like her boy's shroud; to the children it was heaven's smile upon the happy day. Frank drew Florence with him to the door, and very marvellous were the coasting and skating stories with which he beguiled her into forgetting how cold the wind was; and he even coaxed poor Dick, with his chattering teeth, out to gather the " white sugar."

And then the early twilight came down, and the poor and the sick were all remembered in the gentle evening prayer with which Mr. Niles closed the day.

Blessing on this mother. Every young heart shall go to its rest with no throb but of pleasure. Even Jennie— good, observant child as she is — sees not George's pale face as she closes her eyes, and never hears those "rustling wings" which are approaching, like a mighty wind, to the listening mother and Rachel.

The next morning the snow lay deep all over the ground. Now for sleds and sleighs, for real, true sleigh riding !

"New York can't snap its fingers to it," says Frank, as he hurries to harness Billy, putting on a double set of bells; "we will go down to old Rose's, and dig her out. Come, Flossy! wrap up as warm as toast."

And so the children started, but had not left the yard before Frank, happening to turn, encountered Dick's eyes fixed upon him, and with such a longing look that it was impossible for him to withstand them.

Checking his horse suddenly, he called out, "Halloo, there, Myrtle Bush !"— the name he always gave Dick. "Ask mother for the old woollen comforter, and wrap up in it, and you shall come too."

So away they went, and Dick's cracked voice rose shrill and high in his shouts of glee above even the two sets of bells.

When about half way to Rose's hut, they saw a queer little figure ploughing its way along in the same direction. For some time the curious eyes found it impossible to discover who it was, and it was not until they were nearly upon it, that Frank called out, —

"Aunt Hitty, as true as I live! Where in the world can she be creeping to through this walking?"

"Down to look after Rose, to be sure," said Jennie, from under the large buffalo. "We might have known she would be there before us. Can't we take her in, Frank?"

"Of course we can," said Frank, shouting to her immediately.

"Aunt Hitty! Aunt Hitty! Stop. Here comes the Ark — Noah, Shem, Ham, with their wives; Japhet, too; but he forgot his wife; so there is just room for you."

The old family sleigh, huge, lumbering, too heavy for any one horse in the world but Billy, was always called, not only by the minister's family, but by the parish generally, "the Ark;" so Aunt Hitty, with her merry laugh, turned off the road and stood quite still till it came up; then, sliding into the small space squeezed out for her, took both Totty and George into her lap, and wrapped them up in the two ends of her small blanket-shawl, as if they were not more than half as large as she was herself.

Old Rose's black face was seen at the window,

with the nearest approach to a smile upon it which any one ever remembered there, and they all thought of it afterwards, and of the cordial —

"Name of sakes! little missus gwine to come again, and bring um all to look arter ole nigger, are you? snow inside of her house as well as out!"

"But not so cold, Aunt Rose," said Florence, rubbing the negro's cold, wrinkled hand with her soft white one; "see here — my hands are as warm as toast."

"Name of sakes! what a snow flake!" said Rose, turning over the hand and looking at it curiously; "most a-mind to bite a bit right out of it;" and raising it quickly to the mouth Florence felt the aged lips pressed for an instant upon it.

That night old Rose died. When or how no one ever knew; nor did she leave behind a single ground of conjecture as to whether the sweet lessons of piety which the child brought to her had been received; but George Niles said to his father, when he went out to the funeral, that he had much faith in the efficacy of such simple teaching. Jesus, when he set a child in the midst of his disciples, and told them that to be worthy of the kingdom of heaven they must become like it, showed not only his deep knowledge of human hearts, but his knowledge of that kingdom within the veil.

Mr. Niles remembered his son's words as he looked upon the black coffin lowered between the two deep white snow banks, and reverently folding his hands, uttered those beautiful words written alike for the poor, forgotten black sinner and for the purest saint, "I am the resurrection and the life."

CHAPTER XVII.

CHRISTMAS and New Year came hurrying on, and the box must once more be sent to the south; but all are busy, preparing it — all interested. Even the invalid lies on his sofa and watches the work as it progresses, or with his thin, long fingers holds the bright worsted which tassels and ties so many rigolets for the woolly heads so far away.

Old Billy and the good sleighing are constantly in requisition for the nearest town where there are shopping places. Mrs. Niles directs and busies herself about all. One would think, to see how interested she seems, that it was the only care or responsibility she had.

Rachel and Florence recall the box of last year's packing, and Rachel, as she remembers the night scene with Henry Erwin, may be seen to shake her head and mutter to herself, —

"Eh, eh! White boy, for true. No better than worst plantation nigger!"

Little George annoys her by wanting to know if she means him, and only leaves for her comfort.

"Precious little white lamb, no; for true, no. Massa George's own boy! Bress de Lord, not all like in dat are family."

But the packing of the box was the greatest Christmas event. New England does not "set apart the day and hallow it" as she does her Thanksgiving.

Old Puritan ghosts seem to walk coldly out of their graves, and go chattering about, scaring away Santa Claus, with the whole retinue of good fairies; and New Year meets with scarcely a more hearty reception. "This year thou shalt die. Remember your mortality. Time is short, and eternity is long." These phrases shape themselves into speech quite as readily as the more cordial wishes for the "happy new year."

There was a chill in both occasions to the southern child. Mrs. Niles felt it for her, but it was as vain to strive against the true spirit of the time and place as against the sleet and storms of the season. They were both necessary, and if partially concealed, the want of true affection for the days made itself as *really* felt as the block of ice would though hidden under the brightest and softest wool.

"Cousin George! Christmas and New Year are not half as pleasant as Thanksgiving," said Florence, creeping softly into George's sick room.

"No, my little Flossy," he answers, feebly; "but it is not that we are not very glad the dear Saviour was born, only we are not used to keeping it; that is all; and New Year is rather a sad day to us to-day. Did you ever think, darling, that when the next glad New Year comes, some of us may not be here to see it?"

"Are you going to die, as my father did?" asked Florence, suddenly. "You look just like him, cousin George. I see it every day, but I did not think you were so very sick before."

And then Florence, like a frightened child, as she actually was, began to cry loud and violently, resisting every attempt of George to quiet her, and calling, by her passionate wailing, the members of the family to her.

Not a word of reply did she make to the many inquiries; and as the subject was one upon which as yet there had been no intercourse between George and his parents, he could not bring himself so suddenly to speak of it now, and the weeping child was forced away, to sob herself to sleep in her own room. But from this night a change seemed to come over Florence. She never wished to be away from George a moment; but, sitting on her footstool by his couch, or leading him gently by the hand, she was content and quiet; away from him, she was restless, impatient, and so little like herself, that Rachel said to Mrs. Niles, —

"Little missus hear dem coming. She do just so fore Massa George lebe her. De good Lord have mercy on de poor child. She love dat cousin dearly, for true."

And so the angel of death came swiftly in, and one child after another heard his tread, or saw the shadow of his wings, as it fell upon George; and, putting out his thin, trembling hand, the young minister clasped that of his heavenly guide, and his mother knew by his brightening eye, that he now saw the form which never is visible to mortal vision, and from his parting lips she heard the eager words, "Though I walk through the valley of the shadow of death I will fear no evil, for *thou* art with me." And then came the glad song of the Lamb, and, quivering with his last breath, that holy shout of "victory through Christ!"

21

It rung in Mrs. Niles's ear as she closed the eyes
of this first born, this "summer child." It whispered
itself over and over to her, as looking into his grave
she saw the pure snow flakes drop star-like upon his
silent breast. It went home with her, drowning the
rough, whistling, winter wind, the only dirge for the
early dead. It met her as she opened the door of
the desolated house. It prayed for her, and with
her, as kneeling by his bed, with clasped hands, she
faltered out, "Not as I will, but as thou wilt."

This was to have been the glad, sportive, merry
winter! Had death frozen all the life out of it, for
the young, expectant hearts? A little while, a very
little, and the grave darkened over the parsonage,
with a gloom which seemed one with the bleak,
short, winter days, and then Mrs. Niles took hold
of life cheerfully again. The old smile came back,
the dear old familiar words and tones of affection,
and gradually, imperceptibly but surely, life and
warmth returned to the parsonage, and the child's
laugh, Frank's gay, merry words, Florence's sunshine,
and even Totty's spoiled ways, brought the child's
world back; the world of to-day, with no yesterday
and no to-morrow; and George was not dead, but
away, happy, well, and one day they should "all go
to him."

Mrs. Niles must now do her own and the unfin-
ished work of her boy; and blessed be *work!* Necessity is God's comforter to those he loves; in the
busiest hours he comes nearest to their heart. Lessons, work, skating, sliding, coasting, — what an active winter it was! and how quickly the snow banks
began to disappear, and the ice to crack into those

ominous "benders," which all country children love so well; and so spring came, and it was almost impossible to make Florence believe that the two years were past, and she must now choose her home.

So, however, a letter from her uncle Henry informed her, adding that he would be in Grafton ready to take her back to New York with George, and that Ida, Grace, and her aunt, were very impatient for her to come.

Florence read the letter with as much astonishment as if the idea of a return to New York was for the first time in her life suggested to her; then, uncertain and troubled, she carried the epistle to the fountain of all her comfort, her good aunt; and to add still more to her surprise, instead of having it dismissed from her mind the moment she read it, heard, —

"Well, my darling, this is a very serious question for you to decide. You had better think it over for a week, without talking about it to any one; you will then know your own wishes a great deal better than if you are assisted or directed." And in pursuance with this plan, Mrs. Niles forbade her children to mention the subject to Florence.

CHAPTER XVIII.

APRIL came with its buds and its beautiful promises, and with it came uncle Henry and Ida, to accompany Florence back to New York.   Florence
had no rest day nor night, and became at last such
a poor, pale thing, that Rachel said, "New York was
withering her bud (de Lord presarve de child!) way
off where it was; Heaven only know what dat are
would do to her, when she dare, for true."

But "little missus" this time knew her own mind,
and fortunately, when the day really came which was
to bring her city relations, had no fear of either of
them or of the result of her choice.   Dick and she
held many whispered consultations on the important morning, the result of which seemed to make
Dick perfectly beside himself with joy, for though
he had grown since he had become somewhat ac-
climated, to be near as tall as Mr. Niles himself, he
might be constantly seen turning somersaults in the
muddiest parts of the yard; and his white teeth were
about the most conspicuous thing on the premises,
when Frank in the lumber box, with Billy and Katy
doing duty again, drove the visitors to the parsonage.

But we must not linger over these last scenes, for
it would require lengthy description to give any
idea of Mr. Erwin's surprise and chagrin, when Florence informed him of her determination to remain
where she was, giving simply as her reason, that

she was very happy, and couldn't go away from aunt Niles now George was dead.

Ida's vexation at first passed all bounds of politeness; then she became sullen; but at last, as if her heart was so full that it could not and would not brook the refusal, she burst into passionate weeping, and the poor, unloved child pleaded as only an asking, affectionate nature can plead, for some one to fill the "great void." Then, indeed, Florence was moved, and the two little girls, with their arms around each other's neck, sat, and wept, and planned, as if the future were at their own disposal.

Mrs. Niles was grieved for the neglected child, in her softer mood, and so urgently claimed her for the summer if George must return to his mother, that Mr. Erwin, not unwillingly, consented to her remaining; and so Ida became a member of the family at the parsonage.

"Bress de Lord! Glory be to his name foreber and eber!" said Rachel, when the various conclusions were made known to her. "Miss Ida now see, for true, what it is to be in dat ere family, whom de Lord own and bress; and what if she don't seem like one of dem dere little ones? — haven't you faith, old mauma as you are, dat is as big as dat little bressed mustard seed? Eh! eh! of jist sich may be dat kingdom of heaven, cause de same Christ he come to bress um still. So, so, mauma go back now, and tell Cato and dem dere five tother boys, dat it's a bressed privilege to be free, and a bressed privilege to live in dat good old South Carliny. De Lord help us. Little missus she choose, but old mauma she no choose after all. Let de Lord decide; he know best."

Dick, however, had no choice to make. Mr. Erwin talked about a return south immediately for so valuable a hand, but there was a flash in Rachel's eye when he did so, which reminded him of the scene at the rifling of the Christmas box. Rachel had kept her faith with him so far. Henry had returned from sea, and was making what seemed to be a real effort to do better — it would be a pity to have any thing retard it — so he wisely let Dick alone, and after a few business arrangements, and a promise that the negro should be apprenticed to some good trade as soon as he was able to learn it, took his departure for New York, carrying the reluctant, tearful Georgy with him, and carrying with the child many seeds for good, which, carefully implanted by the pious negro, and fostered by a kind, heavenly Father, should bear fragrant blossoms in that godless home.

The night after his departure, the side door opened softly, and putting her little face in the crack, aunt Hitty's musical voice said, —

"Little Pet, I jist looked in, you know, to say I have been working for 'second' people all day; so I am proper tired; but Deacon Ben and Mrs. Drummond, and a lot on um, you know, have set about gitting up a donation party, or some sich thing, cos as how they think this minister of ourn is turned anti-slavery, and is a-going to have the plantation of Myrtle Bush, or Currant Bush, or some sort of a bush, negroes and all, brought up here to Grafton, now little missis — bless her pretty face! — is a-going to stay. I say it's mighty droll, now — ain't it? But you know Deacon Ben must crow, and if he'll crow *for* you, why, it's jist as well as if he crowed agin

you, for all that I know. So good by; and I am
all ready to make the meetin jackets for all of them
boys of Rachel's — I don't know what her last name
is — as well as for this ere colored feller here. I am
a practical abolitionist, you know."

Then she winked to every member of the family,
but most ominously at Florence, and disappeared.
And so was settled all the troubled questions of the
national sin in the little town of Grafton.

THE END.